carrots

A SHELBY NICHOLS ADVENTURE

Colleen Helme

MANETTO BOOKS

Book Cover Art by Damonza.com Copyright © 2013 by Colleen Helme
Book Layout ©2017 BookDesignTemplates.com

Carrots/Colleen Helme. – 2nd ed.
ISBN 1456414143
ISBN-13 9781456414146

Dedication

To my daughters
Erin and Melissa

ACKNOWLEDGMENTS

I would like to thank my family for reading this book as a work in progress and for your continued encouragement to finish the story. I'd especially like to thank Tom, for supporting and encouraging my creative nature. Thanks to my daughters, Erin and Melissa, for your excitement for my books and also sharing that enthusiasm with everyone you know. To Damon for the wonderful cover art! I love it! And last but not least to my fans whose wonderful comments and reviews keep me going. You're the best!!

Shelby Nichols Adventure Series

Carrots
Fast Money
Lie or Die
Secrets that Kill
Trapped by Revenge
Deep in Death
Crossing Danger
Devious Minds
Hidden Deception
Laced in Lies
Deadly Escape
Marked for Murder
Ghostly Serenade
Dying Wishes
High Stakes Crime
Ties That Bind
Grave Duty
Presumed Dead
Devil in a Black Suit ~ A Ramos Story
A Midsummer Night's Murder ~ A Shelby Nichols Novella

SAND AND SHADOW SERIES
Angel Falls
Desert Devil

NEWSLETTER SIGNUP
For news, updates, and special offers, please sign up for my
newsletter on my website at www.colleenhelme.com. To
thank you for subscribing you will receive a FREE ebook.

Contents

Chapter 1

My life changed that day because I didn't have any carrots.

I was driving home when the dark, threatening clouds that had been gathering all afternoon finally let loose, and it began to pour. It was April, so rain wasn't unexpected, but it couldn't have come at a worse time. All I wanted to do was go home and relax, but first I had to stop at the grocery store and pick up some carrots. I planned on making chicken soup for dinner, and everyone knows you can't make chicken soup without carrots.

Luckily, the grocery store was on my way home. I pulled into the parking lot, but all the close spots were taken, and I ended up parking so far away that I knew I'd get soaked. Did I really need those carrots? I turned off the engine and, without the wipers going, I could barely see out the windshield. I waited a few minutes, hoping the rain would let up, but when it didn't, I knew I'd have to make a run for it.

Gathering my courage, I took a deep breath and jumped out of the car. I made a mad dash for the doors, and nearly made it inside, only to find a massive puddle blocking my way. I ran too fast to stop, so I jumped. I barely made it over the center of the puddle before my feet splashed dirty water halfway up my pants and soaked my shoes. My breath caught at the sudden wetness, and I stifled a curse. By the time I reached the doors, not only were my shoes completely drenched, but the splash made it look like I'd wet my pants.

Totally humiliated, I had two choices. Either go back to the car and admit defeat, or take it like a man. I grabbed a shopping cart and marched into the store. Now that I'd made it this far, there was no turning back. It didn't matter that my shoes were squeaking, and water was trickling down my neck. Or that my hair was now plastered to my skull, and water dripped from my nose. Come hell or high water, I was going to get those blasted carrots.

I got to the produce aisle and triumphantly placed the carrots into my cart and stood there. I did it. So why was I feeling let down? Where was the euphoria of accomplishing what I'd set out to do? Then I realized that I'd been through all that for a measly bunch of carrots. What was I thinking? I'd risked life and limb for this? I wiped the rain from my face, and pushed the hair back from my forehead. There had to be something else I needed.

I had a sudden hankering for some Hostess Cupcakes, yummy chocolate goodness with creamy whipped filling inside. Now was my chance to grab a box. I could probably hide them easily enough in the back of the kitchen cupboard with the pots and pans. No one but me would know where they were. While I was at it, why not pick up some more Diet Coke? I hated to run out, and it never hurt to have extra on hand.

When I reached the check-stand, I was feeling lots better. This hadn't been a wasted trip after all. My cart was at least half full. As I placed the items on the black conveyor belt, I noticed the checker had raised her eyebrows. Sometimes the checker can tell what I'm making for dinner from what's in my cart, but not tonight. She rang up my items; carrots, celery, Diet Coke, cupcakes, and potato chips. Then she gave me one of those knowing looks while she scanned the Twizzlers, Cheetos, and candy bars. With a guilty flush, I quickly explained that most of it was for my kids and their friends. It was the truth, but from her smile, I wasn't sure she believed me. Maybe I had gone a little overboard in the unhealthy-foods-department.

As she placed the bags into my shopping cart, someone screamed. My heart skipped a beat, and I flinched to hear an earsplitting boom coming from the area near the bank. I stared in astonished disbelief as a man fell heavily to the floor, blood oozing from his chest. As he fell, he grabbed the rubber mask from the face of the man beside him, and I realized that man had a gun.

Another shot went off, and everyone scattered for cover... everyone except me. My brain seemed to be moving in slow motion, and I stood there with my mouth open like a dummy. How could something like this be happening in my grocery store?

The man with the gun pivoted and saw me staring at him. His eyes blazed with demented zeal, and he fired.

Next thing I knew, someone was holding a cloth to my head and murmuring something I couldn't make out. His face was white, and when he spoke, his voice shook. I tried to ask him what was wrong, but the words just wouldn't come out of my mouth. What was I doing on the floor? What was that awful noise?

I finally recognized the wailing sound of sirens. That seemed to jolt my senses awake, and I reached for my hurting head. I started to sit up and smashed the potato chip bag with my elbow. The bag exploded and sent chips flying everywhere.

The man helping me gasped with horror. I tried to tell him that I hadn't meant to make such a mess, but he wouldn't listen. Instead, he kept trying to push me down, but there was no way I wanted to lay my hurting head on those greasy chips. His face turned a bright shade of red before he finally quit trying and left to get help.

Safe from the potato chips, I sat up and the world started to tilt. Maybe sitting up hadn't been such a good idea after all. I concentrated on taking deep breaths, and was rewarded when everything came into focus. Good. That had to mean I wasn't hurt too bad, right?

My relief turned to panic to feel something wet trickling down the back of my neck. It was warm and sticky, with a faint coppery smell, and my stomach turned into a queasy knot. I clutched the cloth a little tighter and swallowed.

Just then, a young man knelt beside me. He wore paramedic's uniform, and his eyes held quiet confidence. His calm manner soothed my racing heart, especially when he told me I was going to be all right. That was when my eyes got a little misty and it was hard to swallow past the lump in my throat. He didn't laugh or seem embarrassed by my tears, and his concern was so sweet, that I almost began to cry. But, since I didn't want to become a blubbering idiot, I concentrated on getting up off the messy floor instead.

"Whoa, what do you think you're doing?" he asked. "You should stay there until we make sure you're stabilized, and then we'll load you onto a gurney."

Load me? He made it sound like a monumental task, like I was a big sack of potatoes. A crazy fear came over me that if anyone tried to pick me up they'd stagger, or groan. Maybe even pull a muscle. How embarrassing would that be? Not that I was overweight or anything, but I wasn't as slim as I used to be.

"That's okay. I'm really not feeling so bad. It's just a little knock on the head. There's no reason why I can't walk to the gurney."

His mouth quirked and he started to argue, but he didn't have much of a say in the matter when I stood up. His arm came around my waist to steady me, and I was grateful for his help. He was stronger and bigger than I first thought, and, when he smiled encouragingly, I started feeling better. Maybe he could have picked me up after all.

After sitting down, I realized I was still a little shaky, and it had nothing to do with him. At least I didn't think it did. He urged me to lie down, but I felt silly lying down when I wasn't hurt that bad.

His lips pursed with disapproval, and I was just about to relent when my attention was drawn to the man lying on the floor. Paramedics surrounded him, frantically working to save his life. An oxygen mask covered his face, and several white bandages on his chest were soaked in blood. They inserted an IV in his arm, and when they lifted him onto the gurney, the rubber mask fell out of his hand. My stomach clenched, and I didn't feel so good anymore.

"Okay, I'm ready here. Let's see the damage."

I gratefully turned my attention to the paramedic beside me. He had little rubber gloves on his hands, and medical packages laid out ready to use. He gently moved my hand holding the cloth from my head, and I blanched at the sight of all that red blood. My blood. I swayed, but the paramedic must have figured something like that would happen and, with relative ease, maneuvered me to lie flat on the gurney. He was good.

"Don't worry. Head wounds usually bleed a lot, but you're going to be fine. The bullet just grazed your scalp.

You'll need a few stitches, and you'll have a headache and a little pain, but nothing serious. You're very lucky." He staunched the bleeding with a bandage and began wrapping it around my head. "We'll get you to the emergency room, and the doctors will take care of you."

I nodded, grateful I'd taken a shower and washed my hair that morning. Then what he said hit me. The bullet? I'd been hit by a bullet? In the head? Oh my gosh! And they were taking me to the hospital? I blurted the first thing I thought of. "Where's my purse? I can't go anywhere without my purse."

Why was he smiling? "Is this it?" He held it up so I could see it, and my mouth dropped open.

"Yeah. How did you get it?"

"Someone brought it over. Here, I'll put it next to you so you won't lose it. Then we'll put you in the ambulance and take you to the hospital."

"Okay, thanks." I got cold all over and started to shake. The realization that I had nearly died washed over me with freezing clarity. That crazy bank robber had fired a gun and shot me in the head. I could be dead right now. I tried to calm down, but the shaking seemed to get worse.

Concerned, the paramedic patted my arm, and then spoke over my head to someone. "I think she's going into shock." For the first time, I realized there were several people standing around me. One of them put a blanket over me, and took my wrist to check my pulse.

"I'm going to give you something to help you relax, all right?"

I nodded gratefully and hardly felt the sting in my arm. A few moments later, the drug took effect, and settled me down. As they wheeled me to the waiting ambulance, my fear vanished, and I felt a lot better. It had even quit raining, and the air had a nice, fresh smell to it.

Almost to the ambulance, a man in a dark suit came to my side. He smiled encouragingly, and two big dimples magically appeared in his cheeks. I'd never seen dimples like that. When he started to talk they wobbled in and out of his cheeks like little tornados. He looked at me expectantly, and I realized I hadn't caught a thing he'd said.

"Huh?"

He smiled again and repeated his question. "My name is Detective Harris. Did you see the man who shot you? We were hoping someone got a good look at him."

"Oh... yeah... I did." When I didn't elaborate, the detective said something about talking to me at the hospital. "Sure thing," I said, or at least that's what I tried to say. It came out more like, "Shrthn."

While they loaded me into the ambulance, I strained to get another look at his dimples. He kept smiling and those dimples started to spin. I shifted my position to keep him in sight while they closed the ambulance doors. My elbow slipped and I almost fell off the gurney. Thankfully, the paramedic helped straighten me out, and put a pillow under my head. Before I knew it, I was so relaxed that my eyes wouldn't stay open, and I dozed off.

I woke to the glare of bright lights, and realized I was in the emergency room. Two men in green scrubs and funny hair nets wheeled me into a curtained area that gave the impression of privacy, but allowed me to hear everything else that was going on. It was a little disconcerting. A nurse came in and introduced herself, then took my blood pressure and pulse.

When she was done, she asked me about my health insurance. Luckily, my purse was right beside me, and I rummaged through it until coming up with the card. Things were still a little fuzzy, and when she asked me who my next of kin was, I panicked.

"You'd better let me call my husband. I don't want him to worry." Christopher had enough on his plate without me adding to it. He put in long, hard hours at his law firm, and usually stayed late, so I knew I could catch him there.

But the nurse wouldn't let me near the phone. She assured me they could place the call and, after thinking it through, I relented. Besides what could I say other than, "Hi honey, I've been shot in the head, can you come to the hospital and get me?" He'd probably think it was a joke, and I was only saying that to get him to come home in time for dinner.

The doctor was gentle and stitched me up pretty fast. Only I didn't like it when he kept saying how lucky I was. Just an inch or more over, and my brains would be mush. I moved my gaze to look at him when he said that, but his lips weren't moving. "Did you just say something?" I asked.

He smiled, shaking his head. "Just a few more stitches and I'll be done. I know this has been a difficult experience, but you're doing great. Just hold still a little longer."

That was strange. Things must have affected me more than I thought. My head was numb but it still hurt, and I did feel a little out of it. That probably explained it.

"There, all done." The doctor smiled, and I let out my breath in relief. Just then, the nurse opened the curtain and there was Chris, looking stoic and scared at the same time. My heart caught like it always did when I saw him unexpectedly. His dark, wavy hair was slightly mussed, like he'd run his hands through it several times. His face was so pale that it looked like he'd forgotten to shave and his deep brown eyes seemed to gleam with extra moisture. He cleared his throat and smiled, then came to my side and grabbed my hand.

"Hey there." He was trying to sound casual, but I could hear the underlying stress in his voice. "How's she doing?" he asked the doctor.

"Great. We're all done here. I'm going to give you a prescription for the pain and some instructions on how to care for the stitches. I'll be back in a moment."

The moment he left, I threw my arms around Chris, and sudden tears ran down my cheeks. I didn't want to let go of his solid comfort. It took me a minute to get under control, and when we finally pulled apart, I could see the worry lines around his eyes.

He swallowed before speaking. "I didn't know what to think when they called and said you'd been shot. At least they told me you only had a minor injury, or I don't know what I would have done. I'm still not clear on what happened."

"I was at the grocery store getting carrots when a man came in and robbed the bank. I saw him shoot this guy, and then he shot at me. I guess I didn't duck in time."

He hugged me again. "Thank God you're all right."

The doctor returned with last minute instructions and the prescription. I was hoping for another happy shot, and I did get a shot, but this one was for tetanus and hurt like crazy.

As we gathered up my things to leave, the detective with the dimples arrived. When I saw him before, the only thing I'd noticed were his huge dimples, but now I was struck by how good-humored and clean-cut he seemed. Definitely not something you'd expect from a cop. He was built like a linebacker though, so his size was intimidating. Maybe that was why he could afford to be nice.

He introduced the other detective with him, and explained that they were both assigned to my case. The other cop's name was Detective Williams, and he began to question me. I told them everything that happened, except for the smashed potato chips.

"Do you think you would recognize the bank robber if you saw him again?" This was from Dimples.

"Yes, I'm pretty sure I would."

"What did you say?" Detective Williams asked. His brows were drawn down over his eyes, like something I said didn't make any sense. I scanned the other faces around me, and realized that everyone was looking at me like I'd lost my mind.

"Dimples just asked me a question, and I answered it. You did, didn't you?"

"Dimples?" Detective Williams grinned, then cleared his throat like he was trying not to laugh.

"Oh, sorry. I couldn't remember his name, and you have to admit, he's got really big dimples. It's not something you could miss, especially when they spin around like..." I stopped before I made a bigger fool of myself.

Everyone focused on Dimples, and his face turned a bright shade of red. "I'm Detective Harris." He talked to me slowly, like there was something wrong with me. "I've been assigned to your case with Detective Williams." He stuck his hand out, and I took it automatically.

"Shelby Nichols. Nice to meet you," I said, just as slowly. The detective smiled and his dimples got huge again. I choked back a chuckle, and couldn't understand why just looking at him made me a little crazy.

"I was going to ask you if you thought you would recognize him again." Dimples a.k.a. Harris said.

"You did ask me that." At his confused expression I cringed. "Didn't you?"

"No. I was going to, but I hadn't yet."

Detective Williams was growing impatient. "It doesn't matter. I think we understand that she thinks she could identify him." He turned to me. "You're our only lead at the moment since the video feed at the bank only got the back of his head after the mask came off." *It would be great if she could come down to the station and give us a complete description, though. Maybe we could even get an artist's rendering done.*

My breath caught. What was going on? I knew he didn't say the words, but I heard him as if he had. Next, he confirmed it by saying aloud those exact words. The room started to tilt, and I felt the blood drain from my head. I swayed, and Chris grabbed my arm to steady me.

"I think I'd like to go home now."

"Can this wait until tomorrow?" Chris asked. "I think my wife has had enough for one day."

The detectives exchanged glances. "Sure," Dimples said. "We have the general description. Here's my card. I'll call you in the morning and maybe we can set up a time with an artist to get a more complete picture." I watched his face to make sure I heard everything he said. It all came out right. Still, I nodded just to be on the safe side.

I sighed with relief when they left. Chris did too. As he directed me to the car he was worried, and more than a little scared. Just an inch or two to the left and I'd be dead. He'd lose me and what would he do with the kids? Who would make sure they did their homework, and get them to all their practices and games? He couldn't do all that, along with the demands of his job. He'd have to hire a housekeeper or something, and that could cost a lot of money.

What? Where had that come from? I got into the car and tried to stop those depressing thoughts, only to get an instant headache. In pain, I leaned back into the seat and groaned.

"Honey, are you all right?" Chris asked.

"No. Something's drastically wrong with my head."

He chuckled. "Well, yeah. I'm sure those stitches hurt. Come on. Let's get you home."

My brain had to be misfiring or something, and my imagination was running wild. Somehow, I was imagining what I thought other people were thinking. That had to be it. The trauma of getting shot in the head was causing this wild reaction. If I got some good rest, this weirdness was sure to go away.

As soon as we got home, Chris wanted me to go right to bed, but I wanted to see the kids first. Thank goodness he'd called them earlier and explained what had happened.

When we pulled into the driveway, every window in the house blazed with light. Our house was old, but I had fallen in love with it after Chris and I were married. I loved the big front porch and the blossoming cherry trees in the front yard. We'd probably spent more money fixing it up than a new house would have cost, but I knew it was worth all the trouble the moment I walked in and felt safe and warm.

The kids bounded into the living room as soon as they heard us come in. Josh wanted to hear all the gory details. At fourteen going on twenty, it hardly seemed to faze him that I'd nearly been killed. He thought the blood on my shirt and the stitches in my head looked cool. But I could tell it really troubled him, and handling it this way made it easier.

Twelve-year-old Savannah was quiet and subdued. Normally she could talk my ear off, but not tonight. She held me a little tighter than normal, and didn't let go until I reassured her that everything was going to be all right. Her thoughts were jumbled, racing from one idea to the next before the first was completed. I tried to block the noise from my mind and winced. She was so loud. "Can you talk more softly please?"

"Mom, I haven't said anything."

Oh no. She was right. "I'm going to lie down. I think I really need some sleep. Will you guys be okay?"

"Sure, honey. We'll be fine." Chris's brows were drawn together in concern, and Josh and Savannah eyed me with unease. Although none of them said anything, I could practically hear them thinking that I looked terrible. My shoulder-length blond hair was poking up on one side of my head, and I had mascara under my eyes. The blood on my shirt and in my hair, along with my pale face, made me look like a vampire. Or maybe it was vampire food. That seemed to be coming from Josh.

I pasted a big smile on my face, and practically ran to my bedroom. As I shut the door behind me, the barrage of thoughts ceased. Holy crap! What was going on? I was breathing pretty hard, and it took a minute to calm down. I jerked slightly when Chris came to the door, and said he was leaving to get my prescription and something to eat. I told him thanks, and relaxed when his footsteps retreated down the hall. The prescription was what I needed. That, and some sleep, and I would be fine. This craziness would go away.

In the bathroom, I avoided looking in the mirror while I turned on the hot water and wet down a washcloth. When I finally got the courage to look up, a pale wild-eyed version of me looked back. My blue eyes seemed startled, and there wasn't any color in my lips. Kind of like vampire food. My neck and white shirt were covered in blood adding to the effect. Good grief! No wonder they'd looked at me strange.

I spent the next few minutes washing my face and neck, and felt a little better once I was clean. This time when I glanced in the mirror, I looked more like myself, although my eyes still had that haunted look. It was probably because the scene when the gunman shot me kept playing over and over in my head. It was like a re-run that I couldn't get to stop.

I turned out the bathroom light, and, with a calming breath, changed into my pajamas. Sleep was what I needed, and I would be fine in the morning. I crawled into bed and tried to relax, but couldn't do it. I kept seeing the gun pointed at my face, and hearing the crack as it went off. Finally, Chris came in with some water and a pain pill.

"How are you doing?" He sat beside me, his brows drawn together in concern. He thought I looked terrible. "Come here." He pulled me into his arms and gently rubbed my back. "You're safe now." He kissed my forehead, then took my face in his hands and lowered his mouth to mine. The kiss was soft and gentle. Like a broken dam, tears flowed from my eyes. I clung to him and deepened the kiss, needing his warmth and strength.

Breathless, he pulled away. "You really had me worried and I... just don't ever do that to me again. All right?"

"Okay. Sure." I eagerly promised, needing him more than I needed air. The dark images hanging over me were forgotten. "Now get back here and finish what you started."

With a wolfish grin, he took me in his arms.

The next morning, I woke to the sound of the phone ringing. Chris was gone, and for a moment I panicked, wondering if the kids had made it to school. The clock read eight-thirty, and I quickly picked up the phone. My voice cracked, and I had to clear my throat before I could say hello.

"Mrs. Nichols? Sorry, I didn't mean to wake you. This is Detective Harris. Detective Williams and I would like to know if you could come down to the station and help us with an artist's rendering of the suspect."

They didn't waste any time. "I don't know. I just woke up."

"I understand if you're not feeling well. Would it help if we came to your house? We can be there in about forty-five minutes."

"All right... I guess." He thanked me and hung up.

I lay back down, then sat up with a jolt. Forty-five minutes? I should have made them give me at least an hour. What was I thinking? I showered and carefully washed my hair around the stitches since the doctor told me not to get them wet. My head was tender and painful, but I managed to blot my hair dry. At least my dark blond hair was long enough to comb over the stitches, but it took a while to fix it right.

My face was another matter, but I didn't really have time to put on any makeup. At least I'd lost that wild-eyed look. I compromised and applied some lipstick, hoping I didn't look too bad.

As I buttoned up my shirt, the doorbell rang. I hurried to the door, and there was Detective Williams and Dimples, along with a woman I figured was the artist. I invited them in, and the detectives smiled pleasantly. Dimples was surprised at how well I cleaned up. He liked the way my hair covered the stitches, and thought I looked good without makeup. He had no idea my eyes were so blue. I was about to thank him when I realized he hadn't said a word.

I took a step back, and sudden black spots clouded my vision. Williams grabbed my arm, and both of the detectives hurried me to the couch. As I took in big gulps of air, Dimples gently shoved my head between my legs.

"This should help," he said. "You must have stood up too fast or something."

The darkness slowly faded, and the world seemed to right itself. Now was not the time to panic. I managed to sit up, and put a reassuring smile on my face. "Sorry about that. I'm okay now. I guess I'm still a little woozy from yesterday."

"That's understandable," Dimples said, anxiously studying my face. "Are you sure you're okay?"

"Yes," I assured him. He smiled encouragingly, and his whirling dimples instantly caught my attention.

"This is Julie. She's going to do a description for us on her laptop."

It was hard to tear my gaze away from his cheeks. The way his dimples flashed in and out seemed to have a hypnotic effect on me. With an effort I broke the spell, then turned my attention to Julie and gave her a quick nod.

She was a professional, and got right down to business. I concentrated on the questions she asked, and it helped shut out thoughts I didn't want to hear. It also kept me from freaking out.

Every once in a while I could hear Williams suck in a breath, and mild annoyance came through. He was not a patient man. Dimples, on the other hand, was more encouraging. He was basically positive, and that helped a lot. Still, I was having a hard time blocking out some of the random thoughts they were sending.

With all of that going on, it was a surprise to see the artist's finished product. It was basically right, even though I couldn't exactly remember the details. His eyes looked kind of crazy, like something out of a nightmare. Those she got perfect.

Both of the detectives thanked me profusely, and I felt a little guilty at how quickly I ushered them out the door, but darn it, I was barely holding it together. As soon as they left, I shut the door and slumped onto the couch.

What was going on? It wasn't possible to read people's minds. That was insane! How could a simple head wound cause this to happen? Could I hear everyone's thoughts, or just those connected with the robbery?

No, that didn't make sense. Besides the detectives, I'd heard other people as well. Probably even the doctor who sewed up my head yesterday, and last night it was Chris and the kids. At that point, I thought maybe all I needed was a good night's sleep, but now I knew nothing had changed. It hadn't gone away. This was real, and it scared the living daylights out of me.

The phone rang, startling me so much I nearly jumped a foot. When I got my breathing under control, I gingerly picked it up. The caller ID said it was my mom. Would I hear her thoughts over the phone? "Hello?"

"Shelby? Is that you? You sound funny. Are you all right?"

"Oh, sure Mom." I listened to silence, and brightened considerably.

"Well you don't sound fine." Again there was nothing in the pause, and I sighed with relief. "Are you going to answer me?" she continued. "What's going on?"

"Sorry Mom. I thought someone was coming to the door, but they kept walking up the street." I was lying, but it was the only thing I could think of at the moment. "Did Chris call you?"

"Yes, and it's a good thing he did before the paper came. Have you seen it?"

"The newspaper?"

"Oh, never mind," she huffed. "How's your head? Chris said you had to have stitches."

"Yeah, but it's not too bad, although it still hurts some. I'm just a little out of it today, so I thought I'd take it easy."

"That's a good idea. Do you need me to come over?"

"No, not at all. I'll be fine." That came out a little forcefully, but I knew I wasn't ready to face her thoughts.

"Well, call me if you need anything. Don't worry about dinner. I'll fix something, and bring it over later."

"Oh, that's great. Thanks."

We disconnected, and I felt better. At least now I knew I couldn't hear anyone over the phone. I had a sudden vision of being locked in my room, and talking to everyone I knew over the phone, kind of like the people in prison. Yikes. There had to be something else I could do. Maybe all I needed was time. Maybe once my head healed up, it would go away. If I just knew it would get better, I could handle it. Maybe I could make it go away by sheer force of will. The words, "go away and never come back" brought me up short. Where had I heard that before? Now I was driving myself crazy. Get a grip, Shelby.

I wandered into the kitchen for breakfast. I wasn't hungry, but since breakfast is the most important meal of the day, I thought I'd better eat it. I decided to pretend that nothing was wrong. And if it was, maybe there was a bright side to all this. Maybe I could get in one of those poker tournaments, and win a million dollars.

I read the paper while I ate. I was on my second bite of toast when I saw the article. My throat got tight, and I couldn't swallow. There was a picture of me, and the other man who was shot. My picture wasn't bad. I was sitting on a gurney holding a towel to my head, and talking to the nice paramedic. Besides being so nice, he was really good looking.

The other photo showed them loading the man who was shot into the ambulance. All the tubes and medical equipment covered up his face. He looked like he was in bad shape, and I realized that I didn't know if he'd lived or died.

I scanned the article and found out that he was in critical condition. It was a relief to know he was alive, and I really hoped he'd make it. I was surprised to find how thorough the newspaper was. Not only were Dimples and Williams listed as the officers in charge of the investigation, but it also included both my name, and that of the other victim. His name was Carl Rogers, an average guy who just happened to be in the wrong place at the wrong time. Kind of like me.

There were several eyewitness reports, but they were mostly reactions to what had happened. Apparently everyone else had ducked when the shots rang out.

It was hard to believe someone would rob a bank inside a crowded grocery store, but according to the paper, this was the third time in two months this had happened at different stores. Only this time, people got hurt. Poor Carl Rogers. At least my injury was small compared to his.

The phone rang, but this time it was my best friend, Holly. She wanted to know all the gory details, which I felt obligated to tell her. Plus, she would definitely appreciate the cute paramedic part. Talking to Holly was always good therapy. Of course, I left out the fact that I could read minds. I wasn't going to tell anyone about that. They'd think I was crazy, or delusional. Until I told them what they were thinking. Then they'd probably want to stay as far away from me as possible.

I'd barely ended the call when it rang again. This time it was my next door neighbor. When I finished that call, it rang again. It seemed like everyone I knew in the neighborhood had read the newspaper, and wanted to know the whole story. After about the eighth time, I was ready to throw the phone at the wall. I figured an abbreviated version was in line, so the next time it rang, I answered abruptly without checking the caller ID.

"Yes I was shot in the head, but the bullet only grazed me, and I'm still alive. I had to have stitches, but my hair pretty much covers it up, so you won't be able to see any blood. Other than that, I'm doing fine."

"Honey?"

"Oh. Hi Chris."

"I take it you've been getting a lot of phone calls."

"Yeah, only about fifteen or so." I was exaggerating, but by the end of the day it could be true. "But that was the first time I used the shortened version."

"I just thought I'd call to see how you were doing. Did your mom call?"

"Yes, she's bringing dinner tonight. Isn't that nice?"

"Yeah, that's great. Maybe you should turn the phone off."

"That's a great idea. I think I will."

"I'll try and come home a little early. Are you sure you're all right?"

"Yeah, I'm fine. So how early is early?"

"I'll try to be home around five-thirty... unless you need me before that?"

"No, that sounds good." Five-thirty was early for him, and I didn't want to push my luck. We said our goodbyes and I quickly silenced the phone. All that talking had given me a headache, and the stitches didn't feel too good either, so I decided another pain pill was in order. Besides, who knew? Maybe I'd be back to normal after a little nap.

I woke to the back door slamming. That had to be Josh. He always made a grand entrance. "Hey mom! Where are you?" Before I could answer, he was striding into my bedroom full of excitement. He had Chris' brown eyes and my blond hair, and I knew he'd been fighting off the girls since he was ten or eleven.

"Did you see the paper? You're a celebrity! Everyone at school was asking me about it. So did you really see the guy who shot you?"

"Um... yeah. The police came over this morning with an artist for a description."

"Cool. We'll have to be sure and watch the news tonight so we can see what he looks like." Before I could answer, his attention was already wandering. He was hungry, and wanted to play his new video game. He also had a lot of homework that was due tomorrow.

"Why don't you get something to eat, and then start on your homework?"

"I don't have any homework." I arched my brow and narrowed my eyes at him. He frowned. "Okay, I have a little, but I can do it after dinner." He really wanted to play his video game.

"Not tonight. You do your homework first, and then when you're done, you can play your game."

He gave me a sharp look, but reluctantly agreed. As he thought about his homework, he decided he could rush through it pretty quickly. It was a stupid science class anyway. Then he could get together with his friends after dinner.

"And do a good job, or you're grounded from playing your game for the rest of the week, and maybe forever." This time there was anger in his eyes. "What's so stupid about your science class?" I asked.

"What? I never said it was stupid. And how did you know I had homework in science?"

Oops. "It was just a guess. Plus, it seems like you don't like science."

"The teacher's just boring, that's all." He turned to leave, thinking I'd never understand what his life was like, and he wished I would just leave him alone. Why did I have to be so involved in his life anyway? He was old enough that he didn't need anyone telling him what to do.

Wow. That was a surprise. Is that what he really thought? "Hey Josh." I was about to remind him he was only fourteen, but changed my mind at the last minute. "You're a great kid, you know?"

He looked at me like I was a moron, but I wasn't offended because I knew it secretly pleased him. "Whatever. I'm going to get something to eat."

"Okay." I listened to his retreating footsteps, and then took a deep breath. My nap hadn't changed a thing. I could still read minds. And if I wasn't careful, I was going to get in a lot of trouble. How was I going to manage around my family?

Maybe knowing what they were thinking could help me understand them better. But the thing that made shivers run up my spine was realizing I'd know what they thought about me. I mean... really thought. Could I handle it? Especially from Chris?

We hadn't been as close to each other lately. His long hours as a junior partner in a big law firm didn't help. His firm handled all kinds of important cases, which he couldn't always talk about. Now that I thought about it, it seemed like all we had in common anymore were our kids. Most of our conversations were about them, or paying the bills and taking care of the house and yard.

Would I find out that he thought I was boring? Or worse, that he didn't even like spending time with me? I was his wife, sure, but did he see me as anything else? He needed me to take care of the kids and house, but what did he *really* think of me? Was I boring? I didn't think I wanted to know.

I eased out of bed, and hurried into the small room we used as an office. Maybe there was something on the Internet about reading minds that would help me. I googled mental telepathy, and was shocked by all the hits. I even found a how-to book I could buy, but most of the information was based on developing mental telepathy, not stopping it. There were some interesting articles, but nothing more than conjecture. The only thing that looked like it might work was making a hat out of tin foil. I was desperate, but seriously, how would that look?

Savannah came home from dance class, and it was only a matter of minutes before my mother and Chris would be there. Maybe blocking out people's thoughts would be like blocking out background noise. I had done that before, so that was an option. Still, I got out a piece of tin foil just in case.

Chapter 2

Dinner was a disaster.

My mother got there just a few minutes before Chris, and in the process of setting the table and sitting down to eat, I thought I was going to die. With the talking and all the thoughts flying around, I felt like I was drowning in a sea of noise. I never realized how much gibberish everyone had going on in their minds.

My mom thought I looked pale and tired, but what she said was she thought I looked great considering I'd been shot in the head. I guess both things were true, but I was getting tired of hearing about the shot-in-the-head part. It just wasn't that funny to me anymore.

Christopher was genuinely happy to see me looking so good after last night. He was even happier to see the pot roast. When a man's hungry, it's pretty hard to compete with a pot roast. While his attention was on the food, I slipped into the other room and turned on some music. I figured the music would help distract me from hearing unwanted thoughts. I made sure I knew all the words to the playlist so I could sing along in my mind. At least that was the plan.

"Thanks for bringing dinner," I said to my mom. She assured me it was no problem, at the same time thinking about everything she'd had to do to fit it in. It was a lot more work than anyone would ever appreciate, but it was a worthy cause. She just hoped I was all right. She looked at me and smiled, thinking how glad she was I hadn't been killed. She probably would have had to step in, and take care of Chris and the kids.

"So," I said brightly, not wanting to hear any more. "How's everybody doing? How was school?" The kids weren't that talkative, so I turned to Chris. "How was your day, honey?"

It was an effort for him to pull his attention away from his potatoes and gravy. "Good. The case I'm working on will be going to trial next week. We've just about got everything ready."

He took another bite while he thought about an important document that had gone missing. It amazed him how anything ever got done in the office. Brad screwed up the last case, and now it was up to him to redeem them. But how was he supposed to do that when they misplaced important files? Sometimes he just got so angry he could hardly think straight.

I was shocked. None of these thoughts showed up in his expression. He was really angry, and I wished there was something I could do to help. "What is it you're missing?"

That took him by surprise. He wasn't used to me being that sensitive to his comments, and he hadn't said anything was missing.

"Just a file of some information from a witness that was misplaced. I'd like to go over it before the trial. Make sure I'm ready."

That wasn't all of it, but he didn't really want to talk about the case at home. That was one of his priorities, leaving work at work. But he couldn't help thinking about it. Maybe the information was stuck in another file by mistake. He'd have to check it out first thing in the morning. If he could get Kate to help him, he was pretty sure between the two of them they could get to the bottom of it, and she was always willing to help him whenever he needed it. Sometimes even when he didn't.

"Did you know Mom is famous?" Josh asked.

Everyone chimed in about the newspaper article, while I was busy trying to figure out who the hell Kate was. I knew I'd never met her before. Then it came to me. She was the new lawyer they'd just hired. I hadn't been paying attention when Chris told me before, and I had no idea the person they'd hired was a young woman. At least that's how Chris thought of her.

He'd also thought that I was insensitive. He was truly surprised that I was paying attention to what he said. Like I never listened to him. What did he mean by that? Was I really that insensitive to his comments? Did that make me a bad wife? Was Chris disappointed in me? And what about this Kate person? Was something going on with her?

"Shelby?" Mom said. It was strangely quiet.

"Huh?" Everyone was staring at me.

"Why did you put tin foil on your head?" That thought pretty much echoed from everyone.

I must have put it over my head when I was trying to concentrate, and they were being so noisy. With a spasm of embarrassment, I quickly removed it. "I just read about it on the Internet. That it can help head wounds." Josh and Savannah almost bought it, but Mom and Chris thought I was losing it.

"Does your head hurt?" Mom asked, clearly perplexed, but wanting to give me the benefit of the doubt.

I jumped on her explanation. "Yeah, it does. I should probably just take a pain pill, but I don't like to be so out of it."

"You could take some Tylenol," Chris suggested. "Let me get you some." He left the table, worried that the trauma may have affected my reasoning abilities.

They all thought the same thing only with different variations. "Hey, you guys," I smiled. "I'm all right. You don't have to look at me like I've lost my mind or something." I forced a laugh and everyone smiled, relieving some of the tension.

Chris came back with the pills. I smiled while swallowing them, trying to keep things light and cheerful. "Thanks. That should help." I hadn't eaten much, but I didn't really have an appetite anymore. "Will you excuse me? I think I'll go lie down." They all thought that was a good idea, so I didn't feel too guilty about leaving them to clean up.

Once in my room I was far enough away to find it quiet. Whew. I was going to have to work harder at blocking thoughts. It scared me to think that I couldn't be around the people I loved. Reading minds was horrible. There had to be a way I could stop it, or at least block it out. If I couldn't, I just might end up in the loony bin, and that was not an option I wanted to think about.

Chris came in a little while later. He sat on the bed, and pulled me into his arms. His soothing touch calmed me, and I relaxed. I concentrated on how good it felt to hold him, and it helped block his thoughts.

"I've been thinking," he said. "Even though you weren't hurt that bad yesterday, you've still been traumatized. It probably wouldn't hurt to see a therapist about it. I'm sure you're probably feeling vulnerable and scared, and don't even realize it."

I smiled. That was the last thing on my mind, but it was sweet of him to suggest it. I understood that he was trying to explain my strange behavior.

"Why don't you call Dr. Westerman, and see if he can refer you to someone?" he added.

"That's a good idea," I said. "I think this whole thing has kind of stressed me out."

"And it's not resolved. The gunman is still out there. It really makes me mad that they put your name and picture in the paper. Hopefully, once the artist's rendering of the suspect is broadcast on the news, someone will turn him in."

I hadn't even thought about that. "Do you think the gunman would come after me?"

"I doubt it. If he's smart he'll run, but you never know. At least the paper didn't say you were the only eyewitness. Then I'd be worried. Right now he doesn't know how many people can identify him, so I doubt that he'll be concerned about you."

"But I am the only eyewitness. I got a good look at him when everyone else ducked. That's why he shot at me."

Chris tensed. "That's true, but he doesn't know how much the surveillance camera caught on tape, and I don't think Harris would give out that information."

"Who's Harris?"

"You know... the cop with the dimples."

"Oh, right." I'd forgotten his real name. "Dimples."

Chris smiled. "I'll call the police department tomorrow. I want to make sure you're safe. In the meantime, maybe you'd better stay home, or at least don't go anywhere by yourself. Do you think you're still up for the big dinner tomorrow night?"

"The dinner? Oh, I totally forgot. Yes, of course I'm up for it." It was a special dinner from the senior partners in Chris' law firm. When they won a big case, they liked to treat everyone in the office to a celebration dinner. If Kate was there I wouldn't have to ask Chris about her. Then I would know if something was going on. Even though I knew nothing was going on for Chris, she was a different matter entirely.

"Good, because I really don't want to go without you." He kissed me lightly, and then with gentleness, deepened the kiss. I melted inside. He really did love me. When he pulled back we were both a little breathless, and my eyes widened when I caught his thoughts. "I don't want to leave," he said, "but Savannah needs help with her homework."

"I can help her."

"No, you stay here and rest. I'll take care of it."

He shut the door behind him and I relaxed, feeling better. Focusing on other things really did help block all those thoughts. And if there was something more I could do, I was determined to find it. This couldn't be permanent, but until it went away, I had to learn how to make it work.

I rested in bed for a while, but I wasn't sleepy, so I decided to practice my blocking techniques. I wandered into Josh's room where he was playing video games.

"Hey there," I said.

He was annoyed that I was intruding on his game time. "I finished my homework."

"Good."

"So, what's up?" he asked.

"I just wanted to watch you play."

Josh sent me a look of disbelief and shook his head, wondering if I was checking up on him. He couldn't think of any other reason I would suddenly be interested. "There's nothing wrong with this game, so you don't have to worry about me playing it."

"Great, then you won't mind me watching."

He shrugged his shoulders, slightly annoyed, but was soon engrossed in the game. I picked up his thoughts on what he should do next, and concentrated on shutting off whatever it was that let me hear him. After a moment, it began to work. His thoughts faded to an annoying whisper that I couldn't quite understand. Unfortunately, I could only keep it up for about ten minutes because I got a pounding headache. But it was progress, and I hoped it would become easier the more I practiced.

I went to bed soon after that and fell asleep quickly. I didn't wake when Chris came to bed, and was disappointed that I couldn't follow up on those thoughts he'd had earlier. The ones that made me hot all over.

He was gone before I woke the next morning, so I was kind of cranky, but I rationalized that tonight would be different.

I vowed to use my new abilities shamelessly at the party. How else was I supposed to know what was going on at the office? Especially with this Kate person? I smiled, realizing this was the first time I was actually grateful for my mind reading abilities.

The phone rang, and I answered to find Dimples on the other end of the line. After we exchanged pleasantries, he got down to business. "Since the description and drawing went out we've had several tips. We haven't let this out, but we have a suspect in custody. Do you think you could come down to the station and look at a line-up?"

"Of course. When do you want me?"

"Just come as soon as you can."

I rushed to get ready, feeling a big weight lift off my shoulders, and I realized I was more concerned about finding the robber than I thought. I brushed on the minimum amount of make-up for now. Later, before the big dinner, I would take time for the full effect. I still had to figure out what I was going to wear. I had a slinky black dress I'd only worn a few times. It was sexy, but with class, just what I needed for tonight.

Dimples smiled when I arrived, and it brightened my day. He ushered me into the main room where several policemen had their desks. His desk was back in the corner, and he offered me a chair beside it. I tried to block out as much of the noise as I could, and concentrated on Dimples. He enjoyed talking to me, and was looking forward to closing the case. He thought it would look good on his record to make an arrest this fast.

"I hope it works out," I said after I sat down.

"What?"

"That you can make an arrest." Uh-oh. "I mean... it would look good on your record... right?"

Dimples nodded, but his mouth dropped open, and his dimples totally disappeared. He closed his mouth with an effort. "Wow. That was weird. I was just thinking that exact same thing. Do you have ESP or something?"

Should I tell him? Not the whole thing, but maybe a little? With that kind of opening, how could I pass it up? Besides, it would be nice to confide in someone. "You know, I kind of do. You might think this is weird, but sometimes I have premonitions about people. I mean... not all the time of course, but once in a while."

"Really? That's amazing. I've always heard about people who could do that, but I never actually met anyone in person." He studied me for a moment, wondering if I was for real, or just pulling his leg.

"Should we go?" I asked, starting to feel like a specimen under a microscope.

"Oh, yeah. Just give me a moment to get things set up. Can you wait here? It won't take long."

I nodded, and he was out the door in a flash. I hoped I hadn't scared him off. I really liked his dimples, and he seemed pretty nice too.

As I glanced around, I noticed another man who was sitting beside a policeman's desk. Only this guy's hands were cuffed behind him. He noticed me staring, and blew me a kiss. Yuck. The cop told him to mind his own business, and the guy made a face. I wondered what he was in for, and immediately focused on his thoughts.

I heard a string of profanity that made my ears turn red, but then came the real information. He was pretty smug that the cops couldn't hold him. He'd been really careful about fingerprints, and no one would ever know where he'd stashed the goods. The cops had checked his grandmother's property before, and never knew they were standing right on top of it. That root cellar was the best thing he'd ever come across.

I pulled my mind away and took a deep breath. That weasel was in for a rude awakening. I was tempted to go over to the cop and tell him what I'd found out just to see the look on the guy's face, but that wouldn't be very smart of me. Maybe I could leave an anonymous note? No, it was probably better to tell Dimples... in a round-about way of course.

Just then Dimples returned. "Sorry. That took longer than I thought it would. The observation room is this way."

"Um... before we go... you see that guy over there?" I surreptitiously pointed him out, and Dimples nodded. "I got one of my premonitions about him," I whispered. "I don't know what he's here for, but I think he hid some stolen items in a hole or cellar or something on his grandmother's property. You might want to check it out." I could see that Dimples was having a struggle accepting this. He couldn't tell if I was serious.

"I could be wrong, it's just a premonition, but it might not hurt to check."

He could see the logic in that, but how was he going to explain to the other officer how he knew?

"You could just tell him that a neighbor called in because they'd noticed some suspicious activity." Dimples inhaled sharply, and then started coughing. "Are you all right?" I asked.

"Yeah... fine." He swallowed and cleared his throat several times. When his gaze caught mine, he didn't know exactly what to say. Then he called the other officer over and gave him the information, using the reasoning I had given him.

"I don't know how you do it," he said, when the officer left, "but if this pans out..." he shook his head with disbelief. "Come on, we'd better get going."

I followed him down a long hallway and up a flight of stairs. "For your protection you'll be in another room looking through a one-way mirror so the suspect won't see you. We have seven men in the line-up. All you have to do is identify the guy who you think shot you."

He opened a door to a room that was dark inside and framed by a huge window. On the other side about twenty feet away, the men were lined up in a row, and numbers were on the wall above their heads.

Dimples shut the door, and had me sit on a soft chair in front of the window. "Don't worry, they can't see you." He must have sensed the tension that stiffened my shoulders. Through an intercom he told the officer we were ready, and at his command the men turned from one side to the other before facing front again.

I examined each one closely. They were all dressed alike, with the same complexion and dark hair, but number three looked the most like the guy in the bank. Still, I wasn't sure. There was something about him that didn't seem right. But what if it was him and I messed up? "How certain do I have to be?"

"We need to have a positive identification before we can press charges. Unfortunately, the only evidence we have is the mask, but a positive ID would be a step in the right direction. It would help us get a search warrant."

Dimples was pushing for number seven. That guy's hair color seemed too dark, but what if he'd changed it since the robbery? I focused real hard on their thoughts, but the glass was too thick. I wasn't sure it was any of them. "Can you have number three, and number seven, come closer?"

Even then, I couldn't tell. What I needed was the mirror gone, but how could I explain that to Dimples? "I'm just not sure. Is there any way I can look at them without the mirror in the way?" I knew that sounded funny, but Dimples was so eager for me to make an ID that he considered it.

"I can't let them see you." He was disappointed, but then added, "How close do you need to be?" He was thinking about my premonitions.

"I just need to be in the same room. If they all faced the wall so they weren't looking at me, would that work?"

How was he going to explain that?

"You could let me slip in while they were turned for just a few seconds. No one would ever know I was there."

"All right." He couldn't believe he was going to do this. He took me down the hall, and opened the door to the lineup. He left the door open, and asked the policeman in charge to tell them to face the wall. I slipped inside for a second, and scanned their thoughts quickly, lingering on three and seven.

Three was thinking about all the work he had left to do on his desk upstairs, so I knew it wasn't him. Seven was sweating, but not because he'd just robbed a bank. He was running a meth lab in his basement, and was hoping the guys were clearing everything out before the cops got a search warrant. I sighed with disappointment. It wasn't any of them.

I slipped into the hall, and hurried back to the observation room. When Dimples returned, I gave him the bad news. "I'm sorry. None of them are the robber."

Dimples let out a string of profanity, but it was only in his mind so I tried not to look shocked. He led me back to his desk with pursed lips, and kept cursing in his mind. He wasn't taking it well, so I decided to redirect his thoughts.

"But you might want to check out number seven anyway. I think there's something he's real nervous about in his basement." I hoped that was vague enough to make Dimples do something about it.

He sucked in his breath, then scratched his head as he contemplated it. "I don't know. I need probable cause to get a search warrant."

"I think it might be drugs. Has that guy ever been picked up for drugs?" I already knew he had. "Would it hurt anything if I was wrong?"

"Just my reputation." He smiled at me, trying to bring some levity into this weird premonition stuff. It was a little too strange for him, but if I was right, how could he not follow through? Stopping the bad guys was more than a job to him. It was a calling. That was why he had gone into law enforcement in the first place.

We got back to his desk, and he searched my face for signs of insanity. I almost rolled my eyes and told him to knock it off, but instead, I took a deep breath and gave him a confident smile. I decided not to push it. He would do what he felt best.

"I guess I'd better go," I said.

"Thanks for coming down. It's too bad we didn't have him." The phone on his desk rang. "Can you hang on for just a minute?" I nodded, and he picked up the receiver. The conversation wasn't long before he hung up. "That was the hospital. The other victim just died."

"Oh no." The room seemed to shrink around me.

"It's armed robbery and murder now. I've got to go, thanks for coming down. I'll keep you posted."

"Okay." My stomach twisted.

"Oh, and I'll follow up on those 'tips.' I'm real interested to see if they pan out."

"You'll keep it between the two of us, won't you?"

His dimples went crazy when he smiled this time. "I won't tell a soul. Someone might think I was nuts."

I smiled on the way to my car. He didn't know how right he was. On the downside, I felt bad for poor Carl Rogers. I had really hoped he would make it. It was strange to think that he was dead.

I got in my car, surprised to find that it was nearly three o'clock. That visit had taken longer than I realized. All thoughts of the police station fled while I focused on what I needed to do to get ready for tonight. I wanted to look my best, and that meant having plenty of time to fix my hair around my stitches, put on my makeup, and figure out what to wear.

Chris got home late. I was strapping on my black pumps when he came in the bedroom. I sucked in my stomach and frowned. My slinky, black dress seemed a little tight on me, and I wasn't sure I should wear it.

"Hey there," Chris said. "You look nice."

Nice? Is that all? After spending most of the afternoon on my hair and make-up that was all he could say? He turned away and rummaged through the closet looking for his black suit.

"Do you think this dress looks all right?" I asked, calling his attention back to me. "Or do you think it's too tight."

He flicked a glance over his shoulder, then studied me a second. "It's fine. It's a little tight, but it still looks good on you." He figured I must have put on some weight since I wore it last. I wasn't as skinny as I used to be, but everything considered, he thought I looked pretty good for a woman my age, especially after having a couple of kids.

My age? Good grief, how old did he think I was? I was in my mid-thirties and younger than him. Mid-thirties wasn't old. Unless he just thought I looked old. Sometimes women looked older than men, even when they were the same age. Was I like that? I didn't think I had many wrinkles or big bags under my eyes. My skin didn't look sallow did it?

Maybe in this sleeveless dress my arms were baggy. Sure, I wasn't as skinny as I used to be, but I didn't weigh that much.

Suddenly furious, I ran into the bathroom before Chris could see how upset I was. I leaned against the closed door, and took deep breaths to compose myself. Did he really think I looked old? I studied myself critically in the mirror. He was right. I wasn't as young as I used to be. My eyes had a few creases at the corners, but with the foundation I had on, it wasn't too bad. Still, angry tears started to form in my eyes, but I willed them away. I couldn't let tears ruin my makeup.

Wait a minute. What was I thinking? I looked pretty darn good. My hair hung saucily across my well-defined eyebrow and my eyes held that knowing look of how to please a man. Sure I wasn't skinny; but I had curves in all the right places. I was not the girl Chris married. I was a woman, and sexy as hell.

I tried to think rationally. It wasn't his fault he'd hurt my feelings, so it wasn't fair to be angry over something he didn't actually say. At least he didn't think I was fat... then I'd really be mad. Truthfully, I could probably lose a few pounds, but he was nuts if he thought I didn't look good.

I squared my shoulders. I couldn't get this upset over every little thing I heard about myself. Tonight, I had to act like I was normal. I couldn't let my guard down, not even once.

"Sweetie? Are you almost done in there? If we don't leave now we're going to be late."

"Just a minute," I sang out. I pushed down the anger, and replaced it with a little defiance. Then I found the reddest lipstick I had and put it on. Take that "Mr. Looks Fine!"

Chris was sitting on the bed tying his shoes when I came out. This time he really looked at me, and I was rewarded with a low whistle. It must have been the red lipstick. "Oh baby, oh baby," he said with a smile. "Let's go."

On the way to dinner, I told Chris about my trip to the police station. "I'm so disappointed they haven't caught him yet."

"Yeah. I called Harris this afternoon and we talked. He said they were getting tips all the time, but most of them were bogus. He still hoped something would turn up."

"Did he tell you the other man who was shot died today?"

"No." He glanced my way, his brows arched in surprise. "It makes me sick to think that you could have been killed at the grocery store. It also makes me mad. Stupid people like that bank robber should be put away for good." He was thinking of how much he would like to catch the guy and beat him to a pulp, then pump a few bullets into him, and rip off his arms and legs. Wow, he really was mad. It put me in a good mood.

We were only a few minutes late to dinner. While Chris talked to his coworkers, I scanned the room for Kate. I imagined her as the unattractive, serious, brainy type who tried to be as tough and competitive as the men. That way, they wouldn't even notice she was a woman. Or even better, she could be older, and a little on the heavy side. She was happily married, and had a matronly air about her.

All my hopes were dashed when I actually saw the young, flirtatious redhead, who looked like a fashion model for Victoria's Secret. Why did she have to become a lawyer? She wore a spaghetti strap green dress that hit her long legs just above the knee. Her long, auburn hair fell in perfect symmetry over her bare shoulders. I had a vision of her wearing clothes like that to work, and realized this was worse than anything I could have imagined.

As Chris angled me over to meet her, she sized me up in one glance. "Hi Shelby, it's so nice to meet you. I've heard so much about you."

"That's nice." I wanted to add that I hadn't heard a thing about her, but she might take that as a compliment.

"Chris just adores you," she gushed. She was really thinking that I wasn't bad, but Chris could do better. "He's always talking about his wife."

I glanced at Chris. He tried hard not to look at the swell of cleavage above her low neckline and smiled at me, wishing he were somewhere else. He had been dreading this meeting, worried that I would read more into it than there was. Not because of his actions, but because of Kate. She was young and attractive, and seemed to really like working with him. It was a little uncomfortable.

He put his arm around me and drew me close. "Now that you've met her," he told Kate. "You can understand why I like to talk about her. She's an amazing woman."

"Well, I hope we can get to know each other better," she said with a smile that didn't show any warmth. "I'm always looking for new friends. Maybe we could do lunch sometime." She could see how possessive Chris was, but it didn't put her off in the least. Her desire for Chris fell over me like a slap in the face. She wanted him, and it didn't matter that he was happily married.

"That would be great," I said. "How about Monday?" That took her by surprise.

"Uh... sure." Her smile was false, and full of pretense. Deep down, she had no desire to spend any time with me. It was Chris she wanted to spend time with.

"I'm coming into the office to help Chris so that will be perfect." Chris didn't know what I was talking about, but decided to stay out of it. Kate's active mind was already churning with possibilities of how she could use this to her advantage. Maybe she could arrange to be alone with Chris in his office when I showed up.

"What time are you coming in?" she asked, all innocent looking.

"I'm not sure. Does it matter?"

"No, just wondering." She looked at Chris. "Chris and I might be in court, that's all."

Chris was beginning to sense that there was some underlying conflict going on and quickly intervened. "It looks like it's time to eat."

"Oh, you're right." I smiled at him like he was brilliant. "We'd better find our places." I gave Kate a frosty smile, so she'd know I was on to her.

She blinked. "I'd better find my date, but save us a place. It would be nice to sit by the two of you." She wasn't about to let me intimidate her. She was a Lawyer. I was Chris' wife, but, as far as she knew, that was my only accomplishment.

She left before either of us could agree to save her a place, and I felt the same disgruntlement from Chris that I was feeling. "I don't like her," I said, before I could stop myself.

"She's a hard worker." Chris was being diplomatic.

"She's a..." I was going to say slut, but caught myself. "A very attractive woman." That made Chris uneasy. "Is that why you didn't tell me about her?"

"I told you all about her two weeks ago," he said, defensively. He knew he'd covered his bases, and wasn't about to be blamed if I hadn't been paying attention.

"I remember you talking about your new associate, but I had no idea she looked like that."

"Oh? And it would have been better if I'd told you how she looked?"

"Of course not." I certainly didn't want him taking her side. I could tell she bothered him in more ways than he cared to admit. So it was going to be up to me to take care of her. "Let's see if there's room for all of us at Brad and Emily's table."

Chris readily agreed glad to change the subject and anxious to let the episode pass. I made sure we were settled so that Kate had to sit by me and not Chris. When she returned, she was disgruntled that I had out-maneuvered her, but rallied by having her date sit by me so she could see Chris better from her side of the round table. She also wanted him to see as much of her cleavage as possible. She kept leaning over the table, and I had to restrain myself from dumping my ice water down her neck.

Not only was Chris struggling, but Brad was having a hard time too. Emily was grateful Kate was working with Chris, and not her husband. It made me feel better toward Emily to know that she thought Kate was a slut too. Sitting next to me, Kate's date was enjoying the view, and hoping he'd score later.

Disgusted, I withdrew my concentration. I didn't want to hear any more thoughts. I sat back in my chair, and tried to shut it off. The buzz in my mind started to die away until it became an annoying whisper. I could still hear loud thoughts every now and then, but it was bearable. I just wasn't sure how long I could keep it up.

By the time dinner ended, a deep pain that started at the base of my skull began to radiate over the skin of my head to fall behind my eyes. I had to escape, even if it was only for a few minutes. I excused myself from the table, and hurried to the ladies' room. The bathroom door shut and a wall of silence hit me so hard my eyes teared up with relief.

I must have been there for a good ten minutes before Emily came in looking for me. "Oh, there you are," she said. "Chris was wondering if you were all right. He told us about the bank robbery. How's your head?"

"I'm fine. I just needed some time alone. Crowds sometimes get on my nerves."

"I know what you mean." She straightened her dress, and put on some lipstick. "I don't want to alarm you, but I think you'd better get back out there. That new associate, Kate... well she's..." she hesitated, looking for the right words.

"Throwing herself at Chris?" I finished for her.

"To put it bluntly, yes." It was making her sick, and she was grateful it wasn't Brad. Of course Brad wasn't as drop-dead gorgeous as Chris, but for once she didn't mind in the least.

"Thanks for the warning." I hightailed it out of there as fast as I could. Kate's date was at the bar, and she had moved to his chair and was leaning over the table toward Chris. When she saw me approach, she didn't even try to straighten up.

"There she is," she said, with fake concern. "Chris told us about the robbery. Are you sure you're all right?"

She was thinking that it was too bad I didn't die. She could imagine 'consoling' Chris in his grief, and once she had her hands on him it would be easy to seduce him. All it would take was one kiss, and she'd have him begging for more. Especially once he saw her naked. She'd worked hard to get her body to look this good, and now that she'd seen me, she knew there was no competition in that department.

I felt my hands tighten into fists. I'd never hit anyone before, but I'd always figured I could do it if I was mad enough. As I got closer, alarm tightened in her eyes, and she stopped drooling over Chris. She thought I looked kind of crazy, and shrank back into her chair. I stood over her, struggling to get my anger under control.

"Look, honey," Chris said. "It's your favorite. Sit down and have some. It's really good." He pushed the crème brulée toward me, and I let him pull me down into my seat. He could tell that I was furious, and hoped to distract me from making a scene. He didn't understand what was wrong with me, and it scared him. He was also angry with Kate, but he didn't think she knew what she was doing.

I looked into his beautiful dark eyes and let myself relax. "Thanks honey," I said. "It looks really good." I gazed into his eyes for a long moment, wanting him to know I wasn't talking about dessert. He chuckled, suddenly thinking about kissing me right then and there. I couldn't have been more pleased, especially since Kate was watching.

"Well, I'll see you on Monday," she interrupted, trying to get Chris' attention.

"Yes," I answered. "Don't forget our lunch."

"Looking forward to it," she said sweetly, and left to find her date.

Chris knew I was upset about Kate, but it bothered him that I seemed so volatile. He'd never seen me angry enough to almost hit someone. Then it struck him that maybe the stress from the robbery had changed me. Since that incident, I had been acting strange. I wasn't my normal self, and it worried him. He wanted to ask me if I'd made the appointment with a psychologist, but didn't want me to think he thought I was crazy.

I ate my dessert and tried to decide what to do. Should I tell him what was really wrong with me? If I did, how would that affect our relationship? If I didn't, would he know I wasn't being honest with him? Maybe I could say that I was having premonitions, like I told Dimples. How would Chris react to that? Toning down the truth would probably be better than telling him I could read minds. Knowing I could read his thoughts might be too much. I knew I wouldn't like it.

By the time we got into the car and began the drive home, I still didn't know what to do. He didn't either, so he focused on something else. "Kate is kind of hard to take sometimes, but she really is a good lawyer."

I didn't know what to say to that. He took my silence as disagreement and forged on. "She's very professional at work, as well as organized and efficient. And she doesn't seem to mind being the 'go to' person for us." Although when he thought about it, it was probably more for him than anyone else.

"Don't kid yourself." I couldn't keep silent. "She's after you and you know it."

"I do not," he said, offended. "Don't make something out of this that doesn't exist."

"Oh? And the way she's acting doesn't make you uncomfortable?" I had him there.

"Yes it does, but I don't think she knows what she's doing. She's so open and friendly that a lot of men take it the wrong way. She even complained about it to me. I don't think she realizes the effect she has on men."

"Well, that's where you're underestimating her. She knows exactly what she's doing." I couldn't keep the edge from my voice. "She knows how to use her body and looks to get a man, and the man she's after right now, is you."

"What?" There was no way he was going to let me blow this out of proportion. It wasn't fair. "How can you say that? You didn't even talk to her for more than a few minutes. Did she just come right out and tell you?"

"Don't patronize me. This isn't funny."

"I know it's not. I just think you're jumping to conclusions without all the evidence." This was the lawyer in him talking, and once he got going, he was hard to stop.

"Don't you ever have a feeling or a hunch about someone?" I asked.

He considered it. "Sure you can have a hunch about something, but unless it's based on facts, you can be wrong just as many times as you can be right."

"What if I told you that she wished I would have died during the robbery, because it would make it easier for her to worm her way into your life, and your bed?"

"Did she tell you that?" He couldn't imagine Kate saying any such thing.

"Not exactly."

"Then what did she say?"

What could I say? I wanted to tell him the truth, but I didn't think that was wise. In the silence, he began to think that I really needed to see a shrink. He was sure I was about to hit Kate tonight for no reason, and he wondered if I had bottled up my anger over nearly being killed. Or maybe the trauma of the shooting, and the aftermath was making me irrational. Maybe I had a vigilante syndrome of some kind. Something was going on, and he really wanted to know what it was.

"I don't need a shrink, honey. I just need you to trust me about Kate." Oops. I held my breath as he stared at me in shock. He quickly turned his attention back to the road before we hit something. "I mean... I'm sure you're thinking that I'm acting strange, and I really did want to hit Kate, but if you knew what she was thinking, you'd understand." Now I was making it worse. "Not that I knew what she was thinking, but I could tell by the way she'd been throwing herself at you all night. And I wasn't the only one who noticed. Emily thought so too."

Chris took a deep breath as we pulled into the driveway. He couldn't understand any part of my rambling explanation. He thought if I could only hear myself, I'd realize how irrational I sounded. He was more convinced than ever that I needed help. Big time. He gave me a lopsided smile because that was all he could muster under the circumstances.

"That's interesting," he said, hoping to placate my deranged mind. He didn't want to alarm me with an open confrontation, at least not until we got in the house. "Well, let's go inside, shall we?"

"Why? So you can lock me up? I'm not crazy. I mean... I know I've been through a traumatic experience, but it hasn't made me irrational. My mind is working just fine." My heart plummeted, and I was on the verge of tears. I was suddenly desperate, and desperate people sometimes seemed nuts, so I knew I was making a mess of things.

"Calm down, honey." Chris took my hand and squeezed it. "I'm not going to make you do anything you don't want to do. It's just that, ever since the shooting you've been acting different and it's scaring me. I just want you to be all right."

"I am all right," I practically shouted. "Well, no, I guess that's not exactly true. There is something, but I'm afraid you won't like it. That's why I haven't told you." My stomach tightened, but I knew I had to tell him the truth. There was no other way. Not now.

"After I got shot, and they stitched me up, something changed. I don't know how, or why, or what happened, but suddenly I could hear people's thoughts. It was the weirdest thing. And at first, I thought I was going crazy. But it hasn't gone away. It's still there. I can hear what people are thinking."

Chapter 3

Chris thought I was joking at first, then he realized I was serious and began to panic. "That's not possible. No one can read minds. You know, that's not even funny." He didn't believe me, and his panic was turning into anger. Why was I so mad at him that I'd make up some ridiculous story? What was I trying to prove?

"I'm not trying to prove anything, and I know it sounds ridiculous, but please don't be mad at me. Do you think I asked for this? This is the strangest thing that's ever happened to me. It's still hard to take in, but I'm not making this up. I swear!"

"Yeah, right." Chris couldn't take it. His face got that blank look, and he got out of the car and slammed the door, incredulous that I would try to pull something like this on him. He didn't want to think that I was crazy, but he couldn't accept that I had told him the truth either. He shook his head and stalked into the house.

I just sat there with my seatbelt on and watched him go. It felt like all the life had gone out of me, and I couldn't move. I knew I could prove it to him pretty easily, but I didn't really want to. Part of me didn't want to believe it either, and telling him had made me realize how crazy it sounded.

Once I convinced him, what if he decided he couldn't live with it? By telling him had I just made the worst mistake of my life? What if I woke up tomorrow and it was gone? Then he really would think I was nuts.

The front door opened, and Savannah stepped out onto the porch. "Are you coming in?" she yelled. I still felt drained and empty, but somehow mustered the energy to get out of the car.

"Hi sweetheart." I tried to sound normal. "Did you get your homework done?"

She made a face and wondered if that was all I cared about. She had plenty of other stuff going on, but the only thing I ever asked about was her homework.

I almost got back in the car. I was such a failure. Chris was furious and thought I was nuts. Savannah didn't think I cared, and I was sure Josh was upset with me too. I'd nearly lost it at the party, and Chris was probably packing up my clothes to send me to a mental institution. All because of that stupid, murdering robber. Why did this have to happen to me?

"Mom," Savannah whined. "What are you standing there for, come on." I didn't want Savannah to worry, so I pushed my troubles aside, and hurried into the house. I gave her a quick hug, and then asked her what she had been doing all day. Listening to her chatter away, I found a reason to keep going. My family meant more to me than anything, and I wasn't about to let a few problems get in the way. Somehow, things would work out. At least they couldn't get any worse, right?

I found Chris in the study concentrating on the computer. I stood in the doorway until he flicked an annoyed glance at me. "What are you doing?" I asked.

"Just looking things up on the Internet."

"Oh." I would have told him I'd already done that, except he wasn't looking up mind reading or ESP. He was looking up psychosis and schizophrenia. That kind of shocked me. "I'm not psychotic," I blurted, "and I don't have schizophrenia either, so you're just wasting your time."

Oh yeah? He thought.

"Yeah," I said.

He swallowed, and thought in his mind, *so you can just read my thoughts, huh? Well, how about this? I'm thinking about the time we were in Hawaii, and the top of your bikini came flying off when you jumped from the boat.*

I grimaced and said, "Why did you have to pick my most embarrassing moment?"

Because I don't want to believe it's true. How can it be? It's crazy.

"But it is true." I pleaded for him to understand. "I know it sounds crazy, and I don't know how or why it happened. I can hardly believe it myself. All I know is that after I got shot, I could hear people's thoughts."

Damn. He looked at me. "You heard that. Right?" I nodded. *Shit.* "Did you hear that too?" I nodded again. "So you can hear everything I'm thinking?" *How am I ever going to live with this?*

"Not all the time. I've been learning how to block out thoughts. It takes some concentration, but I can do it. And I think I'm getting better at it."

"How does that work?" he asked.

"Well, it's like a switch got triggered in my brain to let me hear thoughts, so if I concentrate on that switch, I can block them out. I did it during dinner tonight, but after a while, it gave me a headache, and I had to leave."

"Is that when you went to the bathroom?"

"Yes."

"Okay." He started to feel better. "So you can control it."

"Uh-huh."

"Let's try it out then. I'll think of something, and you see if you can block it."

"Give me a second." I didn't want to point out the one big flaw in his plan. That I could lie. I wanted him to trust me. "Okay, go ahead." I concentrated really hard and waited. I thought I could hear a really bad rendition of The Star Spangled Banner.

"Did you hear that?" he asked. *You did, didn't you? This is stupid. You could just lie and tell me it worked.*

"Try it again," I interrupted. "Only sing something different."

He rolled his eyes, and I concentrated really hard. This time I got a low buzz, but that was all. When I opened my eyes, I smiled at him. "I didn't hear it. What did you sing?"

"I'm not telling." His brows furrowed together. He was serious.

"Deal. You know, I did have one other idea I haven't tried yet. I'll be right back." I ran downstairs and got my bike helmet.

When Chris saw me, he started to laugh. "Is that why you had tin foil on your head the other day? You thought it would block out thoughts?"

"I thought it was worth a try."

He laughed harder, and couldn't seem to stop. I guess it was kind of funny, but he was getting hysterical. Then he glanced at me with my helmet on, imagining how funny I would look wearing it all the time and laughed even harder.

He held his stomach, and tears leaked from the corners of his eyes. Every time he looked at me, he laughed again. "Honey, you should see yourself."

I decided I'd better take off the helmet before he died of laughter. I guess the strain was getting to him, because it took him a while to calm down. "We should probably go to bed," I suggested. He didn't say anything. "Okay?"

"Didn't you hear me?"

"Nope, I've still got my shields up."

"That sounds like something out of Star Trek." He started to chuckle again. "Shields at fifty percent and holding," he mimicked.

"Please!"

"All right," he sighed, taking a deep breath. "I'll stop. Just do me a favor. Keep your shields up around me. Okay? I need some time to adjust, and I need to know you're not listening to everything I think."

"Believe me. I don't want to hear your thoughts." His eyes widened. "Not that they're bad or anything. I'd just rather not know."

"That's fair. I mean, I don't think I'm thinking bad things, but if I have to watch what I'm thinking all the time, it will drive me insane."

"I understand." I sat on his lap, and ran my fingers through his hair. "This can't last forever. Who knows, maybe tomorrow it will be gone." He put his arms around me, and the tension quietly drained away. I nuzzled his neck before finding his lips. His desire washed over me like an aphrodisiac, and took my breath away. Before long, I couldn't tell where his feelings ended, and mine began. I only knew I was suddenly flooded with throbbing passion. I couldn't get his clothes off fast enough.

He pulled back, a little stunned. What was going on?

I smiled. "I think this might be a fringe benefit that you won't complain about."

He groaned. "Oh baby, oh baby."

Over the weekend I learned what most men thought about. Food, sports, and sex. Not necessarily in that order. I tried hard to block out everyone's thoughts, but it wasn't as easy as I'd hoped. I'd slipped up enough that Chris was growing weary of guarding his thoughts.

On Monday morning, he actually looked forward to going to work, and getting away from me.

It hurt my feelings. "I hope you have a great day at work away from me." I probably shouldn't have said that.

He sucked in his breath. "Shelby..."

"It's okay. You're right. You need a break from me, and I need to work on blocking thoughts so we can get through this." Now Chris felt bad.

"Go," I said, trying to make it up to him. "I'm fine. Oh, and don't forget that I'm coming in today. Remember? I'm going to lunch with Kate."

"Yeah, right. You know I think it's a bad idea."

He actually said what he was thinking. "Yes. But don't worry. I can control myself." I kissed him, and then pushed him out the door before he could protest. We were both walking a fine line, and I didn't want it to get any worse.

After I got the kids off to school, I decided to go jogging for half an hour. I'd sort of wasted the weekend, and if I was really going to diet, I'd better exercise too.

Halfway through my workout, I ran out of energy. Noticing another jogger behind me, I tried to keep up the pace, but he was gaining, and my lungs were on fire.

I rounded the corner to a busy street and started walking, expecting the jogger to pass me at any minute. But when he didn't, I glanced back to see if he was still there. He walked about half a block behind me, and something about him seemed familiar. Had I seen him before? Curious, I looked again, but he was leaning over to tie his shoe, and I couldn't see his face.

I turned forward, and a seed of unease crept up my spine. It was probably nothing, but until they caught the robber, I couldn't help feeling a little bit scared. Maybe I shouldn't be out in the open like this.

A rush of adrenalin kicked in, and I decided to run home, but before I got my legs working, the man blew past me at a fast pace. It startled me so bad that I didn't look up in time to see his face. But I could still study him from behind.

He was tall, at least six-three, and seemed to have lots of muscles. His dark hair curled a little and was long enough to brush the collar of his t-shirt. He was thinking that it was too bad it was such a busy street, and he'd have to figure out a different route next time.

Those were harmless thoughts, right? So why did that creep me out? He kept his pace steady, so that by the time I turned down my street, I could barely see him. I shook my head, knowing I'd probably let my imagination get the best of me, and hurried home.

All that exercise had given me an appetite, but there wasn't anything in the fridge to help me lose weight, so I decided to make a quick run to the grocery store for a case of slim-fast.

As I entered the store it hit me that the last time I'd been here I got shot, and someone else had been fatally wounded. I paused and took in my surroundings. The bank was open for business. There wasn't any crime scene tape, or blood on the floor, or potato chips scattered everywhere. Everything was back to normal. Everything except me.

People passed by me, wishing I would get out of the way, and wondering why I just stood there. Hadn't I ever seen a grocery store before? That broke the spell, and I grabbed a cart, then made my way to the aisle with the slim-fast, knowing it didn't do any good to think about the past, especially when there wasn't much I could do about it.

I concentrated on the dieting aids instead, finding lots of them to choose from. In fact, there were so many that I couldn't decide which program to go with. Maybe one tasted better than another? I finally bought several different kinds, figuring I could try them all, and then stick with the one that tasted the best.

I'm not a superstitious person. Still, I went to the check-out that was as far from the bank as possible. No need to tempt fate. The checker was thinking that I sure had a lot of food for someone on a diet. It was expensive too, but I really wanted to get those extra pounds off.

There she is.

Of all the random thoughts, that one caught my attention, and tightened my stomach with unease. Who was thinking about me? Just then a store manager came up and smiled. "How's your head?"

"Uh... better, thank you." Was it his thoughts I'd heard? I couldn't tell. I looked around but couldn't spot anyone staring.

"Glad to hear it. That was such a terrible thing to have happen. Who would have thought that someone would rob the bank in a grocery store? We have better security now, so something like that shouldn't happen again. Can I help you out to your car?" He'd found out my husband was a lawyer, and was hoping I wouldn't sue the store.

"Sure, that would be great." I knew it would help him feel better, and even though I didn't need his help, it was nice to have company. Not that I was afraid or anything, it was just unsettling to be at the scene of the crime. I mean, the person who shot me could be here right now, and I'd never know.

When I got home, I didn't have a lot of time to get ready, especially if I was going to get to the office before noon. Chris wasn't happy that I was going to lunch with Kate, but if he knew I was doing it for his sake, he'd totally understand.

There was a message on the phone to call Dimples, but that could wait until I got to Chris' office, and it would give me something to do with my time. I quickly showered, but then ended up standing in front of my closet with no idea what to wear.

None of my clothes were the kind a lawyer would wear. Mostly jeans and t-shirts. I finally pulled out a pair of black cotton-cable leggings, and paired them with a red, scoop neck, tunic sweater that I accented with a black belt and black heels. Red is a power color, and with a touch of red lipstick, I felt confident and in control.

It was just after eleven-thirty when I arrived at Chris' office. Even though I expected Kate to be there, it wasn't pleasant to see her working so closely with Chris. She put on a distracted air, like she was too involved to pay much attention to me, but inside she was pleased I'd found her standing so close to Chris. She looked beautiful in her gray tailored suit and white blouse. The skirt seemed a little short, easily showing off her long legs. She also wore a pair of glasses that added an extra allure to her features.

Nervous guilt flowed from Chris. He wasn't happy that she was standing so close to him. It almost looked like I was right about her, and he didn't seem to like that. "Hi, honey," he said. "We'll be a few more minutes, and then you and Kate can go to lunch."

"That's fine. I have to call Dimples, so take your time."

I walked to the other end of the office, and punched in Dimples' number on my cell phone. I didn't want Kate to think I was bothered by her presence, so I gave them plenty of room.

While I was on hold for Dimples, I glanced out of the third story window. Across the street, a man was casually leaning against a light pole. As he looked up at me, our eyes locked. He was tall and muscular, with tan skin, and wavy dark hair that was slicked back behind his ears. His face broke into a huge grin, before he quickly disappeared into the crowd. Had he just smiled at me?

"Hello... hello... is anyone there?" Dimples asked.

"Dimples! The strangest thing just happened. I saw a man jogging this morning, and now I think I just saw him again."

"Shelby? Where are you?"

"I'm at Chris' office. He was standing across the street, and saw me looking out the window."

"Did you get a good look at him?"

"Yes... but it's not the robber. I don't know who this person is."

"Then it's probably nothing."

"Yeah, I guess not." I hated to let it go, but he was probably right. "What did you need to talk to me about?"

"It's just a hunch, but I wanted you to know. Yesterday I spoke to Carl Roger's doctors. They were really surprised that he died. Everything was looking so good, and then the next thing they know, he's dead. Sometimes that happens, but I just can't help wondering if someone helped him along. I mean, besides you, he was the only other person to see the robber's face."

"So... you think the robber did it?"

"I could be wrong, but it doesn't hurt to check. We should get the autopsy results in a few days. Anyway, I just wanted to warn you to be extra careful, just in case."

"You think he might come after me?"

"I don't know. It's a possibility that's crossed my mind, but it's not likely. I'm not trying to scare you. I just want you to be careful."

"Okay. Thanks. Are there any other leads?"

"Yes. We're checking out every lead we've got. It's the same M.O. from the other bank robberies, so we're comparing them, and getting a profile put together."

I wished I could read his mind over the phone so I'd know what was really happening. "So you'll call if anything turns up?"

"Yes. I'll keep in touch. In the meantime, if you see anything suspicious, let me, or Detective Williams know."

I assured him I would, and we disconnected. I gazed out the window and shivered, knowing there was probably a killer out there looking for me. I knew the killer wasn't the man I'd just seen, but it seemed strange that I'd seen this guy twice in one day. Wasn't that something suspicious? This guy probably didn't have anything to do with the robbery, or Dimples would have said something, right? So why was he watching me from the street?

"We're finally done," Chris announced. "And I'm supposed to be in court in fifteen minutes so I've got to run." He gathered up his papers and gave me a quick kiss before walking out the door. "Talk to you later."

"So, where do you want to go?" Kate asked. She smiled pleasantly, but was thinking I looked pretty good in red. It didn't make her happy, but she didn't let it bother her too much, especially since she knew she looked a lot better than I did.

I smiled back, trying not to show how much her thoughts angered me. The conceited little brat...she didn't look that good. With great diplomacy on my part we finally decided on the Italian restaurant down the street.

It was within walking distance, so we made small talk until we got there. After we were seated, she ordered a small dinner salad with the dressing on the side. Not to be outdone, I ordered the same thing with low-fat dressing and a Diet Coke.

"Nice glasses," I said.

"Thanks. I don't really need them, but it helps my image." She smiled. "It's hard for most people to see that there's more to me than my looks. The glasses help them realize I have a brain."

"Oh, right." She made me sick, but I decided to agree with her. "I'm sure it's difficult being a lawyer who looks like a super model."

She smiled brightly. "You're so right. That's what I like so much about working with Chris. He sees beyond my looks, and actually gives me the respect a real colleague should have." It was also what made him so attractive to her. He was the first man she had been attracted to who hadn't been interested in her, and that made him a real challenge.

"What made you want to become a lawyer in the first place?" I asked, wanting to get her mind off my husband before I did something crazy, like grab her around the neck and choke the breath out of her.

"I wanted to help people." But she was really thinking about the billable hours and her Uncle Joey, who'd paid for her schooling in return for her expertise. Uncle Joey had a lot riding on her, and she didn't want to let him down. He paid well too, but that was something no one was supposed to know about.

Naturally, I was dying to know what kind of business Uncle Joey was in.

"So, what do you do?" she asked. She was guessing that I hadn't even finished college. It didn't help that she was right.

"Chris and I have two kids, so I spend a lot of time seeing to their welfare. With school and sports and all their activities, it's a full-time job. I'm also involved with the PTA and my church."

"That's great," she said, thinking how boring it sounded. How could Chris be satisfied with a nobody? "It's nice to see a stay-at-home mom, but don't you ever wish you had your own career?"

"I am actually thinking of starting my own business," I confessed.

"Oh? What?"

"A consulting agency."

"What kind of consulting?" she asked.

"All kinds," I said, confidently. "I have a talent for finding out things, and I think I could use that to help people."

Kate tried hard not to laugh. Did I even know what I was talking about? A consulting business? With what credentials? It would be the only consulting business on record without any clients. Poor Chris, he really deserved better.

The little jerk! It was getting hard for me to keep my cool. She needed to be put in her place, and her constant thoughts of Chris were the last straw.

"Take you, for instance," I continued. "Right now you're trying hard not to laugh at me. You think I'm a nobody, and you're after my husband because he's the first man who hasn't been overcome by your charms and fallen at your feet."

She was speechless. How had I figured that out? She covered it with a show of anger and indignation. "That's slanderous and you're completely wrong. You don't know a thing about me."

"You can think that if it makes you feel better, but I'm warning you. Stay away from my husband."

"Or what?" She narrowed her eyes, calling my bluff.

"I'll tell everyone about Uncle Joey." She turned white, and I was afraid she was going to faint. We locked eyes for a moment before she dropped her gaze to her lap. I had won this round.

Kate stood and placed her napkin on the table. "I guess I'm not so hungry after all." She threw some bills on the table, and then in a low, hard voice said, "This isn't over."

As she stalked out, I allowed myself a small smile. Then I sighed, wondering what I had just done. I wasn't sure I wanted her for an enemy. I mean, who was Uncle Joey anyway? Maybe he was a hit man, and I'd just signed my death contract. My stomach churned. I didn't have much of an appetite either, so I paid the bill, and started back to Chris's office.

With dread, I realized that, as much as I didn't want to, I had to see Kate again. I really needed to get her thinking about Uncle Joey, so I'd know who he was, and if he was someone I needed to watch out for. I also needed to tell Chris about Dimples' phone call and the guy I'd seen twice today.

When I arrived at the office there was no sign of Kate and, to be honest, relief swept over me. Chris hadn't come back from court yet, but a client waited for him in the outer office. The client looked to be in his early forties, and was dressed in a suit. He was thinking about a surveillance camera, and worrying if it was convincing enough to convict the hoodlums who'd cased his shop. I nearly gasped aloud at the staggering amount of insurance money he planned to get, but was saved from making a fool of myself when Chris walked in.

"You're back fast," he said. "How was lunch?"

"Fine. I can see you're busy. I just wanted to tell you I was going home."

He raised his eyebrows and thought, *That bad huh?*

"I'll tell you all about it tonight." I quickly left before the client could wonder about our one-sided conversation. As I passed Kate's office, I could hear her talking on the other side of the door. There were a lot of pauses, so I figured she had to be on the phone. I thought she may have said, "Uncle Joey," but I wasn't sure. The conversation ended, and I decided I'd better get out of there before she caught me listening.

I took the elevator to the parking garage and hesitated, trying to remember where I had parked the van. As I walked across the garage, I heard the familiar catch of an engine as it started. Bright headlights caught me in the face, blinding me. With squealing tires, the car peeled out of the parking space, and came barreling straight for me.

Chapter 4

In the split second before the car hit me, I dove to the side, my mind registering that I knew that face. With dawning terror, I realized it was the bank robber, and he was out to kill me. I rolled across the ground and slid into a parked car. The killer's car screeched around the bend, and I scrambled to get up before he came back to finish me off.

With shaking hands and jelly for legs, I ran back to the elevator and pounded on the call button. "Come on! Come on!" The car rounded the corner toward me, and still the door wasn't opening.

Just as the car pulled up next to me, the elevator doors swished open. I dashed inside and punched the buttons while the robber pointed his gun at me. Before he could get a shot off, the doors slid shut, and I nearly collapsed. Taking huge gulps of air, I slumped against the wall and tried to calm my pounding heart.

In no time at all, the doors slid open and I nearly screamed, thinking I hadn't gone anywhere. Luckily the elevator had moved up a floor, and I realized I had pushed the buttons for all the floors.

I nearly sobbed with relief, but tensed every time the doors opened, wondering if the robber would be waiting there with his gun drawn. When the doors finally slid open on the third floor, I bolted into Chris' office. Luckily, he was alone. He took one look at me, and knew something terrible had happened.

I was so upset I could hardly speak. "He was there... in the parking lot... waiting for me... the robber... he tried to run over me, and then he pulled a gun. It was horrible!"

Chris held me for a moment, then gently pushed me into a chair. "I'll call Detective Harris," he said. "He'll know what to do." He punched in the numbers, and I calmed down a little while they talked, then Dimples wanted to talk to me.

"Are you sure it was him?" he asked.

"Yes. Who else would want to see me dead?" A mental image of Kate popped into my mind, but I dismissed it. She wouldn't try to kill me. At least not yet. If she was smart she'd wait and see if that maniac robber could do it for her.

"Okay, I'll be right there. Stay where you are."

As if I would go anywhere. "He's coming here," I told Chris, and finally started to calm down. As I went over everything that had happened with Chris, Dimples burst into his office.

"What kind of car was he driving?" Dimples asked. "Did you see a license plate number?"

"Umm, no. I think it was black, and on the small side. It happened too fast to see a license plate."

"What kind of car?" When I hesitated, he prompted, "Toyota? Honda? Ford?"

"I don't know cars that well, but it could have been a Honda." At this, Dimples started to get frustrated. His only lead and all I could tell him was a black, on-the-small-side car?

"I'm pretty sure it was black, but it might have been dark green or dark blue," I said. His anger escalated. "You have to remember that it's dark in the parking garage."

I hurried to put up my mental shields, since I didn't want to hear all the swearing that was going on. At least Chris was trying to control his. I couldn't say the same for Dimples. He called in an APB for a small, black car, possibly a Honda, and possibly speeding away from the downtown area.

"All right." Dimples turned to me, trying to be professional. "We have to believe that the killer knows who you are, and where to find you. We can handle this one of two ways. For your protection, we can take you to a safe house for a few days, or, we can put an undercover policeman in your neighborhood to watch the house, and hope the killer comes back and we catch him."

"Using Shelby as bait?" Chris asked. "I don't think so."

"You have to remember that we have practically no leads. Usually by now, we're flooded with calls. But with this case, it's almost like anyone who knows anything is afraid to talk. And there's something else you should know, we think that the other victim didn't die of his wounds. It looks like he was suffocated."

As the implications of that sank in, I made up my mind. "All right, I'm willing to be bait," I said. "But you're forgetting one thing. I've got two kids. What about their safety?"

"I think he only wants you, Shelby. You're the only one who can identify him. I think he'll lay low until the right opportunity comes along."

"Like when I'm out jogging alone?"

"No," Chris jumped in. "I will not let you use Shelby this way. Even if I have to take her out of the country, I'm not going to jeopardize her safety. You're the one who needs to find the killer before anyone else gets hurt."

My heart swelled, but Chris wasn't thinking straight. I didn't want this to drag out forever. I wanted to get on with my life, and finding the killer was the only way. Besides, I had a big advantage. I could read minds. I'd know when he was around. I could make it work.

"Wait, Chris. I think Dimples is right. I want to end this, and I think drawing out the killer is the best way."

Just then, Dimples got a phone call. While he spoke into his phone, I caught Chris' thoughts that I had truly lost my mind, and he wasn't about to go along with any of it.

"They just pulled over a black Honda for speeding through a stop light," Dimples announced. "The driver matches the description. I think it's our man." He rushed out of the office, assuring us that he would call as soon as he knew anything.

"I hope that's really him," I said. "Wouldn't that be great? Then we wouldn't have to worry anymore." Chris was still mad that I was willing to put my life in danger. How could I do that to him and the kids?

"You know, it's not my fault that my life is in danger, but sitting around doing nothing wouldn't solve that. It would just make me crazy. What if they never caught him? How long would I have to put my life on hold? That would be worse."

Now Chris was mad that I'd heard his thoughts. "I thought you weren't going to do that."

I almost denied it, but that would just turn into a big argument. So now what was I supposed to do? "It's silly to argue over this, especially if they've caught him. Let's call a truce and give Dimples some time to do his job. I'll put my shields up so you don't have to worry about what you're thinking. All right?"

Chris took a deep breath, and tried to curb his anger. "Fine," he said, and walked over to sit behind his desk. He picked up some papers and started going over them, still angry, but trying to get over it.

A few minutes passed, and he acted as if I weren't there. I couldn't let him get away with that. "It would help if you gave me something to do."

He knew he was being a jerk, but it was hard to deal with the situation when he was so mad. "I suppose you could key the notes from my interview with Mr. Hodges into my computer for me."

"Was he the guy that was waiting for you earlier?"

"Yes." Chris' stomach growled. He'd missed lunch, and it was all my fault.

"Okay. Give me your laptop, and I'll do it while you go get something to eat." Uh-oh, I did it again.

I thought you said your shields were working?

I acted like I didn't hear that. "Since you're leaving, I'll just sit at your desk." He opened a file and showed me the interview, then moved toward the door.

"Don't go anywhere until I get back," he ordered.

"Okay," I said, trying to look agreeable.

After he left, I took a deep breath, and settled back into his nice, comfortable chair. I hated to admit that I was grateful he was gone, but I needed some time alone so I could regroup. My knee and arm hurt from my fall, and my pants were torn. I lifted the torn material away from my knee and saw blood. It didn't look too bad, so I left it to clean later, and started sifting through his notes.

As I read through them, I realized something didn't add up with Chris' interviews. Mr. Hodges owned a jewelry store that had been broken into. The kids caught on the surveillance tape denied breaking in. They admitted to looking around his shop, but that's all. The search for the jewelry in the kids' homes and personal effects had been fruitless. Mr. Hodges identified them as the robbers, saying he had scared them off that night when he came back to check on something, and the surveillance camera backed him up.

I accessed the video on Chris' computer and realized that the video only showed them entering his store before everything went black. It seemed suspicious to me that they hadn't even tried to disguise their faces. None of the jewelry had been found in pawnshops or anywhere else for that matter. I tried to remember what Mr. Hodges had been thinking when I heard him earlier. He was worried that the video feed would be convincing. He was also excited about the huge amount of insurance money he would get.

Could this be a set-up? The only way I'd know for sure would be to listen to both Mr. Hodges and the kids, but I could do that. This was exciting. I could actually use my new ability for something useful. It would help Chris, and he would be grateful enough that maybe he wouldn't mind so much that I could read his mind.

I finished up, feeling proud of my deductive investigation. When Chris returned, he listened to my explanations easily enough, but wasn't happy with my conclusions.

"I'll have to think about it before I involve you. What you've given me is enough to go on for now, but it will be difficult since my client is Mr. Hodges. I'm working for him you know."

"Oh, I see what you mean."

"This is also Kate's case. I'm just helping her with it."

I didn't like hearing that. "Yes, but if he's the one who stole the jewels from his own store, he should be caught."

"I agree, but we have to be careful how we handle this." He was thinking about client-attorney privilege and all that.

"Right. Well, I still think I should listen to him. It couldn't hurt."

"Let me think about it." He really didn't want me involved, and it bothered me that maybe there was something going on that he didn't want me to know about.

"Are you listening to my thoughts again?" he asked.

I mentally jerked away. "Uh... well, a little. Sorry."

"A little?"

"I know, sorry." I concentrated on putting up my mental shields when the phone rang.

Chris answered, and I could hear Dimples on the other end. He ended the call and turned to me. "They got him. He wants you to come down to the station to identify him."

"Does he think it's the robber?"

"He sounded pretty positive, but he didn't say for sure. How about I walk you to the van? As much as I'd like to go with you, I've got a lot of catching up to do here. You'll be okay without me, right? If it's not him, I want to know. I want to be included in where we go from here with the police." He still wasn't sold on the idea that I should act as bait.

"Sure, that's okay. I just hope it's him." All the way to the car, I kept my shields up, but it was hard, especially since Chris didn't say much, and I wanted to know what he was thinking. We talked about the kids for a minute, but when the elevator doors opened into the garage, I automatically moved behind Chris. Unreasonably nervous, I held onto his arm. He helped me into the van, then leaned over and kissed me.

"It'll be okay," he said, sensing my anxiety. "Call me as soon as you know anything."

I drove away with him watching, and the tension began to fade. So far, so good. No deranged killers aiming guns at me, or trying to run me over. I sighed. What the heck was I so worried about anyway? The killer was in custody, right?

As I turned onto the street, I began to relax. The police station was only a few blocks away and soon, this horrible chapter in my life would be over. I checked the rearview mirror, and did a double-take. There he was. The man I'd seen while jogging this morning, and again from the window of Chris's office. My spine tingled, and I shivered with apprehension. Three times in one day? This couldn't be a coincidence.

Intent on watching the man behind me, I totally missed the car zooming through traffic until it came right at me. As the driver turned the wheel I yelped, then braced myself against steering wheel as he smashed into the front end of my car. The impact sent both our cars flying off the side of the road and into the parking meters.

The grinding crunch and shattering glass still rang in my ears as I glanced out of my broken window. I stared in confused horror to see the killer, who was supposed to be in jail, jumping out of his car and aiming his gun in my direction.

As he fired the first shot, I quickly ducked, and scrambled to get out of my seatbelt. I frantically pushed at the button until it unlocked, and I dove toward the passenger side door. With strength born of desperation, I manhandled it open, and crawled out.

Gunfire erupted, and I fell to the pavement on my hands and knees, trying to keep low. I heard the crunch of glass, and knew he was coming around the van to finish me off. Terrified, I lurched to my feet, and took off running.

I dodged around the building for cover, and ran as fast as I could down a secluded driveway. I heard his footsteps pounding on the pavement right behind me and willed my legs to move faster, but he was gaining. As his arms closed around me, I screamed in terror.

We tumbled to the ground, and I twisted to get away, but he pinned me tightly with his body. He loomed over me, and his face froze in a mask of rage. As he brought the gun to my head, I knew it was over. Suddenly, a loud crack boomed and he jerked from the impact. A rapid stream of blood gushed from his neck, and the gun slipped from his weakened fingers. His eyes widened in surprise and he toppled over.

I couldn't breathe. What had just happened? Was he dead? Who killed him? Was I next? The man who'd been following me all day came to my side. He pushed the killer away from me with his foot, and holstered his gun. I finally got some air into my lungs, and tried not to get hysterical. My rescuer pulled me to my feet. With his arm holding me securely, he walked me away from the dead body.

I shook so badly that I didn't notice the direction we were headed. When I finally realized he was taking me into the parking garage, instead of back to the street, I started to protest, but he clamped his hold firmly, and in a no-nonsense voice, told me to keep walking.

As he pushed me into the driver's side of an unlocked car, I heard sirens in the distance. All of a sudden, my dazed brain started to function, and I tried to get out. Before I knew how he did it, my wrists were in handcuffs, and shackled to the passenger door.

He jumped into the driver's seat and I found my voice. "What are you doing?" He didn't answer, so I tried again. "Who are you?"

"Let's just say I'm a friend of a friend."

"You just killed that man. Why did you do that?"

He was thinking that he'd just saved my life, so what did it matter. Then he smiled politely and explained. "Just doing my job."

My heart stuttered with paralyzing fear, and I nearly wet my pants. "Your job? You mean like... like..." I couldn't finish.

"A hired gun? Yes, you could say that." There was a hint of pride in his voice. "Although I use the term loosely. You see Shorty back there was getting out of control, and my boss was afraid he'd spill his guts if he ever got caught. I knew the only way I'd find him was to keep an eye on you, and look what happened. It paid off." He smiled like he'd just won the lottery. "Under normal circumstances, I would have disappeared, but it seems my boss has taken a sudden interest in you."

"Me?" I squeaked. "Why? I didn't do anything."

"Babe, I just follow orders, but don't worry too much. He's not an unreasonable person." He was thinking that I'd be lucky to get out of this alive.

"Who's your boss?"

"You'll find out soon enough. I'm taking you to meet him right now." Then he started singing a country western song in his mind, something about escaping the devil on the long road to hell, and I quickly put up my mental shields.

I sat there in a daze. I had just escaped death, but what was going to happen now? I tried not to panic, but my stomach started twisting. I jerked on the handcuffs, but that was an exercise in futility. Fear made my stomach roil, and since I didn't want to throw up, I decided to accentuate the positive. I was still alive. That was good. And there had to be a chance I could survive. A hired gun wouldn't save me, just to kill me, right?

I glanced at him, trying to ascertain if he was the type that could kill a helpless woman in cold blood. There was a scar over his right eyebrow and his chiseled features seemed carved from stone. His size alone was intimidating, and I cringed at the realization that there was nothing soft about this guy.

We drove across town, and soon pulled in front of a large estate. The security guard opened the gate and waved us through. We drove about half a mile to the huge mansion sitting on top of a small hill. An armed guard dressed in black hurried from the house. He opened my door, and I nearly tumbled onto the pavement. The hired gunman threw him the keys, and he unlocked my cuffs.

I could have bolted, but I didn't feel like being tackled again. Instead, I squared my shoulders, and walked with all the dignity I could muster toward the house. I kept my shields up, not wanting to know my fate. I had already faced death once, how much worse could it get?

The large foyer opened into a beautiful room decorated with antique furniture and huge oil paintings. Flower arrangements dotted the mahogany tables, and Persian rugs covered the beautiful hardwood floor.

All this opulence rolled over me as I continued down the hall. We stopped in front of a door, and were soon admitted into a smaller, but no less elegantly appointed study. At once, the man sitting behind the desk rose to greet us with an interested smile. He was tall and well built, dressed in a dark, expensive business suit and gray shirt. He looked to be in his mid-to-late sixties, and had a beautiful mane of silver hair that contrasted starkly with his black, bushy eyebrows.

"Ah," he said, and came toward me. "You must be Shelby."

How did he know that? I dropped my shields and got a shocking revelation. "You're Uncle Joey?!"

He laughed indulgently, but really hated me calling him that, and I knew I'd made a huge mistake. "I'm gonna die," I mumbled.

The hired gunman mentally agreed with me, and it suddenly made me mad. Since I couldn't tell him to shut up, I sent him a killer look. You know... the kind I reserve for when my kids are misbehaving. It must have had an effect, because he was struggling not to feel guilty, and he hadn't felt that way in years.

"Please Shelby, sit down. Ramos, why don't you pour Shelby a glass of water? I'm sure she's thirsty after her ordeal." He thought the garbage in my hair added a certain charm to my torn pants, and dirty sweater. I smoothed out my hair, delighted when a glob of gunk fell onto his floor.

He glanced sharply at my smug face, and I wondered if I had just made another mistake. I sat up straight, and tried to look innocent, although I was furious with Kate for getting me into this.

"Thank you Ramos," Uncle Joey said. "Please wait outside. I have something important to discuss with Shelby. You might say it's a matter of life and death." He smiled at his stupid joke, and I shrank back in my seat.

"When Kate called me this afternoon she was pretty upset. I don't like to see her upset. Her face gets all splotchy. It must have something to do with her complexion. You know how redheads are. Anyway, she posed an interesting question. One that I'm hoping you have the answer to."

"What?" I couldn't fathom what he wanted of me.

"How did you know I was involved in Kate's life? Who told you about me?" At the puzzled expression on my face he continued. "Whoever you're protecting, it won't do them any good, so you might as well tell me, and save yourself a lot of trouble."

My stomach twisted, and a feeling of doom settled over me. What in the world was I going to tell him? He looked at me expectantly, so I thought I'd better say something. "What makes you think Kate didn't let it slip?"

He smiled chidingly. "Kate knows better than that. The only person who might have checked into her background is someone from her office. Your husband maybe?"

I blanched. "No. He doesn't know anything." Uncle Joey raised his brows. He hoped he wouldn't have to do something too drastic, like rip off my thumbs.

Yikes! Would he really do that?

"Look," I said, frantically. "I really don't know anything. I don't know who you are, or what you do, or who you do it to, or anything." I was babbling, but I couldn't seem to stop. "I don't know how you're involved with Kate, except that you paid for all of her schooling, but that doesn't mean anything. A lot of times an Aunt or Uncle will help with a niece's education, right?"

Uncle Joey scowled. He was thinking that he wasn't her uncle, and it bothered him that I kept calling him that. He only allowed Kate to use it to keep her happy and ignorant. "You're not answering my question. I'll give you one more chance." He smiled, but anger simmered under that calm exterior. "You'd better tell me the truth now, while you've still got all your fingers."

I swallowed. He was serious. "And after that are you going to kill me?"

"Of course not. All I need is a name, then you'll be free to go to your home in the avenues with your husband and two children."

My blood ran cold. He knew all about my family and me. He was thinking he didn't want to kill me, but at this point, he didn't have a choice. Once I gave him what he wanted, he'd have Ramos take care of it. Make it look like an accident. Like that brunette that got on his nerves. He couldn't remember her name, something like Amanda. Then he realized that getting rid of me would make Kate happy, and that seemed to help him make up his mind.

Something inside me snapped. It must have been the part about making Kate happy that did it. "You dirty, rotten liar! You have no intention of letting me go home. You're going to tell Ramos to make it look like an accident. The same as what's her name Amanda. And then you have the gall to think that killing me will make Kate happy? Well, I've got news for you. Chris wouldn't want Kate even if I was dead! And just what makes her so special anyway? I mean... if you're not her Uncle, then who are you?"

Uncle Joey's eyes bulged. No one had ever talked to him like that before. Then he seemed to grasp what I had just said. "You... how...?"

I was still shaking with indignation, but I took a quick breath, and pulled myself together. "I read your mind."

"That's impossible." He didn't believe me, despite the overwhelming evidence.

"I used to think that too. But I can hear your thoughts just as plain as if you were speaking aloud. Right now you're thinking one of us is crazy, and it had better be me."

His mouth dropped open in wonder, and he stared at me like I had just grown two heads. Then his eyes tightened with speculation, and he began to envision all of the things I could do for him. Useful things, like finding out who was cheating or lying to him. His mind whipped through half a dozen different scenarios, too fast for me to catch them all, but leaving no doubt as to what he wanted from me.

"Oh no, you don't." I panicked. "I won't do it."

His mouth turned into a self-satisfied smile, and his eyes gleamed. He knew he had the upper hand and relished it. "Maybe not for your own life. But what about Chris and your children? I think you'd be willing to do anything to keep them safe."

The cruelty of his words was like a punch in the stomach. He wouldn't hesitate to follow through on his threat, and it sickened me. I slumped in my chair, defeated and drained. I couldn't let him hurt my family.

Then somewhere deep inside, an idea blossomed. There had to be a way I could turn the tables on him. He couldn't guard his thoughts any better than anyone else. At some point, I would catch him. It might take a while, but if I had to play this game, somehow I'd figure something out, and nail him to the wall.

I squared my shoulders and looked him directly in the eyes. "It doesn't look like I have much of a choice."

"I'm glad you understand." He was giddy with joy, and didn't seem to mind that I knew. "Think of it as insurance. And if things work well between us, I'm more than happy to compensate you for your time."

"I don't think I want your dirty money."

"That's what they all say, but sooner or later you'll come around." He kept chuckling at his good luck, and it was making me sick, so I decided to throw a damper on things.

"There's something you should know. This mind reading thing just started a few days ago. It happened after I got shot during the robbery your friend 'Shorty' pulled. I don't know how long it's going to last. Some morning I might wake up and it will be gone."

Under the circumstances, he didn't think I was telling the truth. "We'll deal with that when, and if, it happens. For now, we've got to get you back to your family without anyone knowing where you've been. I'll make a few phone calls and have Ramos drop you off at the hospital."

"The hospital? Why?"

"Listen carefully. We'll say it happened this way. After the killer was shot, you got hysterical and ran from the scene. You were afraid that the man who killed the killer was after you, so you hid inside a dumpster until you felt safe enough to come out. That's when Ramos found you wandering the streets. Thinking you were nuts, he gave you a ride to the hospital, where they figured out who you were and called the police." He settled back in his chair, immensely pleased with himself. "Stick to that story, and everything will be all right. Got it?"

"I guess." I hated this, especially the being-nuts-part.

"Good. I'll call you when I need you, and I'll try to keep our appointments during the day when your kids aren't home. Less explaining that way."

"You're not going to tell anyone else about my mind reading skills are you?"

"Of course not. We'll keep this between the two of us. It'll be our little secret." Ugh. He was making me sick. He got my cell phone number, and made me promise to keep my cell phone on and with me at all times.

Then it was over, and I actually walked out of there alive. Ramos helped me into the car. He was impressed that I was still alive too, and wondered what kind of bargain I'd made with the big boss. After shadowing me for the last few days, he couldn't think of a single thing. It kind of hurt my feelings, and I wanted to tell him that I wasn't totally worthless. But in view of all that had happened, I decided to keep my mouth shut.

At the hospital, Ramos pulled the car around back. A man standing in the shadows came out rolling a wheelchair. Ramos insisted I get in, and while I was complaining, the other guy stuck me with a needle. I yelped. How did I not see that coming? The next thing I knew I couldn't seem to keep my eyes open.

Through a hazy fog, I somehow ended up on a bed in the emergency room. It wasn't long before my mind cleared, and Dimples arrived, followed by my frantic husband. The doctor came in behind them. As Chris hugged me, the doctor explained that I was in a state of shock, and they had given me a sedative to calm me down.

Other than that, and a few bruises, I was just fine. They'd cleaned the cuts and scrapes on my knees, along with the blood splatters they'd found on my neck and face from the shooting. I was appalled at the ease with which Uncle Joey had organized this. How many doctors did he know anyway?

"Can you tell us what happened?" Dimples asked the million-dollar question.

As succinctly as I could, I explained the car accident, and how the robber tried to kill me by ramming my car and shooting at me. I stayed as close to the truth as I dared, telling them a man I barely glimpsed killed him and I fled, thinking that man was after me.

They seemed to accept that things were fuzzy after that. I kept to Uncle Joey's story, and the hospital's records backed me up, which I have to admit was freaking me out. They released me soon after my explanation, and I was eager to get out of there.

Chris was subdued on the way home. He felt guilty about what had happened to me. After the close call in the parking garage, he should have taken me to the police station himself. It was hard to believe that this was the third time I'd nearly been killed.

"Hey," I said, wanting to find the bright side. "It's not your fault. Look at it this way. At least that guy won't be after me anymore." My comment was met by silence and I cringed.

"I keep forgetting you can 'hear' me," Chris said. He wasn't happy about that either.

"Sorry," I quickly apologized. "Whatever they gave me at the hospital makes it hard to concentrate. I'll have to work on that."

"No, it's okay. You just rest. It's been a hard day. We'll be home in a minute."

I wanted to reassure him that he would never have to come to the hospital to get me again, but now that I was involved with Uncle Joey, I couldn't guarantee anything.

All at once, I wanted to tell Chris the truth about everything. It would feel so good to share this awful predicament with him. But I held back, knowing I couldn't risk it. Chris would probably confront Kate, and it could only get worse from there. Maybe later, once I got something on Uncle Joey, Chris could help me.

We got home, and I stifled a cry of pain when I got out of the car. My whole left side was bruised from the car accident, and my knees and elbows were scraped from being tackled. When Chris offered me a pain pill, I gratefully accepted, and let the drug ease me into a restless sleep.

Chapter 5

The next morning, I stayed in bed until after ten. I would have lounged around longer, but my stomach growled with hunger. After eating breakfast and taking a quick shower, I was starting to feel almost normal. The sun was shining, and it was a beautiful spring day. Maybe things weren't so bad after all.

The phone rang and I tensed. Then I realized Uncle Joey would only call on my cell phone, so there was nothing to worry about.

"How are you feeling?" Chris asked.

"Better," I replied. "At least I slept well. I just didn't want to get up."

"It's been a rough few days."

"Yeah, no kidding." That was an understatement, and I hoped to never repeat days like that for the rest of my life.

"You remember the jeweler we talked about yesterday? Mr. Hodges?" Chris asked.

"Sure." It seemed like years had passed since then.

"He's coming by at three o'clock today, and I wondered if you wanted to come and sit in on our conference. It might help you get your mind off your troubles. Plus, I think it would be beneficial to know what he's thinking. Might as well put your new abilities to work, you know?"

"Right," I replied, although I wondered what made Chris change his mind. Yesterday he didn't want me involved. "I can come, but you're forgetting that I don't have a car."

"Yes you do. I got a ride to work and left mine in case you needed it."

"Oh? Who picked you up?" His pause made me suspicious, and my heart lurched.

"It was Kate," he admitted. "She doesn't live too far from us, and since it's practically on her way, she was glad to pick me up. You really should have seen her yesterday. When I told her you'd disappeared, her face went white as a sheet. This morning, when I called and told her what had happened, she was happy to help out."

"I'll bet." I couldn't keep the sarcasm out of my voice.

"Shelby, I don't think you need to worry about her anymore. I think whatever you said yesterday made a big impression."

Right, big enough that she'd called Uncle Joey on me and nearly got me killed. Of course, I couldn't say that to Chris. "I don't care. I don't want you going anywhere with her." My tone of voice must have warned him how mad I was, because he didn't argue with me. "I'll come in at three, but I'm going to leave your car with you, and get me a rental."

"I don't think our insurance covers that," he objected.

"I'll call them and work it out."

"But I'm pretty sure they don't cover it." When I didn't reply he continued. "Why are you being so stubborn about this? There's nothing going on."

"See you soon." I ended the call, not wanting to discuss how stubborn I was. If he only knew what was really happening, he'd understand.

I called our insurance company, and found out that Chris was right. If I wanted a rental, I'd have to pay for it myself, which in my estimation was better than Chris riding with Kate any day.

As I searched the Internet for rentals, my phone rang again. This time it was Dimples. "Can you come down to the station and make a statement? I promise it won't take long."

I really didn't want to go, but since I was going downtown anyway, I might as well get it over with. "All right, but it will take me at least an hour to get ready." He thanked me and disconnected.

I resumed my search, and cringed when the phone rang again. At this rate, I'd never get out the door. I was tempted not to answer it, but the caller ID said it was from Thrasher Development Inc., and I'd never heard of them. "Hello?"

"Hello Shelby." My stomach dropped. It was Uncle Joey. "How are you today?" When I didn't answer he continued. "I take it you're surprised to hear from me."

By then I'd gotten my breathing under control. "I thought you were supposed to call my cell phone, not the land line."

He chuckled. "Yes, well since I knew you were home alone, I didn't think it mattered." He let that sink in. "I have a question for you. Does this mind thing work over the phone?"

"No," I said, quickly.

"So you have to be in the same room?"

"Pretty much. I've never really tested how far away I can be, but it's harder the further away I am. And it doesn't work through glass."

"I see. Then you'll just have to come to the meeting I've got set up for tomorrow morning. I'll need you in my office at ten-thirty."

"That's going to be difficult," I said, glad to have a reason to refuse him. "Yesterday my car got totaled by a murderous killer, and I don't have any transportation until I get a new one."

"Don't worry about it," he said after a second. "I'll take care of it."

"What do you mean by take care of it?" After yesterday, I didn't particularly like the way he took care of things.

"I'll have someone drop off a car for you until you get another one. Do you need it today?"

What was I supposed to say? If I agreed, I could tell Chris it was a rental, and I had figured out a way to get the insurance company to pay. That way, he wouldn't need a ride from Kate, and it wouldn't cost me anything. "Chris left me his, but I was going to take it back to him at his office around three this afternoon."

"Then I'll have a car waiting for you in his parking garage. Inside the car, I'll leave instructions for your visit tomorrow. Anything else?"

"Yes." I decided I'd better tell him what was on my mind before I lost my nerve, especially since he was being so accommodating. "When I help you out, I was wondering if I could be hiding somewhere in the room where no one can see me. Maybe I could talk into a mic, and you could wear an earpiece or something. That way I could tell you what they're thinking while you're talking to them."

"Hmm… that's a possibility, but depending on the circumstances, you might just have to come with me, and give me your impressions later."

"But when it's in your office, I could get situated ahead of time, couldn't I?"

"Let me think about it." He disconnected before I could say another word.

I sighed, and tried to relax my shoulders. If I had to be involved with Uncle Joey, the fewer people who saw me the better, and if he wouldn't let me hide, a disguise might be just what I needed. A wig and some glasses would probably do the trick. Besides, I'd always wanted to see how I'd look with a different hair color and style. As long as it wasn't red.

As I drove to the police station, I wondered how Uncle Joey was going to accomplish the logistics of getting me a car. Of course, after pulling strings last night at the hospital, I had no doubt he could do it. My stomach churned, I was in way over my head. How was I ever going to get out of this? Even more important; how was I going to get out of this alive?

I got to the police station right after lunch. Dimples was glad to see me. He felt guilty after yesterday's fiasco, and was glad I hadn't been killed. If only he knew. He told me the killer's name was Tony Palmatti, and he had a record a mile long.

"Did this guy have any ties to organized crime?" I asked.

My question took Dimples by surprise. "I haven't really looked into his background. Why do you ask?"

Now it was my turn to squirm. "Oh, I don't know. With his record, there might be some ties to other unsolved crimes. That would be good, wouldn't it?" Dimples nodded and I plunged ahead. "Is organized crime very big here?"

"Let's just say we know it's here, but unfortunately, we've never been able to get to the man on top."

"Do you know who he is?"

"Why are you so interested?" he asked.

"I was just wondering if all those things you see on TV shows are based on fact," I said, hoping it sounded reasonable. "So do you know who the big boss is?"

"We have an idea." The name that popped into his head was Joey "The Knife" Manetto.

My heart sank, but it was what I'd expected, only not "The Knife" part. I wondered what he did to earn that nickname. I shook my head. Better not to even go there. I put on a happy smile like nothing was wrong. "Good. Well, I guess I'd better get going."

"Hey, thanks for coming down. Oh, by the way, you remember that guy you had a premonition about?" I nodded and he continued. "Well, you were right. He really did have a meth lab in his basement."

"Oh, that's great... I mean not that it's great he had a meth lab, but that you caught him."

"I know what you mean," Dimples smiled. "It made me wonder if maybe you wouldn't mind coming down here once in a while to help with some of these hard cases. You know... the ones without any leads? What do you think?"

"Sure," I replied. Just watching those dimples zoom in and out was enough to keep me around, but on the practical side, I might as well help the good guys too.

Dimples was grateful, and said he'd give me a call when something came up. It gave me hope that when I had something on Uncle Joey, I could call on him, and he would help me no matter how crazy I sounded.

I left feeling happier than I had all morning, and I had plenty of time to do some shopping before the meeting with Chris and Mr. Hodges. I found a wig store and, after trying on several different styles and colors, decided to go with a chin-length wedge-cut wig that was almost black and had bangs. It covered the shape of my face, and the bangs made my eyes look bigger. I wore it to the jewelry shop so I could get some fake glasses that matched. It crossed my mind that Kate looked good in her glasses, but that didn't have anything to do with why I wanted to wear glasses.

I loved the black frames I found. And, looking in the mirror, I even felt a tiny bit wicked in my new disguise. It must be true what they say about wearing a mask. That it gives the wearer a sense of freedom. It might be fun if the reason for wearing it in the first place didn't turn my stomach. All at once, my little shopping trip didn't seem so fun anymore.

I stashed the wig and glasses in the trunk of the car before I left for the office. I got there a little early, and couldn't help the shiver of fear when I pulled into the parking garage. Was it just yesterday that I nearly got killed? I looked around, wondering if Uncle Joey had left a car for me, and if so, where it was.

I got out of my car and made a beeline for the elevator. When the doors closed I sighed with relief, then jerked in alarm when they suddenly swished open again. Ramos stood there, holding something in his hand. I froze for a moment, thinking it was a gun, and this time, he was going to kill me.

"Hey babe," Ramos took in my white, frightened face. "Didn't the boss tell you about the car?"

"Ye...s," I managed to whisper.

"Okay," he said slowly. "Here's the key." He stretched his hand toward me and I flinched.

"Th... thanks." I reached for the keys, and tried to smile away my nervous reaction. Ramos felt genuinely sorry for me, but he couldn't really tell me not to worry. He was thinking that if he ever had to kill me, he would make it quick, and promised himself that I would never see it coming.

I suddenly wanted to puke. All over him. And he thought he was being considerate? Give me a break. "Which car is it?" I asked, trying not to sound upset.

"The black one, over there," he pointed it out.

I nodded. "Okay, got it." The smile I gave him didn't reach my eyes. I quickly punched the button, and it amused me to see him jump out of the way when the elevator doors slid closed. It was a small consolation, but I'd take it where I could. I pocketed the keys and wondered if all of Uncle Joey's cars were black. Probably.

I opened the door to Chris' office and froze. Kate stood real close to Chris, with her hands on his chest, and her face only a few inches from his. My breath caught, and hot anger rushed through my veins. What the hell did she think she was doing?

"Excuse me?" I said.

Chris jerked back, his eyes bulging with guilt. Kate's lips curved in satisfaction a moment before she turned her innocent gaze on me.

"Hi Shelby," she purred. "Chris lost a button, and I was trying to sew it on for him. He sure has a hard time standing still."

It didn't take mind reading powers to see where she was headed. "Oh? That's nice of you to come to his rescue," I gushed. "Here, let me finish." I swiftly situated myself between her and Chris, keeping my back to her. The needle had fallen from her fingers when Chris jerked away. I nimbly picked it up, and continued sewing on the button.

Kate backed away. "I'll go get my notes, and then we can go over a few things before Mr. Hodges gets here." At least Kate knew when to retreat, although I could still feel satisfaction emanating from her.

I took a deep breath and counted to ten before I said anything to Chris I'd regret. He kept his silent, but was thinking that I'd never understand or believe him, and saying something would only make him look guilty when he wasn't.

"I'm not mad at you dear," I began. "Kate knew exactly what she was doing. It's part of her scheme to come between us. We'll just have to make sure it doesn't work."

Why did saying that annoy him? Then I realized I wasn't blocking out his thoughts. Oops. I glanced at him, hoping he'd cut me some slack.

"Don't look at me like that," he muttered.

"Like what?"

"Like you're afraid I'm mad or something."

"But you are mad."

Between Kate's shenanigans and my mind-reading, he was mentally tearing his hair out. He had doubts that Kate had 'accidentally' pulled off his loose button, but he wasn't about to tell me that. Unless, of course, I had just read his mind and knew anyway.

His left eyebrow lifted questioningly, and I decided to play dumb. "Here's your keys, I got a rental." I dropped the keys into his hand and continued before he could ask any questions. "I stopped by the police station and filled out a report. Apparently the killer had a record. He may even have ties to organized crime." The door started to open and I whispered, "But don't say anything about this to Kate."

Chris nodded, more confused than anything else. He was beginning to wonder if all the excitement hadn't been too much for me, and I should have stayed home for another day. Kate entered with Mr. Hodges, and Chris introduced us, explaining that I was taking detailed notes for them.

Kate flicked a glance at my notebook and pen, somewhat suspicious, but decided it didn't really matter whether I was there or not. She would proceed as planned. She asked Mr. Hodges several easy questions before dropping the bombshell.

"Mr. Hodges, after seeing the evidence and hearing your account, I would be remiss if I didn't tell you that I think you're lying. There's too many things wrong with the video to support the case. The video looks 'doctored' to me, and that alone would throw suspicion on you. We can probably determine that your store was robbed, but I'm not sure the video feed will be enough to convict the defendants."

Mr. Hodges sucked in his breath, thinking he'd been caught. Then he tried to cover it with indignation. "Somebody robbed my store. Maybe it wasn't those kids, but somebody did it... and it wasn't me."

"Of course not," Kate said smoothly. It was the reaction she'd wanted, but she kept her elation to herself. "The police took photos and fingerprints at the scene. I just received word that a set of prints matched those of one of the defendants. We don't have enough evidence to hold the other two, but with the fingerprints, the video, and your testimony, we'll have a strong case. I'm not sure we'll get a conviction, but I believe it will be enough to convince the insurance company that the jewels were stolen."

She waited a moment while that sank in before asking her final question. "Isn't that what you wanted?" She had him there.

"I need that money to continue my business," he replied. "Otherwise, I'll go bankrupt."

Kate smiled. "Good, then that's what we'll work toward." She stood, signaling that the meeting was over. "I'll get everything together, and get a court date set as soon as possible. I'm sure you'd like to get this settled quickly."

"Yes, that would be wonderful." Hodges stood and beamed at her, his luck was holding out. She was just the person he needed to handle his case. And to top things off, she was real easy on the eyes. He usually didn't like lawyers, but he would make an exception for her.

Easy on the eyes? Give me a break.

"I have a few papers for you to sign in my office, and then we'll be done for the day." Kate expertly maneuvered him out the door. She was thinking that when she got him alone, she'd remind him of his obligation to Uncle Joey, and how much it was going to cost for thinking he could hold out on him.

Poor Hodges. If he was linked to Uncle Joey, no wonder Kate was handling the case. I lost the rest of her thoughts when her office door closed and I almost fell off my chair. I didn't realize how far I'd been leaning over.

"Well?" Chris asked.

Crap. What was I going to say? I couldn't tell Chris about Hodges apparent involvement with Uncle Joey. Or Kate's either. "That was interesting," I hedged. "It looks like he's happy about having Kate for his lawyer. He thinks she's 'real easy on the eyes.'"

Chris let out a huff. "What about the jewels? Did he steal them?"

"You know; he didn't really think about that. He was more interested in getting the insurance money."

Chris looked at me expectantly. *Go on*, he thought.

"From what I could pick up," I continued. "I think he set it up."

"That's what I thought too." Satisfaction rolled off him. "But unless we can find the jewels, we can't do anything about it."

"That's true," I quickly agreed, grateful he wasn't asking anything about Kate.

"Kate would probably agree as well," he said. "But she's a real stickler with the facts, and she won't do anything to jeopardize her client. I'll talk with her... see what she thinks." He almost said 'feel her out,' but luckily, he caught himself.

Since I wasn't supposed to be listening, I let it go. "Okay. Well, if you don't need me anymore I guess I'll head out. I'm kind of tired."

The only thing I'd written in my notebook was 'Uncle Joey' but it was covered with little doodle marks. Still, I didn't want Chris to see it, so I quickly ripped out the page, crumpled it up, and threw it in the garbage.

Chris walked me to the elevator, and said he'd be home soon. I kissed him goodbye and left. It wasn't until I got to the parking garage that I remembered I didn't have a car. Or rather I did, but it wasn't mine. It came to me all at once that Uncle Joey was sinking his claws into me just like he had with Mr. Hodges. Soon, he would own me, lock, stock, and barrel. A sense of doom settled over me. How was I ever going to get out of this?

I found the car by pressing the unlock button, and seeing which car started blinking. When I opened the door, I noticed the manila envelope on the front seat. Inside were detailed instructions of how to get to Uncle Joey's office, what time I should arrive, and even the clothes I was to wear in a bag on the floor. Curious, I pulled them out. First came a short black skirt and black stockings, followed by a black v-neck sweater, and black leather boots. All in my size. Now how did he know that?

I sighed, it must have been intuition that I got a black wig and black glasses... which I had left in the trunk of Chris' car. Hopefully, he wouldn't open it. I figured I could sneak them out later, and realized it was just one more thing I had to worry about.

Driving home, I tried to come up with different scenarios that would get me out of working for Uncle Joey. Being on the inside, something was bound to happen. Although I wasn't sure putting him in jail was good enough to keep my family and me safe. He seemed to have far-reaching friends. Maybe someone at the meeting tomorrow would be thinking about how he wanted to get rid of Uncle Joey, and I could help him out.

I shuddered, wondering if that would be classified as murder. I couldn't be involved in murdering someone, even if it was Uncle Joey. No, somehow, I had to turn the tables on him. I wasn't sure how, but I would figure something out.

It was the only way out of this mess.

Chapter 6

The next morning was rainy and gray. It suited my mood perfectly. The only thing good that happened was that I had lost five pounds because of all the stress. I think I'd rather have the pounds.

I'd managed to get my wig and glasses out of Chris' car the night before, and decided it was time to get ready for the meeting. Dressed in black, with the wig and glasses in place, I looked like one of those spies in the movies. I felt ridiculous and way out of my league, but what could I do?

My back doorbell rang, and I froze as I heard it opening. "Hello?" my mother called. "It's just me. Are you decent?"

What was my mother doing here? "Just about," I yelled. "Give me a minute and I'll be right there." I pulled the wig off and threw the glasses on the dresser. Then I whipped off the skirt, and pulled on a pair of jeans. Mom was coming down the hall when I came out of my bedroom. "Hi mom, what's up?"

"I just brought over some soup for your dinner tonight."

"It's ten o'clock in the morning."

"I know, but I had some time." From her thoughts, I knew she was really mad. "I just heard that you were nearly killed again from Gloria Lundskog down the street. She's the one whose son is a policeman. She knew all about it. Why didn't you tell me? It was so embarrassing that she knew about it, and I didn't." She paused for breath. "Are you all right? How's your head? Did you get hurt? What happened?"

I took a deep breath. "I didn't tell you because I didn't want you to worry, especially since I'm fine. I didn't get hurt or anything."

"Gloria told me that the robber who was chasing you got shot and killed. Right in front of you. She said you were lucky to be alive. Can't you see why I'm upset?"

"Yes. You're right. I should have called. I don't know what I was thinking, except that I probably wasn't. I'm sorry, but everything's fine now. In fact, I was just leaving for a ten-thirty appointment. Can I call you when I get back?"

"Why is your hair all plastered down against your head like that?" she asked. "Especially for an appointment. It looks funny."

My hands flew to my head. "Oh, I was thinking of wearing a hat so I didn't fix my hair." I needed to leave. Now.

"Where are you going?"

"I'm interviewing for a job at Thrasher Development. It's just something part-time, to keep me from getting bored. Anyway, I'll tell you all about it later. Okay?" I walked her to the door. "Oh, and I haven't told Chris about this job yet, so please don't say anything. I thought I'd wait until I decided if I wanted it before I told him."

She arched her eyebrow at me, wondering what I was lying about.

How did she always know? "I've really got to go," I begged.

"Okay," she grumbled. "Don't forget to call me."

"I won't." I practically shoved her out the door, and ran back to my room. I quickly changed and pulled the wig back on my head, taking a minute to adjust it, then I grabbed my glasses and boots. I'd have to put them on in the car.

My heart pounded with anxiety by the time I got onto the freeway. I had fifteen minutes to get there, and it usually took twenty-five. My knuckles had turned white by the time I exited the freeway, and I practically had to peel my hands off the steering wheel at the first stoplight. But I'd made good time.

I turned into the driveway of the parking garage right at ten-thirty and my heart fell. The door was shut. How was I supposed to get in? A car honked behind me, and I nearly jumped out of my skin. I let my foot off the brake and pulled in closer. Something on the car must have triggered the door, because it began to roll up. I took a good look in my rearview mirror, and recognized Ramos. He had a puzzled look on his face, like he didn't know it was me, and I smiled, pleased that my disguise was working.

I found a parking space and put on my boots and lipstick, then straightened my wig. I reached for the door, but it suddenly opened, and I let out a yelp.

"Whoa, babe. It's just me." Ramos said. "Thought I'd help you out of your car since you were taking so long." He pulled the door all the way open and smiled politely, then his smile got bigger. He was enjoying the view of my legs under the short skirt, so I got out as fast as I could. Then I had to lean in to grab my purse. He enjoyed that view even more.

"Stop that!" I whirled around, catching him by surprise.

"What? Uh... sorry." Despite his words, he flushed with guilt, and that puzzled him. It was something he was starting to feel more and more, mostly when he was around me. "What makes you think...?"

"Women's intuition," I answered.

"Oh." That was something he didn't want to touch with a ten-foot pole. "By the way, I like your hair. Did you color it?"

"No, it's a wig." He was confused, so I rushed to explain. "I don't want anyone to know who I am."

"Oh," he said, then smiled and let out a chuckle.

"What's so funny?" But I already knew. He thought it was a little late for that, but he'd give me points for trying. He couldn't wait to see Manetto's reaction when he saw me in the wig and glasses. I was a little ditzy and unpredictable. It made him smile. He liked that.

"Nothing," he answered. Then he felt bad when he realized how hard it was going to be to kill me.

"Oh for Pete's sake!"

"What?"

"Never mind, let's just go."

We took the elevator to the twenty-fifth floor, and entered the big double doors to the suite. I was surprised to find the outer room beautifully decorated in earth tones and wood paneling. The colors made the light fixtures on the wall and ceiling sparkle with warmth. Photographs dotted the walls, and green potted plants added color. The waiting area was comfortably situated with black leather chairs, a coffee table, and a bookcase.

I hadn't expected it to be so nice. In fact, I was thinking it would be in the basement, with a bunch of wooden chairs surrounding a bare hanging lightbulb. The chair under the light would have straps and ankle restraints. And it would be very dark.

"Hello." A woman's cheerful voice broke into my morbid thoughts. "You must be Shelby. I'm Jackie, Mr. Manetto's secretary." She came around her desk and shook my hand with a gracious smile that took me off-guard. How could this nice, classy lady work for someone like Uncle Joey? She must not know what he really did. "You can go in. Mr. Manetto is waiting for you."

Ramos took my elbow and guided me toward another set of double doors. If he hadn't been holding my arm so tight, I might have tried to run. My heart pounded with sudden dread, and it was hard to breathe. What was I doing here? What made me think I could handle someone like Joey "The Knife" Manetto? So what if I could read minds. Since he knew my secret, he wouldn't let his guard down around me. How stupid could I be? My breathing came fast, and I thought I might be hyperventilating.

"Easy babe," Ramos pulled me to face him, his voice low and calm. "Don't be scared, he's not going to hurt you. I don't know what kind of arrangement you have, but he'll keep his end of the bargain. It's how he does business. You'll be fine as long as you don't double-cross him." Now why didn't that make me feel better? "Let me give you some advice." He leaned in close and whispered. "He hates it when people grovel. Whatever you do, don't grovel. Okay?"

I could hardly believe what I was hearing. Ramos held back a smile and tried to be serious. The fear inside my stomach uncoiled. "You're pulling my leg, right?"

"Not really, but at least now, you don't look like you're going to faint."

"I wasn't that scared." He nodded with exaggeration, and I conceded. "Well maybe a little." I took a deep breath. "I'll sure be glad when this is over."

Uncle Joey was sitting behind a large cherry-wood desk. The huge office was distinctly masculine, and reminded me of a throne room with Uncle Joey as the main focus. Wood wainscoting framed the honey-beige colored walls, which were accented by golden light fixtures. A rich creamy carpet covered the floor. There was a burgundy leather couch along one wall, with a small conference table and chairs in the corner. This room was even more beautiful than the other one. A bank of windows let in the morning sunshine, and it was bright and pleasant.

"Nice." I couldn't help being impressed.

Uncle Joey stood to greet us, and smiled indulgently, taking in my wig and glasses. "I'm glad you like it. Thrasher Development is a thriving business. One I'm very proud of." He turned his attention to Ramos. "Thank you for escorting Shelby. If you'll greet our guests, we'll join you in the conference room." Ramos nodded and left.

Uncle Joey returned his attention to me, amused by my disguise. "We're meeting with several of the men I do business with. I don't trust any of them completely, and I'm sure they don't trust me, but I figured it couldn't hurt to know if they have any hidden agendas, or secrets. Anything that would be helpful for me to know."

"Right," I said, wondering how I was going to keep it all straight. "How many of them are there?"

"Five. Will that be a problem?"

"I don't know. I should be able to handle it, but I've never done anything like this before, or with this many people."

"Just do your best. I'm going to introduce you as my personal assistant. Here's a notebook and pen. Do you have any questions?"

I swallowed. I had a ton of questions, but none I could ask him. "No."

"Good, then let's get started." He led the way to the conference room, extremely pleased to have my talents at his disposal.

A long rectangular table was situated down the center of the conference room. One wall was covered with windows, giving a breathtaking view of the city. The men were seated at the far end of the table, leaving the head seat open for Uncle Joey. He greeted them pleasantly, then introduced me as his personal assistant.

As he seated me beside him, I flushed when I 'heard' a few stray thoughts about my figure. One didn't think I was Joey's type, while several others wondered what else I did for him. I wanted to disappear, but at least none of them thought I was fat... that was good.

Uncle Joey didn't tell me their names. Apparently I wasn't important enough to know. Their interest in me dropped when they started discussing business. I let my guard down slowly, and drew a diagram of their seating arrangement on my notebook with corresponding numbers. I was worried that I wouldn't be able to tell who was thinking what, so I tried to tune in to one person at a time. It was hard work, especially with so many of them. Most thoughts centered on the discussion, and it was hard to get past that layer to what their inner thoughts were.

I started with number one. He was an older, bald guy who sweated a lot. He kept wiping his head and face with a handkerchief. These meetings made him uncomfortable, because he didn't like to know everyone else's business. He had too many things of his own to be concerned about. He'd rather deal with Manetto alone. He didn't always agree with how they did things, but he kept his mouth shut. In a year or two, he would retire and let his nephew handle his assets. Maybe his nephew would have the guts to get rid of Manetto, since he couldn't do it. They shared too many secrets.

That could be something I could use, and I made a mental note that number one would like to get rid of Uncle Joey.

The next guy had a medium build and brown hair, and he wore glasses. He was very businesslike on the outside, but his thoughts came in quick short bursts. Underlying them all, one thing was perfectly clear. He hated Uncle Joey. He was also defensive about something. I wondered what Uncle Joey had on him. It must be something bad.

It looked like number two also wanted to get rid of Uncle Joey. I pulled my mind away, and took a deep breath. This was starting to wear me out, and I could feel a headache coming on. I hoped I could make it through the rest of them.

I took a moment to relax, then focused on number three. He was a younger man, probably in his early thirties. He was very agreeable, and really wanted to make a good impression on Uncle Joey and the rest of the group. He was thinking hard about coming up with some great ideas, and genuinely wanted his end of the business to work.

It surprised me. Finally, someone on Uncle Joey's side. Without warning, I got a flash of him burying a knife in Uncle Joey's back. I dropped my pen, and it bounced off the table with a thwack. Conversation halted, and everyone looked at me like I'd just committed a cardinal sin. I smiled uneasily, and bent over to retrieve my pen while the shock wore off.

I began to wonder if anyone even liked Uncle Joey. This was bad. What would I tell him? There were only two guys left, but after this, I didn't know if I could keep a straight face while I listened to them.

I inhaled through my nose, and concentrated on number four. He was dark and good-looking with brooding brown eyes. When I listened to him he was thinking about the basketball game coming up. He wanted to make sure he got good seats for the playoffs. His mind turned to the woman he'd been with last night. With his lips, he traveled up the length of her long legs...

I pulled away as fast as I could, but couldn't help the crimson flush that spread over my face. I closed my mouth, and kept my eyes down, not sure I could ever look at that guy again.

When I got my composure back, I noticed Ramos studying me from his perch by the door. From what I could gather, he was trying to figure out my role in all this. Why was I involved? What did I have to offer that made Manetto want me in this meeting? All of a sudden my head felt like it would burst. It was almost too much. At least there was only one more person to listen to.

I switched my concentration to number five, hoping to get this over with quickly. This man was smooth and self-assured. He radiated confidence and leadership, and his thoughts were completely centered on the business. In fact, he was so intense, his concentration never faltered, and it almost seemed like he was acting out a role. I listened intently, but he never let down his guard. He was good.

The meeting began to wind down, and I knew I had to try number four one more time. I didn't think Uncle Joey would be satisfied with a basketball game, and I wasn't about to tell him the other part. This time, he was actually paying attention, and I sighed with relief.

Uncle Joey was giving him an assignment and, as he agreed, he was mentally wishing "The Knife" would treat him more like an equal. Remembering the humiliation "The Knife" had heaped on him last week when he messed up flooded him with anger. He hated Joey with a passion hot enough to kill. I jerked away, amazed that none of this anger showed on his face. Were they all acting out parts?

The meeting soon broke up and I stayed in my seat, grateful they were leaving. Filtering through so many random thoughts had worn me out, and I had a monster headache. As soon as they were all out of the room, I lowered my head onto the table, closing my eyes and reveling in the silence.

I wasn't sure how much more of this I could take. I also didn't think I'd found out anything useful. How was I supposed to tell Uncle Joey that most of them wanted to kill him? Of course thinking about it, and doing it were two different things. How would he take it? I wasn't sure I wanted to be the bearer of that kind of news. It put me in a quandary. What should I tell him, and what should I keep secret?

Before I could decide, Uncle Joey returned and, unbidden, I found myself having some of the same nasty thoughts about him that came from the others. I slapped my hands over my mouth and coughed to cover the insane laughter that bubbled up. Then I spoiled it by nearly choking.

"Are you all right?" he asked. "Ramos, bring Shelby some water."

"I'm fine," I said, clearing my throat and slamming my mental shields tight. Ramos handed me a glass of water, and I quickly drank it down. "Thanks."

"Well?" Uncle Joey asked. "Did you find out anything? Does anyone hate me?"

His question took me by surprise, and I worked hard to hold back my sarcastic response. It took all of my control not to roll my eyes. "Um..." I cleared my throat, striving to stay in control and not laugh in Uncle Joey's face. "Do you have any Tylenol or aspirin? I have a really bad headache."

"I think there's some in the medicine cabinet in my bathroom."

"Oh great. I'll be right back." I jumped up and nearly collided with Ramos who stood beside the door. "Which way is the bathroom?"

He looked behind me at Uncle Joey. "There's one in Mr. Manetto's office."

"Thanks." I made a beeline for the office. When I found the bathroom, I locked the door behind me. I hurried to the sink and soaked a washcloth in cold water. Then held it to my forehead. The cold shock had the desired effect of bringing my sarcasm under control, and I finally let out my breath. Whew! This was harder than I thought.

At least I hadn't ruined my chances of staying alive by laughing in Uncle Joey's face. Now I had to decide what I was going to tell him. They all hated him, but I hadn't heard any plots against him. That was the truth without all the graphic detail. That should be fine, right?

I found the aspirin and filled up my glass with water to wash them down. After taking a calming breath, I hurried back to the conference room to face Uncle Joey. Ramos studied me, his expression grave. I let down my shields and found that he didn't think I was going to last much longer. What did he mean by that?

Anxious, I switched my attention to Uncle Joey. He wasn't sure what to make of my behavior, but I hadn't fooled him one bit. He knew I'd been holding back laughter and it rankled. No one ever laughed at him and lived to tell about it.

He excused Ramos with a nod and gave me a piercing look. "Shall we continue?"

"Yes." This was going to be tricky. "Um... I think you already know the answer to your question about anyone hating you. Right? I mean... a man in your position has to realize that when you have a lot of power, others can be resentful. And when you coerce people into doing things against their will, they're not going to like it either. Or you, for that matter. So when you asked if anyone hated you, I thought you were being sarcastic. You know?"

"I see," he said, stony faced, his mind curiously blank.

He wasn't responding in the way I hoped, so I tried a different tactic. "So, let me show you the diagram and what I found out. Number one is the sweaty bald guy. He doesn't like these meetings. He'd rather meet with you alone. Oh, and he'll be retiring within the next year or so. He'll probably turn his share of the business over to his nephew. Out of all of them, I think he's the one you have to worry about the least."

"Why is that?"

"Because he's getting too old to actually kill you, and he wants to spend more time with his family."

Uncle Joey scrubbed his face with his hands. "So everyone else wants to kill me?"

"I wouldn't necessarily say that, but I would have to say that they don't like you very much. Whether it's enough to kill you, I don't know." While he was digesting this I decided to hurry the process along. "Take number two. He's got a good head for business and he's a quick thinker. I'd say he's doing a good job for you."

Uncle Joey perked up at this. "Yes. He gets his job done and he does it right."

"There you go." I was trying to be as positive as I could. "I don't know what you're holding over his head, but he's not very happy about it. Maybe you could cut him some slack about that. I bet he'd be more loyal to you if you did." Uncle Joey didn't respond, so I continued. "But that's just a suggestion. You can do whatever you want."

I nervously chewed on my bottom lip. "Let's see, number three here is kind of young. Is he a relative or something? Wait. Don't answer that. He really wants to make a good impression on you, and he is committed to making the business succeed. He's another good worker and more committed than you may know."

"He definitely has ambition," Uncle Joey agreed.

"Yes, and that's why you'll have to watch him. He might get it in his head to take over before you're ready. It might help if you decided who is going to take over the business and take that person under your wing. Then maybe the others wouldn't be so focused on you." He smiled, and the first stirrings of hope swelled in my heart. Maybe I would survive after all.

"I know what you mean, but I don't want my choice to cause any problems. It's not exactly someone they're expecting."

An image of Kate came to his mind and I quickly squelched my response. I had to act as though I didn't know he was considering her. "I understand. It was just a thought." I tightened my shields. There were some things I just didn't need to know, but it was probably a little too late for that. "Let's move on to number four..."

"Wait a minute. You know who I'm considering as my successor now, don't you?"

Damn. "Oh, no. I have my shields up real tight. You don't have to worry about me listening to your mind. I think the less I know the better."

"What do you mean about shields?"

"I've found that I can block people's thoughts. It's something I had to learn right away, or I would have gone nuts. You just don't know what it's like to be in public and hear things. All kinds of things. It can be mind-boggling. Plus, it always gives me a bad headache. Kind of like today. Keeping my mind open and trying to focus on your people really took a lot out of me. So after the meeting, I put my shields up. I need to let my brain relax for a bit."

He just looked at me in disbelief, then shook his head, thinking he wasn't sure he believed me, but decided to let it go for now. "Go on."

"Where were we? Oh, yes, number four. He's the one I had to go back to because all he could think of..." Oops, what was I saying? "was the basketball game." I knew my face had turned red again, but I tried to ignore it.

"He's quite the Romeo, isn't he?" Uncle Joey smiled at my discomfort. "So, did he have anything else on his mind that I should know about?"

I was really glad he clarified that statement. "Yes. I think he wants to do a good job for you. He seems willing enough. He'd like to be treated more as an equal, but he's mad about something that happened last week. I don't know what you did to humiliate him, but he's pretty upset about it."

"I expected that," Uncle Joey said. "But he'll get over it."

Maybe, or he would just try to get even, and that would work in my favor, right? I wasn't about to tell Uncle Joey that. I quickly moved on.

"Number five is a mystery. He was so focused on your meeting that I couldn't get anything from him. He never let down his guard. Not even once. He seems very capable."

"Yes, he is." Uncle Joey frowned.

"Well, that's everything then. I probably need to get going." I stood and gathered my things. "You're not going to kill me now are you? I mean, you wanted me to tell you the truth, didn't you?"

Uncle Joey came to his feet, a smile on his face. "Of course I want the truth, and I appreciate your work today. It gave me a good idea of what you can do, and where we can go next."

"Right." I didn't like the sound of that.

"The more I think about it, the more I realize that I'll probably need you to come to some meetings with one person at a time. I could get lots more information that way. Why don't you plan on coming back tomorrow? Say ten o'clock? It'll just be for an hour or so."

"Tomorrow? Are you..." I wanted to say, kidding me, but it died on my lips. Uncle Joey just smiled that certain way of his when he knew he had me over a barrel. "Uh... sure. Fine."

"Don't be upset. You're doing great."

And he wondered if anyone hated him? "I'll be here at ten."

"Good. How's the car? Do you need anything else?"

"No, I'm good."

"Excellent, see you tomorrow." He escorted me to the door, and I hurried out of the suite.

When the elevator doors closed, I leaned against the sidewall, totally drained. What an experience. How was I ever going to be able to do this? And now I had to come back tomorrow. Ugh! I had to find something on Uncle Joey soon. I didn't think I could handle much more of him.

With the parking garage filled with black cars, the only way I could find mine was to hit the unlock button. As I walked toward the car, I noticed a man talking to someone in a dark corner. I glanced up and recognized number five, but I couldn't see who he was talking to. The hairs on the back of my neck stood up, and I knew he had spotted me. I pretended I hadn't seen him and hurried to my car. Uncle Joey would probably want me to eavesdrop, but I hated the idea of being an informer when he wasn't watching. I also didn't care to be alone in a parking garage with any of these people.

I opened the car door, and was about to get in when I heard my name called. It was him. Double damn! What was I going to do? I was really beginning to hate parking garages.

"Hello!" he called politely. Walking quickly to my car, he wondered if I had seen who he was talking to.

"Oh... hi," I said casually. "I wasn't sure who you were for a minute."

"Uh, yes it is dark in here. They should put more lights around." He paused, then decided to turn on the charm and smiled. "Well, I just wanted to say it's nice to have you as part of the team, and I'm looking forward to getting to know you better." He was really wondering if I was related to Manetto, since that was usually how it worked. Unless Manetto had something on me, if that was the case, he really felt sorry for me.

"Um... thanks, except I'm not exactly glad to be here," I answered, taking a chance.

"Oh, I wondered. Listen, I know it may seem presumptuous of me, but if you have any concerns that you can't take to the boss, maybe I can help you. In the meantime, try not to worry; things aren't always what they seem." He smiled, then turned and disappeared into the maze of parked cars.

What did he mean by that? If he wasn't what he seemed, what was he? Was he an undercover cop? Would that help me or just make everything a whole lot worse? Maybe he was planning to kill Uncle Joey. Now that was something I didn't want to know, because if he was, I wasn't about to stop him, and that probably made me a bad person.

I hurried home, anxious to get out of my wig and glasses before the kids got home from school. I had just enough time to shower, which was a good thing, given how much I'd been sweating at the meeting. I stowed my wig and glasses in a box, which I stashed in the back of my closet, and tried to forget about Uncle Joey.

After Chris got home, that wasn't easy. "Did you say the insurance agreed to pay for the rental?" he asked. "I was looking at the car in the garage, and it doesn't look like a rental to me."

"Of course it's a rental," I said. "Rental companies don't want their cars to look like rentals anymore. You know that. Nondescript, black cars are what all the rental companies seem to have these days. Speaking of which, I called our insurance about my car. It was totaled, but the insurance company said they'd send us a check today. It's a good thing we had comprehensive on it. Anyway, I thought maybe we could go looking for new cars tonight."

My request had the intended effect on Chris. He hated looking for cars, and forgot all about my rental. "Tonight? I'm not sure I have time."

"That's too bad. I really need a car."

"If you want, you can look tomorrow. Then if you find something you like, you can show me." He really hated car shopping.

"Okay, that should work. How's the case with Mr. Hodges?"

"Kate's taken over all of the paperwork, so I'm not as involved. I still think he took the jewels, but unless we can find them, I don't think it will matter. There might be a way if you were able to listen to him."

"Yes, but he's not going to think about where he hid the jewels unless you ask him where he hid the jewels. People just don't think about that sort of thing unless it's already on their minds. It makes my job more difficult than you realize."

He paused and studied me.

"What?" I asked. "You'll be happy to know my shields are up, so if you have something to say, say it."

"You just sounded like you were complaining. You know, like you'd had a hard day reading minds."

"Ha, ha, very funny." That was too close for comfort. "If you want me to try listening to Mr. Hodges again, it's fine with me."

"Sure. If there's another chance, I'll call you in."

The rest of the evening went smoothly, and I felt almost like my old self. I could pretend that hearing an occasional thought or two was no big deal. I could handle that. It was being coerced into helping the bad guys that rankled, although if Ramos hadn't killed the bank robber, I'd probably be dead. It all came down to Kate's interference. If it weren't for her, I wouldn't be in this situation. Of course, that wasn't completely true. It all began because I'd stopped at the grocery store for some carrots. Who would have thought that could be dangerous? It was enough to make me want to stay home for the rest of my life.

Chapter 7

I made sure I got to Uncle Joey's office early since I didn't want any surprises. I wore my wig and glasses, but decided I was going to wear my own clothes. All except for the boots. I really liked them. Then of course, I had to wear black to match the boots, but this time I wore black pants instead of the short skirt. If Uncle Joey didn't like it, that was just too bad.

Ramos greeted me with a sad smile, thinking he was going to miss me unless I came up with something good. Good for what? "Mr. Manetto's waiting for you in the surveillance room." For some reason, he thought I was in trouble, and fear sent a shiver down my spine. He led me down the opposite hall to a small, dark room. Inside were several monitors showing different views of the building. Uncle Joey sat at the control desk.

"Shelby, come in. I want to show you something."

I moved behind him and my stomach dropped. There, on the monitor, was me talking to Number Five in the parking garage yesterday.

"What were you two talking about?" Uncle Joey asked.

"Nothing. Seriously. I was getting in my car... see? And number five saw me and came over to welcome me into the business. That's all." When Uncle Joey didn't say anything I continued. "I saw him talking to someone, and when he saw me, he came over."

Uncle Joey's eyes lit up. "Now we're getting somewhere. Did you see who he was talking to, or hear what they were saying?"

"No. I wasn't even sure it was number five until he came over. The other person was in the shadows, and too far away to hear, but now that you mention it, he did seem nervous, and relieved that I hadn't seen who he was talking to." I was surprised at how fast I spilled my guts. At least I stopped before I told him about the 'things not being what they seem' part.

"That's good to know. If you remember anything else, I want to hear about it."

"Okay," I agreed, relieved to have that over with. Uncle Joey didn't seem too concerned, and I was mad that Ramos had scared me. I glanced over at him and glowered. His brows rose in bewilderment, and he wondered what he'd done to make me mad. He couldn't figure me out, but he knew something strange was going on.

Uncle Joey's secretary interrupted us. "Your client is here to see you Mr. Manetto. I told him to wait in your office."

"Thank you Jackie. Come Shelby, I have someone I want you to meet. This should be relatively easy for you."

Easy? How did he know what was easy and what wasn't? After a quick stroll down the hall, Uncle Joey opened the door to his office, and his client stood to greet him. I took one look at his face and jerked back out of the office, accidentally smacking Ramos in the stomach with my elbow. His breath came out with an "oof," and I twisted to face him, my heart racing with panic.

Ramos took me by the upper arms, and practically lifted me out of the doorway, then beckoned to Uncle Joey, who had missed the whole thing. "Excuse me, Mr. Manetto, there's an important matter you need to take care of."

Uncle Joey made his excuses and came back into the hall, closing the door behind him. He was annoyed and puzzled at my behavior.

"I know that guy," I whispered, wondering what Mr. Hodges was doing here. "I met him in Chris' office. Chris and Kate are handling his case, and I met him there a few days ago, or maybe it was only yesterday." So much was happening, it was hard to keep anything straight. "Anyway, he's seen me! The real me. I can't go in there."

"But you're wearing a disguise," Uncle Joey said. "He may not recognize the real you under your wig and glasses."

Was he serious? "Yes he will."

"I guess we shouldn't chance it." Uncle Joey was having fun with me, and I had to squelch the urge to hit him. He wondered if he could hide me in his office, but wasn't sure how to get Hodges out first.

"I think that's a good idea," I said, then glanced at Ramos, hoping my comment made sense. "Maybe you could show him the view from your window while I find a place to hide. I know! I can hide in the bathroom. With the door open, I should be able to hear everything."

"Excellent." Uncle Joey smiled. "Ramos, see that she gets in all right."

"Yes sir." Ramos didn't have a clue what was going on, but he wasn't about to let that stop him from doing his duty.

Uncle Joey went back in his office, and left the door open. After they had moved to the window, Ramos nodded and I ducked into the bathroom. Luckily, the door was ajar, and I gently pushed it open and slithered inside. I let out my breath that I'd made it, and sat on the floor beside the door.

Ramos stepped inside the office, and asked Uncle Joey if there was anything he needed before closing the door. Uncle Joey then ushered Mr. Hodges back to his seat. Without missing a beat, he began.

"I understand your store was robbed a few weeks ago. As your benefactor, I hope you'll be able to recover the value, if not the jewelry, that was stolen."

"Yes, it was a terrible loss, but my lawyers are confident that I'll recover the money from my insurance company. You don't need to worry. You won't be out a dime."

"You've got a good case?"

"Yes. The surveillance camera caught them on tape, and there were fingerprints on the glass that matched those of the thieves. Plus, I have very good lawyers. I suppose I have you to thank for that."

"I'm glad they're working out for you. As you know, I take care of my investments. What about the jewelry? Has any of it turned up?"

"No, I'm afraid not. I've checked the pawnshops myself, but I haven't found anything."

"Hmm... I wonder where someone could hide jewels like that."

"Just about anywhere, I guess." Hodges immediately thought about the safe he had concealed in his house. It was in a dark room painted a dull mushroom color, and a tall lamp stood in the corner. A photograph of a boat with him and someone else hung over the false opening. The carpet was dark and seemed worn.

"Wouldn't the thieves sell them to a broker, rather than a pawnshop?"

Mr. Hodges grew uneasy. "Certainly, if they knew what they were doing. But these guys were amateurs. They probably don't know what to do with them."

"I know someone who buys and sells specialty items like jewels. He knows just about every dealer in town. I could have him look for your inventory if you like. All I need is the same list and descriptions you gave to the insurance company."

"Sure, that would be great. I think I have a copy here in my briefcase." Mr. Hodges was starting to sweat now, but he could change his plans, and go through someone he knew in Mexico. The man wasn't as reliable, but it didn't look like he could get past Mr. Manetto otherwise.

"Wouldn't it be something if the jewels showed up after you got the insurance money?" Uncle Joey asked.

"Well, naturally, I'd have to give it back. No one else would want to insure me if I didn't." As if he cared. Once he got the insurance money and cashed in the jewels, he'd have enough to live comfortably. He could open a nice little tourist shop on the coast of Mexico and do all right for himself. He'd be away from his creditors and the government, as well as Manetto.

All he needed to win was a good case, and Kate had assured him of that. She thought she had him over a barrel by demanding he check in with Mr. Manetto. Lucky for him, she didn't know how much insurance money he was going to get.

"Ah, here they are." Mr. Hodges said, and handed the stack of papers to Uncle Joey. It was only a partial list, the same one he'd given the police. The list he'd sent to the insurance company had twice as many items on it. "Could you make a copy for yourself? That's the only one I've got."

"Of course." Uncle Joey called his secretary on the intercom and, when she came in, he gave her the papers to copy. "I was just thinking the other day that it's been almost ten years since I got you started in the jewelry business. You've done well for yourself."

"Thanks. It's a tradition I hope to continue." It would be a relief to get out from under Manetto's thumb. He hated Manetto and all the 'favors' he had to do for him. This plan was the only way out. If Manetto found out about the extra money and jewels he'd kept over the years, he was a dead man.

The meeting ended. I waited while Uncle Joey ushered Mr. Hodges out of his office. Before Uncle Joey came back, I needed to decide how much I should tell him. I hated bringing down Mr. Hodges when he was just trying to get out from under Uncle Joey. On the other hand, he wasn't exactly a stellar citizen either. Uncle Joey would probably want to keep all the insurance money after he found the jewels, and Hodges would be left with nothing. But what did it matter to me?

Uncle Joey returned with a devilish gleam in his eyes. Somehow he knew Hodges had lied to him. "So, what did you learn?"

I had to tell him the truth. "I know where he hid the jewels. Or at least I saw the hiding place in his mind. They're in a hidden safe in one of the rooms of his house."

"Do you know which room?"

"I couldn't tell. I only saw it in his mind. I'm pretty sure it wasn't his bedroom. Maybe it was the living room, but somehow I doubt it. It could be—"

"Here's what you're going to do," Uncle Joey interrupted, losing his patience. "I'm going to send you and Ramos to his house for the jewels. I don't want Hodges to know I've got them until he looks for them and finds them gone, but we need to act fast. He's headed for a meeting with Kate, and I'll see if she can keep him for an hour. That should be enough time to get the job done.

"What?" I was shocked. "You want me to break into his house?"

"Yes." He was dead serious.

I could hardly believe this was happening. How could he ask me to do this? "But this wasn't part of my job description. You said all I had to do was sit in on some of your meetings, remember?"

"Shelby." His tone was low and dangerous. This was his show, and he was going to run it his way. If I didn't like it, that was just too bad.

"Fine." I snapped. "But if I get caught—"

"Nothing's going to happen," Uncle Joey said. "Ramos is very good at what he does. You'll be fine."

I was seething, but I kept my thoughts to myself, thoughts that included whacking Uncle Joey over the head with something very hard. Uncle Joey smiled in a conciliatory way, wanting to placate my anger. "Think of this—"

"As an investment." I finished, and put on a false smile. He was going down. Now all I had to do was figure out how.

Uncle Joey called Ramos in, and explained that he and I were going to break into Hodges house. Without even raising an eyebrow, Ramos left us to get ready. I was expecting him to protest having me along, and it kind of freaked me out to realize that Ramos did whatever Uncle

Joey asked, whether it made sense or not. He would kill me without a second thought, and it made me feel weak and vulnerable.

A few minutes later, I was sitting next to Ramos in his shiny black car. It was a sportier version of mine, and sitting next to him, it reminded me of a sleek black panther. With Ramos's dark coloring and imposing figure, it fit him perfectly. It helped that he had changed his clothes and was wearing all black, just like me. I guess when you're in the business of breaking and entering, black is a pretty good color to have your employees wear.

I decided to be as friendly and nice as possible. A little kissing up was the only thing I could think of that might improve my chances of surviving. "So, was it you who picked out my clothes?"

A smile slid over his face and he nodded. "I do a lot of things you wouldn't expect in my line of work."

"How did you know my size? Even my shoe size. Does Uncle Joey have a file on me with all that personal information?" It kind of made my heart shrivel just to think about it.

"He has a special file, but the information is for his eyes only. I don't think he has anything on you, at least not written down. I picked out your clothes and shoes. I've got a pretty good eye for things like that."

"Oh." I squirmed in my seat, feeling uncomfortable. "Well, I really like the boots."

"Yeah? That's cool."

It struck me that Ramos was a lot savvier than I had given him credit for. Back at the office, when he'd seen that I knew who Hodges was, he acted quickly, and diverted a disaster. He was observant of what was going on around him, and always seemed one step ahead of everyone else.

Right now, he was trying to figure out my place in Uncle Joey's organization. Most of the time, he didn't care about those things, but he kind of liked me, at least enough to feel bad if he had to kill me. He wondered why Uncle Joey included me in his meetings. Bringing in an outsider was something the boss had never done before. He also wondered how I knew where Hodges had hidden the jewels. It didn't make any sense. What was it about me?

"Did you bring anything to eat? It's almost lunch time." I had to get his mind off that train of thought.

"There's some bottled water in the back seat. Help yourself. Maybe we can get a bite to eat after we're done." He started humming along to the radio, and turned up the volume.

How someone like him liked country music was a puzzle to me. It just didn't seem to fit him at all. In an effort to understand, I tuned into the beat and pretty soon I was nodding my head in time with the rhythm. It was an upbeat song, which surprised me. Maybe that was why he liked it. I would have thought a trained assassin would go for the dark, heavy-metal stuff. Of course, Uncle Joey's office wasn't anything like I thought it would be either. There was a lot I had to learn. Except that most of it, like stealing, wasn't what I had in mind.

How had it come to this? I was actually going to break into somebody's house and steal from them. Of course, in this case maybe it was different. Stealing jewels from someone who'd already stolen them wasn't exactly wrong, right?

"There it is," Ramos said. We drove slowly past a small house, then kept going around the corner. "We'll park here." He didn't want to be obvious in case Hodges showed up early. "Just follow my lead. The main thing is to act like you have every right to be there. No furtive glances. We'll walk straight to the house, and follow the driveway around to the back."

I swallowed, then got out of the car. Ramos pulled a small backpack out of the trunk, and we walked casually up the street. I found it hard to understand how two people all dressed in black, and carrying a backpack, wouldn't draw attention. My heart sped up as we approached the house. It was a pretty quiet neighborhood. Hopefully no one would see us. I was trembling by the time we got to the back door. The yard was small, but at least it was private. Ramos picked the locks, and we were inside before I knew it. He was good.

"Wait here," he whispered. He relocked the back door, and disappeared through the kitchen.

I held my breath and listened. Did Ramos think someone might be here? Maybe Mr. Hodges lived with his mother, and she was in the house. I shivered with dread, then jerked when Ramos reappeared. "All clear," he said.

"We're alone?" I whispered.

"Yeah, come on. We've got to hurry." He thought I looked like a nervous wreck. My face was pale, and I was crouching down by the floor like a frightened rabbit. It wasn't that big a deal.

With all the dignity I could muster, I stood up straight, and followed him through the house. I studied each room for the paneling and the photograph I'd seen in Hodges mind, but came up with nothing. We went over the house a second time with no success, and my chest tightened with panic. Had I misunderstood?

"Could it be in the garage?" Ramos asked.

"No. It was a larger space than that, but darker, like there were no windows. Almost like a basement."

Ramos stilled, then hurried to the hallway, and pulled open a closet door. Only it wasn't a closet. Steps trailed down into the darkness. He flipped a switch, and the basement lit up. At the bottom of the stairs I saw the wood paneling and the photo. With relief, I eagerly pointed it out to Ramos.

He carefully tugged on the photo, and it swung open revealing a small safe. Did I say he was good? "This is an old model, so it might take a while."

"Can I do anything to help?"

"Just be quiet." He opened his pack and put on some rubber gloves. With his ear next to the safe, he turned the lock, listening for the tumblers to fall.

I checked my watch, knowing we'd been there about fifteen minutes. With the twenty-minute drive, we should still have plenty of time to get away before Hodges came home. As long as Kate did her part.

My cell phone rang and I about wet my pants. I forgot it was in my pocket. I dug it out as fast as I could. "Hello?"

"Hi honey," Chris said. "What's going on? You sound funny."

"Nothing. I just... the phone was in my pocket and it startled me."

"Why are you whispering?"

"I'm... at the library."

"Oh. Okay. Anyway, I'm calling because Harris from the police department has been trying to get a hold of you."

"Who?"

"You know, Dimples. I told him I'd try your cell phone. He said you offered to help him with some of his cases, and he wanted to talk to you. What's going on? Did you tell him?"

"You mean about..." I stopped quickly, realizing that Ramos was listening. "Can I call you right back?"

"Did you?"

"Not exactly. Look, I really can't talk right now."

"Just go outside."

"I can't. I'm standing in line with a bunch of books." Just then, Ramos pulled open the safe, and began to load his pack with jewels. Sudden inspiration struck. "Hey, is Hodges there? I mean, has he come in today?"

My question was met by silence. Maybe I shouldn't have asked. "Actually he was here," Chris said slowly. "But he left about twenty minutes ago. Why?"

"Crap. Uh... I've got to go." I ended the call and turned to Ramos. "We've got to go."

"Did you just hang up on your husband?" Ramos asked. "That's not good."

"No, you don't understand. He said Hodges left his office about twenty minutes ago." Just then my phone rang again, and I nearly dropped it. I did the only thing I could think of, and turned it off.

Ramos shook his head, thinking I was making a mess of things. "Come on." He took the stairs two at a time and flipped off the light before I got to the top. He opened the door, but before going out, closed it again. A second later I heard the back door close, and understood why. Hodges was home.

We sat at the top of the stairs, barely breathing. We could hear Hodges' footsteps as he walked through the kitchen, and down the hall. As he came closer to the door, I held my breath. I felt Ramos tense beside me, ready to spring on Hodges if he had to. The footsteps kept going, and a door closed.

Ramos was trying to decide if we should make a run for it. He would if it wasn't for me, but he was afraid I might trip or something and Hodges would catch us. Uncle Joey wouldn't like that, so we stayed. Then he thought about going back down the stairs, but in the dark, he was afraid I might trip, or knock something over, and Hodges would catch us.

Geez, did he think I was a klutz or something? He finally decided we were safe enough where we were because Hodges probably didn't go down in the small basement very often. We sat on the stairs for a long time, listening to Hodges move around the house. I finally relaxed, realizing that if Hodges ever decided to open the door, he'd have Ramos to deal with.

While we waited, Ramos worried that I'd say something and give us away. After a while, when I didn't say anything, he wondered what was wrong with me. He couldn't figure me out. His thoughts were driving me crazy, so I put up my shields and tried to decide what I was going to tell Chris.

He'd want to know why I'd hung up on him. Twice. Then he'd want to know why I wondered where Hodges was. I certainly wasn't ready to tell him the truth. I needed more on Uncle Joey before I could do that. Of course, by the time I got out of here, it might be the middle of the night. Chris would probably call Dimples, and the entire police force would be out looking for me. I might as well tell Ramos to shoot me now.

My legs were starting to cramp when Hodges finally left. I sighed with relief and checked my watch. It was nearly five. Ramos opened the door and cautiously looked out, then disappeared. I was so eager to leave that my feet got tangled up, and I tripped over the top stair. I stumbled into the hallway, sending the basement door crashing into the wall.

Ramos came running, and when he saw me sprawled on the floor, he started to laugh. He tried to hold it in, but the harder he tried, the more he laughed. He finally took pity on me and helped me up. "Are you okay?"

"Yeah." I was pretty embarrassed, but I had to admit it was funny, and once I started laughing, it was hard to stop. I think the stress was getting to me.

"Good, 'cause we should really go now." He kept chuckling every once in a while, then thanked his lucky stars he hadn't decided to make a run for it. He knew I'd trip over something. I almost told him that maybe he had ESP or something, but I held my tongue. I was in enough trouble already.

We made it to the car and started the drive back to the office. I reached into the back and got out two bottles of water. Not only was I thirsty, but my stomach was rumbling with hunger.

As if he could read my mind, Ramos pulled off the road to a drive-through window at a fast food joint. "Want anything?"

A burger and fries sounded really good, but it was almost dinnertime and I was on a diet. "I don't know. Well... maybe. No, I'd better not."

Ramos crooked his brow, then ordered two of everything. "You'd better eat something," he said. "I'm hungry, and it's not polite to eat in front of someone, especially when their stomach is growling as loud as yours."

"Well, maybe I'll have some fries, and a coke... as long as it's diet." His logic made sense to me. The food smelled heavenly, and I dove in before we'd even left the drive-through. Ramos maneuvered into a parking space to eat his burger, and when he was done, pulled back into traffic. I ended up eating the extra burger too, but it was small, and I'm pretty sure I'd left most of the fries for Ramos.

Feeling much better, I settled back into my seat. Soon we came to the downtown area, and Uncle Joey's office wasn't far. My wig was beginning to itch, and I wanted to pull it off. I probably could now that we were done, but I was afraid of what my hair looked like. Still, it would be a relief not to have it on. I reached up and froze. We were stopped at a red light, and the car next to us looked familiar. I glanced over, and there was Chris.

He glanced my way and I jerked my head toward Ramos. "Don't look now, but the guy in the car next to us is my husband!" Naturally he looked.

"Did he see you?" Ramos asked. "It looks like he's trying to get a better look at you."

I panicked for a moment, then felt silly when I realized I was wearing a disguise. "Wait a minute. He won't recognize me with my wig and glasses on."

"Babe," Ramos said. "You're not wearing your glasses. You took them off, remember?"

I glanced down at my shirt where I'd hung them. In a flash I grabbed them and put them back on my face. The light changed, and we pulled out with Chris keeping pace. "Is he still looking this way?"

"He keeps looking over, but don't worry, I'm going to take a left at the next light."

I didn't relax until we'd left Chris behind. I was hoping to get home before him, but that was impossible now. Still, I needed to get home as fast as I could. As soon as we pulled into the parking garage I was ready to jump out of the car, but Ramos grabbed my arm.

"Wait a minute." The shock of his hand on my arm sent shivers down my spine, and I was suddenly aware of how dangerous and strong he was. "Mr. Manetto will want to see you before you leave."

I blinked and came back to my senses. "Oh come on," I whined. "I've got to get home. You've got the jewels. Can't you tell him what happened?"

Ramos hesitated. He was finding it hard to follow orders when it came to me. That was risky. He'd made it a point not to get attached to anyone he might have to kill, but I was starting to get under his skin. That wasn't good, especially when I looked at him with those big blue eyes. Something inside got soft. He sighed and let me go. "All right. You can go."

"Are you going to get in trouble?"

"Me? I can take care of myself." It was his reputation he was worried about. He didn't want anyone to think he was losing his touch.

"Thanks. I owe you one." I quickly slid out of the car and hurried away.

"Shelby," Ramos called.

"What?"

"Your car's that way." He pointed in the opposite direction.

"Oh, yeah. I guess I got turned around. Thanks." I had no idea which car was mine, but I didn't want Ramos to think I was a total moron. As I walked, I dug the keys out of my purse and clicked the unlock button, then sighed with relief when the headlights blinked, and I hadn't passed it up. I really had to get my own car.

I opened the trunk, and grabbed the sack I'd stashed for emergencies. Inside was a shirt, a comb, and a brush. I slid into the driver's seat, and pulled off the wig and glasses. It felt heavenly to brush my hair, and I pulled it back into a ponytail. After checking the garage to make sure no one was watching, I quickly changed my shirt, then stashed everything in the sack, and put it back in the trunk.

It was almost six thirty when I finally pulled into the driveway. My stomach twisted, and I was sorry I'd eaten that burger and fries. I walked in the back door with my senses wide open. If I ever needed to know what Chris and the kids were thinking about me, it was now.

"Hello," I called, trying to sound confident.

I walked through the kitchen and living room before I realized no one was home. That's when it finally registered that I hadn't seen Chris' car parked in the garage. I hurried back to the kitchen and found the note he'd left for me on the table. It was short and precise, telling me that I had forgotten to pick up Savannah from dance practice. Crap! Was it Thursday already? Chris had gone to pick her up, and was stopping for pizza on the way home. The last part was hard to read, but I finally made it out. It said, "Turn on your phone." Oops.

I tidied up the kitchen while trying to come up with a reasonable explanation that he would accept. All too soon the door opened and they were home.

"Hey there," I greeted Savannah. "Sorry I forgot to pick you up. It's been a crazy day."

"That's okay," Savannah said. "Dad came." She was wondering what was wrong with me lately. I never used to act so weird. "I'm going to go change."

As soon as she was out of earshot, Chris said, "Now would be a good time to put up your shields because I'm sure it would not be good for you to know what I'm thinking right at this moment."

"O-kay," I said slowly, realizing that he was probably right. I concentrated on blocking his thoughts, but it didn't take a mind reader to see how upset he was.

"Savannah called your mother to see if she knew where you were before she called me to come and get her. Then your mom called to make sure I was picking Savannah up. She mentioned that you told her you'd had a job interview, and maybe you were at work."

Uh-oh. She wasn't supposed to tell Chris that. I suddenly didn't know what to say. I was a terrible liar, but how could I tell him the truth?

"Shelby? What's going on?"

Maybe some of the truth would be a good place to start. "When I went out to lunch with Kate, she made me feel like a nobody. You know I never finished college, and I guess I wanted to do something important. I saw this job at Thrasher Development and decided to apply. I was going to tell you, but I wasn't sure what you'd think with everything else going on. I went in today for some training, and it wasn't supposed to take long, but I came across Mr. Hodges name and spent some time looking at his files."

"What does Thrasher Development have to do with Mr. Hodges?"

"The company owns a lot of real estate downtown, and leases to small businesses. Mr. Hodges' jewelry store is one of them. I found his home address, and decided to drive by his house."

Chris' jaw tightened and his whole body went rigid. "Don't tell me you were snooping around."

"I thought it might help your case to find the jewels, but don't worry, I didn't break in. I just looked around the house from the outside."

"What? You went to his house and looked in his windows?" Put that way, it sounded really stupid. "I can't believe you'd do something like that. What's gotten into you?" How could I answer that? "At least I understand now why you hung up on me. Did he come home while you were there?" He said this in jest, not really expecting it to be true.

"I'm sure he didn't see me."

Chris almost choked. "I certainly hope not." If I had done something like that, what else had I gotten into? "And now you have a job? Why didn't you talk to me about it first?"

I jumped to defend myself. "It was just something I did on a whim. It's not that big of a deal. I only go in now and then when they need me. Normally, I would be home long before the kids." My shields slipped and I caught Chris' frustration with me. What did I need a job for when I had agreed to help him in his office?

"This was something I wanted to do that I actually got paid for." As soon as the words left my mouth, I knew I shouldn't have said it.

Chris's gaze snapped to mine and I flinched. "You never complained before," he said with deceptive calm.

Oh boy, I was making a mess of things. I wished I could just tell him I was working for Thrasher Development because if I didn't, Uncle Joey would probably kill me. "I'm not complaining. Really. Where's Josh?"

"I don't know, and you're changing the subject." When I didn't answer he continued. "What aren't you telling me?"

"What makes you think I haven't told you everything?" That was probably a stupid question, but I didn't know what else to say.

"Because this isn't like you."

He was sure making this hard. I guess it was the lawyer in him. "I've told you everything. Except about Dimples. I told him I had premonitions about things once in a while, and offered to help him if he needed it."

"So you're helping Dimples, and working at some big shot real estate company?" His voice got louder. "And the reason you're doing it is because Kate made you feel bad?"

My breath caught, but what could I say? When he put it that way it seemed pretty selfish and petty.

When I didn't deny his allegations, he took a step back. "I know what's happening. Now that you have this mind-reading ability, you've decided to use it to make a name for yourself. You see this as a way to really do something with your life." He shook his head in astonishment. "I guess I never realized how much you resented not finishing college and having a career."

"No. That's not exactly true—"

"Think about it." He cut me off. "Look at what you're doing. It's the only thing that makes sense to me. I never realized how much it meant to you or how unhappy you were."

"Don't say that. I'm not unhappy. You and the kids mean everything to me. Maybe sometimes I've wondered what a career would have been like, but I've never regretted marrying you and having a family. Never."

The tension in him loosened. "I guess I never thought about what you gave up because you were so hellbent on marrying me. It was your idea, you know." This was a sore spot with me and he knew it. As far as he was concerned, it was me who pushed us into getting married when he thought we were too young.

"You don't regret it, do you?" I asked softly.

"No... I just don't understand what's going on right now. It's frustrating, and I'm not sure I like the change. You've always been here, and I guess I've taken that for granted. Now you're taking steps to change our lives without telling me, and I don't like it."

Guilt from my dishonesty swept through me. I wanted to tell him everything so bad it was like a physical pain. But I couldn't. I had to let him believe his conclusions because it was safe. I couldn't risk the truth.

"I'm sorry. I should have told you about the job, and I'm sorry I hung up on you today. It won't happen again."

"Okay." Chris was trying to sort everything out. He needed order in his life. He liked having a plan, and knowing what was going to happen. "We should probably work out our schedules so Savannah doesn't get left again. And I would appreciate you calling me if something comes up."

"Of course. I know we can work this out."

"Good." Something still didn't seem right to him. "Is there anything else? I almost feel like I'm missing something."

I let out a nervous laugh. "You're probably just hungry."

"Yeah." He tried to smile, but the feeling wouldn't go away.

I put up my shields, uncomfortable with my deception, and how it was affecting him. I couldn't tell him anything yet, but at least I knew he wasn't giving up on me. If I could find something on Uncle Joey, I could explain everything to Chris, and he could help me figure it out.

In order to do that, I had to take things into my own hands. Waiting around was only getting me deeper into trouble. That meant I had to take some risks. Maybe I could tell Dimples. I wondered how closely Uncle Joey was watching me. He seemed to know things, like when I was home alone.

It didn't matter. Tomorrow I was going to take action. Uncle Joey had to have some secrets I could hold over his head. What was his relationship to Kate? She believed he was her uncle, but I knew he wasn't. He just went along with it. Why? Was he protecting someone?

That night, Chris astonished me by blocking most of his thoughts. There was a distance between us that hadn't been there before. It was almost like he knew I wasn't telling him the whole truth, and it bothered him more than he let on.

Later, after he fell asleep, I snuggled next to him and he put his arms around me. At least in sleep he forgot that he didn't completely trust me anymore. I finally drifted off myself, but even then, my dreams were troubled.

Chapter 8

The next morning I wanted to stay in bed. I hated deceiving Chris. What made it worse was that part of him knew I was deceiving him. He was trying to repress those feelings, but since I could read minds, he had a suspicion that I knew he felt that way. It complicated everything, and I hated the distance it created between us.

Chris left for work with a stilted peck on my cheek, and relief to get away... from me. I felt terrible and almost went back to bed, but Savannah reminded me that it was my turn to drive the carpool to school. That meant it was Friday already. Where had the week gone? Would my life ever get back to normal? At least my head was practically healed, and the bruises were finally fading from my hip and knees. That was positive.

When I got home, I was reading the paper and nearly had a heart attack when I turned the page. A photograph of the bald, sweaty guy from Uncle Joey's meeting was set below the headline titled: "Restaurant Owner Murdered." The name under the photo was Johnny Falzone. A second photo showed police tape around a restaurant where the murder took place. The article went on to say that Falzone was shot in the head at point-blank range sometime during the late evening hours. The police gave no motive, but stated it was a well-known fact that Falzone was linked to organized crime.

I sat back in my chair in shock. Who had killed him? Why? My blood turned cold when I thought of Ramos pulling the trigger. I knew he was a hitman, but he had killed the robber to save my life. This was different. It was cold-blooded murder. Had Uncle Joey ordered it? It didn't make any sense. This guy was the only one I thought wasn't a real threat to Uncle Joey.

I knew I had to find out all I could about the case. This might be the break I needed to get something on Uncle Joey, and the best place to find the information was at the police station. As long as I was in the same room as the detectives working on the case, I was sure to pick up something, and since Dimples called me yesterday, I had the perfect excuse. I quickly called Dimples' number, but all I got was his voice mail.

Thinking there was no time to lose; I showered and was soon ready to pay the police department a visit. I decided to wear my short black skirt and boots with a black blouse that was accented with silver threads. With this type of look, I could almost pass as a reporter or someone more professional, and it would be a lot easier to get the attention I needed.

On a whim, I grabbed some jeans and a t-shirt, and put them in the trunk. My wig and glasses were stuffed in a bag from yesterday, and I carefully arranged them in the extra space of my makeup kit. It was a cute little box, and no one would suspect there was a wig in it. I decided if I was going to be serious about this, it was time to think like a professional, and have everything I might need handy.

Ready to leave, my confidence blossomed. I was on a mission, and for the first time in a long time, I was in control. After this, I could tell Chris everything. Uncle Joey was going down, and my life would be my own.

When I arrived at the station, the sergeant made me wait while they found Dimples. There was a lot going on, but I could only pick up snatches of information from a few of the policemen who passed through. Their thoughts were pretty random, but underlying them all was a sense of excitement. This was a huge case. Most of the department was working on it in some way or another.

Finally, Dimples came out of a back office and waved me over. He was preoccupied, and motioned me to follow him back to his desk. In the rush, he had forgotten all about calling me yesterday, but he was still happy to see me.

"Shelby. Sorry to keep you waiting, but things are a little hectic around here with the double homicide." His dimples still mesmerized me, and I almost missed what he said.

"Double? I saw in the paper that one guy was killed, but nothing was said about a second person."

"We didn't find the other body until this morning. You see, the first man, Johnny Falzone, was shot in the back room of his restaurant. We found the second body in the freezer."

"Eww. Who was it?"

"We just got a positive ID. He was Falzone's nephew." Dimples looked around warily and lowered his voice. "I'm probably not supposed to be telling you about this. Did Chris tell you I called yesterday?"

"Yes, and since it was too late to call you back, I just decided to drop by today. But if this is a bad time, I can come back later."

"That's okay. Things are hectic but I have time to tell you what I needed. Yesterday we caught a burglary on video. Well, not who did it, but we got a clear picture of the getaway car. We traced the license plate number to the owner, a guy who has several prior arrests. When we brought him in for questioning, he denied knowing anything about it. We've kept him here, but we couldn't find his car, so unless we find something more concrete, he'll probably go free. I was hoping to get your input before that happens."

"Sure," I agreed. "Is he here?"

"Yes, but his lawyer just arrived. We can probably talk to him, but his lawyer will be present. Will that be a problem?"

"I don't think so. Just make sure you ask him good questions. Like, where are the stolen items, and who are you working with. Stuff like that. I'll get a clearer picture that way."

Dimples lips tilted up, but the smile didn't quite reach his eyes. He was questioning his sanity about asking for my help. It still seemed awfully crazy that I could get premonitions about people. If it hadn't worked before, he still wouldn't believe it.

"Okay," he said, wondering if he was nuts. "We'd better hurry. I'm lucky you showed up when you did, or he would have left before we could question him and you could... uh... do whatever it is you do." He trailed off, suddenly feeling foolish. "Why don't you wait in the interrogation room, and I'll go find him and his lawyer. It's right through here."

He ushered me into a small gray room with a rectangular desk and four chairs. He left and I sat down, realizing that this room was more like what I had expected to see at Uncle Joey's office. After a few minutes, I started to get a little claustrophobic and hoped he'd hurry. At least there wasn't a two-way mirror hanging on the wall. Then I noticed the video camera in the upper corner, and realized I was on display. Now they would have a permanent record that I was here spying on them.

Even though I didn't have a thing to feel guilty about, I jumped when Dimples opened the door and held it open. Two people followed him in, and my heart skipped a beat to see Kate. She was the lawyer? This was worse than terrible. This was a disaster. How was I going to explain why I was here?

She did a double-take when she saw me, and the man following behind bumped into her. She ushered him past her with an angry jerk of her head. "I don't know what you're trying to pull Harris, but this woman is not a detective." Kate narrowed her eyes, wondering what the hell I was doing there.

Dimples froze before putting two and two together. "That's right. You work with Shelby's husband. I thought you looked familiar." With her looks, she was someone he wasn't likely to forget, and he remembered seeing her the other day at Chris' office. It finally hit him that he was in deep trouble. He scrambled for an explanation, but I jumped in before he said anything.

"It's okay, Kate. I'm here as a consultant. I told you I was going to start a consulting business, and helping the police is part of what I do." I tried to sound as professional and competent as I could.

"The police pay you for this?" She didn't believe me.

"Not yet. Right now it's on a volunteer basis."

She inwardly sneered and sat down, motioning her client to do the same. She turned to him. "You don't have to answer any of their questions." He nodded, and I was grateful that at least he wasn't anyone I knew.

Kate couldn't get over the fact that I was there. It didn't make sense that I could be involved. She wondered if Chris knew, then she thought he probably didn't, and wouldn't it be satisfying to tell him before I did? I had to bite my tongue to keep from retorting that he knew all about it, even though that was stretching it.

She relaxed, knowing she had the upper hand as long as her client kept his mouth shut. Besides, she wanted to see what I was up to. I couldn't find any trace in her mind that she knew I was involved with Uncle Joey. He probably hadn't said anything to her. That was a plus, right?

After we were all seated, Dimples fidgeted in his chair. He was worried. I wasn't supposed to be there, and if Kate wanted to, she could complain and he'd be hard pressed to explain my presence. He'd probably get fired.

I caught his eye and nodded encouragingly. It was the only way I could tell him that Kate wasn't going to rat him out. He took a deep breath, and began the questioning.

"What were you doing at seven a.m. yesterday morning?"

Robbing the store, you idiot. After Kate nodded, he answered, "Getting ready for work."

"Where is your car?"

Safe from you. "I don't know."

"When did you notice it missing?"

Never. "When I left for work."

"Why didn't you report that it was stolen?"

He waited for Kate's nod, before smugly giving his rehearsed answer. "At first, I thought that maybe my brother took it. Sometimes I let him borrow it. I had to ask him before I could report it stolen, and it took me a while to track him down. Before I could make the report, you guys arrested me."

"We haven't arrested you," Dimples clarified. "We're just holding you for questioning."

"Well the questioning's over." He stood belligerently, nearly knocking over his chair. "I'm outta here."

Kate stood as well. "If you have any more questions you may contact me."

"Can you guarantee that he won't bolt the first chance he gets?" Dimples asked.

"Why should he? My client is innocent, and you haven't charged him with anything. Unless you want a lawsuit for police harassment brought against you, I suggest you get busy looking for his stolen car."

Kate and her client walked out the door. Before it closed she poked her head back in. "Oh, and next time Shelby participates, I suggest you make sure it's approved. I'd hate to see you lose your job over something so unnecessary. The next person might not be so understanding."

I sucked in my breath at her insult, wishing I could hurl something insulting back. Me... unnecessary? I'd show her.

"So, was it worth it?" Dimples asked.

"Being insulted by her? I don't know if I liked it very much."

"No, I mean did you get any premonitions?"

It took me a moment to change gears. "Oh, that. Yes. He did it. I couldn't get a good impression of where he hid the car though. It seemed like it was in a dark place, but that's all I could pick up."

"So, the guy's guilty?" Dimples was surprised I was so sure about it.

"Yes, guilty as sin. Maybe if you keep a close watch on him he'll get careless and lead you to his car. The stolen items are still in it."

"That would be great. I'll try to get somebody on it, but I don't know if we can spare the manpower. This double homicide has priority, and the chief's got everyone he can spare working on it."

He was thinking that the owner of the restaurant had ties to Joey "The Knife" Manetto, and it would be nice to bring him down. His contact had hinted that someone in the organization was rocking the boat, someone close to Manetto, and doing it behind his back. This double murder was a message to the boss. Whoever killed them wanted Manetto to know he had competition. That he was no longer in control. It had all the signs of a takeover.

"Anyway," Dimples said. "Thanks for coming down. You were very helpful. I'll see if I can get someone to watch him."

"Watch him? Oh, yeah... sorry, my mind was somewhere else."

He figured it was because of Kate. "Kate doesn't seem to like you very much."

"It goes both ways." I wished I could confide in him, but now wasn't the right time.

"I'd better get back to work." Dimples stood. "Thanks again for your help."

"Sure, anytime." I preceded him down the hall, and noticed Kate with her client, gathering his personal effects. She wasn't in any hurry, and I picked up that she was trying to gather information on the killings. Dimples was planning on escorting me out of the station, but I wasn't ready to leave yet. "I can find my own way out. I'm sure you're busy. If you need anything, just give me a call."

"Okay, great. Thanks."

I continued toward the door, but when Dimple's thoughts went back to the homicide, I took a little detour around the corner. Glancing down the hall, I quickly froze. A man standing with his back to me seemed familiar, but I couldn't place where I'd seen him before. He turned his head, and I caught a glimpse of his profile. It was Number Five. What was he doing in the police station?

I was too far away to pick up his thoughts, and I wasn't sure I should risk walking past him. Even without my wig and glasses, he might recognize me. Before I could make up my mind, he stepped into an office, and closed the door.

Without thinking about it too hard, I hurried down the hall to see whose office it was. The sign on the wall said Detective Barker. I could hear low voices inside, but couldn't understand what they were saying.

Not wanting to get caught eavesdropping, I retraced my steps. Kate was gone, and I decided I might as well leave too. I'd learned several things, but they seemed to bring more questions than answers. Maybe the informant Dimples was talking about was Number Five. But why would he risk being seen in the police station? Maybe he really was an undercover cop. Or maybe Detective Barker was on the take.

In the parking lot I was thinking so hard, I didn't see the car that had pulled up next to me until the window rolled down. "Hey, babe." I nearly jumped out of my skin. It was Ramos. "Get in."

He suddenly looked like the Big Bad Wolf. He saw my surprise and smiled reassuringly, but he was not happy with me. What was I doing at the police station? As if things weren't bad enough with the murders. He hoped I wasn't informing on the boss. He really didn't want to kill me. "Mr. Manetto wants to talk with you. That's all."

"For now." I finished his thought while a surge of anger rushed through me. Here I was at the police station, with cops only a few feet away, and I couldn't even ask for help. I grudgingly opened the door and got in. Ramos winced when I slammed it shut.

"Did you kill them?" That took him by surprise. "I mean, I know you're a hired gun, but I just hate to think of you killing those men in cold blood." It was out before I could think that maybe asking him wasn't such a good idea.

Something inside of him closed up tight. "You're right, I am a hired gun. That's what I do, and don't you forget it." I'd made him feel guilty again, and he didn't like it. He wanted to know what I was doing at the police station, but it wasn't his place to ask, and he realized he was getting too involved, and that wasn't good. It got in the way of doing his job.

"Maybe you should find another line of work," I suggested. "I'm sure there's lots of other things you'd be really good at."

That was the last thing he thought I'd say, and his mouth quirked up in a half smile. "You're joking, right?"

I smiled, glad the tension was gone. "Oh, I don't know. Lots of people get stuck in one thing, and forget they have other talents they could put to good use. Especially once they've made enough money to live comfortably." I added that last comment when he thought of all the money he'd have to give up.

Speculation gleamed in his eyes, and he wondered again what I did that the boss found so valuable. "I didn't kill them."

The tension across my shoulders eased. "Thank you for telling me." I smiled to let him know I meant it. He nodded and I plunged ahead. "What does Uncle Joey want?"

He growled under his breath before answering. "I don't know, but if I were to guess, it has something to do with you being at the police station right after two of his men are killed."

"How did you know that's where I was?" He didn't answer, but he thought of the GPS in my car. "That's a..." I almost said tracking device before I realized he hadn't spoken. "That's a..." I tried to cover, but I couldn't think of anything to say that would make sense. Ramos just stared at me, willing me to say global positioning system so he'd know if his suspicions were correct.

"What I'm trying to say is, I'll bet you've got something like a tracking device on the car Uncle Joey loaned me. Right? So he can keep track of me?"

Ramos nodded, unsure if that was a good guess or something more. I decided I'd better keep my mouth shut, and try to figure out what I was going to tell Uncle Joey. Since I was at the police station, would Uncle Joey think I was the informant? Of course, maybe he didn't even know there was an informant.

Maybe I should have told Dimples everything. Then at least if something happened to me, he'd know who did it. Now it was too late.

We pulled into the parking garage, and my stomach sank. Ramos was hoping I hadn't outgrown my usefulness. Somehow I knew things, and he thought Manetto would be nuts to have me killed, but unfortunately, it wasn't up to him.

Did that mean he was on my side? I didn't think so. It also meant he was getting awfully close to figuring out what I did. I'd have to be more careful.

Uncle Joey waited for me in his office. He shut the door firmly behind me, closing me in like a lid on a coffin. I almost started to plead for my life, but then I remembered that Ramos had told me Uncle Joey hated it when people groveled, and I snapped my mouth shut.

Uncle Joey hadn't said a word to me, and I realized he had far more troubling things on his mind than me. He was angry, and grieving for the loss of one of his own. Someone was threatening his empire, and after he found out who it was, he was going to rip his balls off and then stick a knife...I quickly put up my shields, and tried to keep the revulsion from showing on my face.

"Please sit down," Uncle Joey said congenially, "and tell me what you found out at the police station."

My mouth dropped open. Was that it? I was suddenly glad I hadn't groveled. "They found a second body this morning. Mr. Falzone's nephew was in the big freezer." He took that rather well. Maybe he already knew.

"Do they have any suspects?"

"No, but they think..." I faltered. If I told him, would I be informing on the informant? "They think it's an inside job." Hopefully he'd think that meant inside the restaurant, and not inside his organization.

Uncle Joey perked up. "What made them think that?"

I had no idea, so I improvised by trying to make it sound like I misunderstood the question. "Maybe because it was after hours, and there wasn't a forced entry, so at least one of them knew the killer." That made sense to me.

Uncle Joey sighed. I hadn't fooled him. He knew someone had double-crossed him. He hoped it wasn't me. "So, why did you go to the police station?"

"One of the detectives working on my case called. He needed me to fill out some paperwork. All they were thinking about was the double homicide, so that's how I got my information."

"I see," Uncle Joey said. "You didn't tell them anything about me then?"

"Do you think I would tell you if I did?"

He actually smiled. "No."

"I didn't, but now I'm not sure I did the right thing. If something should happen to me—"

"Shelby," he soothed. "I'm surprised. You're very valuable to me, and with this double murder, we've got our work cut out for us. Someone close to me is trying to undermine my organization, and you're the best one to help me figure out who it is."

"Lucky me," I said under my breath.

He ignored it. "I've called an emergency meeting. Soon everyone will be here, and I'm counting on you to find out if anyone in my organization is behind it."

I thought his plan was seriously flawed. What made him think I would tell him the truth? It wouldn't bother me to be out from under him, although I didn't like the thoughts of people dying. But if it meant I wouldn't die, maybe it wasn't so bad. It started to bother me that I could even think such a thing. When had I become so callous? "When did you say they would be here?"

"Some have arrived already."

"Oh, no! My wig and glasses are in the trunk of my car, and it's at the police station. I can't let anyone see me without my disguise."

Uncle Joey didn't care. He thought my disguise was unnecessary anyway. "That's too bad, but you'll have to do without it."

"If I can't wear my disguise, I'll have to hide in the room where they can't see me."

"Shelby, at this point I'm not going to waste time on something that doesn't matter, and your disguise doesn't matter." That last part was said rather loudly, and Uncle Joey was a little surprised that he had lost his cool. He paused to gain his composure, and I saw my opening.

"I'm sorry you feel that way, but I really can't go in there without my wig. Besides, don't you feel a little funny about leaving one of your cars parked at the police station? What if someone realizes it's not supposed to be there, and they run a license plate check? When they find out it belongs to you, they'll figure out some reason to impound it, and come snooping around here. I don't think you need that right now." Things were getting out of hand and I was desperate. If I could just get inside the police station, I was ready to tell Dimples everything.

He closed his eyes, wondering if I knew how much I exasperated him. "I'll send Ramos for it—"

"I'll go with him. Someone's got to drive it back, and I've got the keys." I hurried out the door before he could stop me. Ramos was standing guard, and I grabbed his arm. "We have to go back for my car." I tugged at him, but it was like trying to move a brick wall.

Uncle Joey paused in the doorway, smiling at my futile attempt to get Ramos to move. "Get the car and come straight back," he said to Ramos. "Don't let her out of your sight." To me he said, "I want you in my conference room in half an hour whether you have your wig on or not." With that announcement, he shut the door in my face.

"It's never good to mess with the boss," Ramos said, but he was secretly impressed that I dared. "Move it."

It was a quick trip to the police station, mostly because Ramos was all business. I was a bad influence on him, and he wanted to keep his distance. It bothered me at first until I realized that it actually meant that I was a good influence. I couldn't help smiling at that, and even though he noticed my smile, he chose to ignore it.

The bigger problem was finding a chance to talk to Dimples. I knew it was a long shot from the beginning, but if I could just convince Ramos to drop me off, I might have an opportunity. Before I could get out of the car, Ramos caught my arm. "I'll follow you back."

"You really don't have to. I'm not going anywhere else."

"Neither am I, babe." He smiled, but this time it didn't reach his eyes. They were cold and predatory, kind of like when he shot the bank robber.

"Oh, all right." I didn't mask my annoyance as I got out of the car, but for some reason, I couldn't slam the door this time. I marched over to my car, but that one look had undermined my confidence, and I knew now was not the moment to try anything. Ramos had a job to do, and this wasn't the time to push him. I just hoped that if he ever got the order to kill me, he wouldn't do it, or at least he would hesitate long enough so I could get away.

I pulled out of the parking lot, barely glancing at the doors to the police station, knowing Ramos was watching me closely. At least now I had my wig and glasses. Thank goodness I had been thinking professionally this morning and they were in the trunk.

I turned into Uncle Joey's parking garage with only ten minutes to spare. I grabbed my stuff out of the trunk, and made a beeline for the elevator. Ramos was running to catch up when the elevator doors began to close. He wasn't going to make it unless I stuck my foot in the door. I waved instead, and the doors closed, cutting off his startled curse. I didn't feel too bad though, because now I could put on my wig without an audience.

I quickly went to work, and smoothed it into place as the doors swished open. Uncle Joey and Number Five stood together talking in the hall, and both of them turned to look at me.

Number Five smiled, faintly amused, and Uncle Joey quickly directed him to the conference room before turning to me. He tried to hold back a smile, but couldn't do it. "You'd better look in a mirror before you come in. But hurry, everyone's here."

As I started down the hall, Ramos stepped off the second elevator, and nearly ran over me. He opened his mouth to tell me off, but quickly changed his mind. "The bathroom's that way." I knew there was something wrong with my wig, but it couldn't be that bad.

When I saw it, I nearly died of embarrassment. Part of my hair was sticking out one side, and the wig was crooked, with the bangs off center. I looked like I'd been in a bad accident. So much for trying to hurry.

I finally got everything straightened out when my cell phone started ringing. The sound echoed in the bathroom, and it was so loud that I dropped my make-up kit trying to answer it before Ramos came running. "Shit."

"Shelby?"

"Chris?"

"Why are you swearing? You never swear. What's going on?"

"I never swear in front of the kids, but sometimes I swear. Like now."

"What's wrong?" he asked evenly.

I clamped the phone to my shoulder, and started grabbing my lipstick and mascara. "I dropped my make-up kit, and now all my make-up's scattered all over the bathroom floor. Damn! My eye shadow is broken into a million pieces."

"Where are you? Kate told me she saw you at the police station. She asked me about your 'consulting business' and I didn't know what to say. What was she talking about?"

"She probably loved that."

"Shelby."

"Well she would! There's more to her than you think, but I can't explain right now, I'm at work, and I'm supposed to be in this meeting. They're all waiting for me, and I don't want to get in trouble. I'll call you when it's over."

"You mean you're at Thrasher Development? Right now?"

"Yes. I've really got to go. I'll call you later."

"No, wait! I'm not through talking to you. You said yesterday that you'd never hang up on me again. Remember?"

He had me there. "Well, sure. I'm not hanging up on you, but I've got to go. I promise I'll call you as soon as the meeting's over. Okay?"

I heard a heavy sigh before he answered. "Fine. Just don't forget." Then he hung up. The silence seemed louder than normal, and I hoped it made him feel better to hang up first. Not that it mattered to me... ha-ha.

I decided to leave my make-up kit in the bathroom and, after a glance in the mirror to make sure everything was in place, I stepped into the hall. Ramos stood next to the door like a statue, and I knew he'd heard everything I'd said to my husband.

"Better hurry." He motioned me down the hall. "Here's a pen and a pad of paper."

I took them with a big sigh and entered the conference room. Everyone turned to look at me, and the room went dead silent. Uncomfortable, I quickly took my seat next to Uncle Joey. The negative energy directed my way hit me like a ton of bricks, and I would have staggered if I hadn't been sitting down.

"What's she doing here?"

"Don't worry about her," Uncle Joey said. "She's not your concern. What is your concern, is who killed Johnny. I want some answers, and I want them now."

Although the room was silent, my mind was suddenly bombarded with shouts of anger and distrust. Some of the distrust was for me, but mostly, it was directed toward each other and Uncle Joey. Many of them were thinking that it was someone else sitting at the table, but I couldn't pick up a guilty thought anywhere. If I had to guess at that moment, I'd say that none of them were involved.

"I am grieved by the loss of my good friend Johnny Falzone," Uncle Joey began. "And I intend to find the person responsible for his death. I have reason to believe that it was an inside job. Someone who knew Johnny well. Perhaps one of you."

They all rushed to deny it, and I had a hard time sorting through their thoughts. I jumped from one to another, searching for the guilty party. The only one who didn't seem concerned was Number Five. This made sense if he was an undercover cop.

Uncle Joey directed the discussion to their enemies, and who would gain from killing Johnny. This seemed to calm everyone down. He asked if anyone knew about Johnny's business and if there was someone he'd angered recently.

They covered all the possibilities and scenarios, but came up with nothing concrete.

I zeroed in on Number Five, hoping to find out if he worked for the police, but he was as closed as ever, almost like he was hiding something. I figured that was as close to the truth as I was going to get.

"I want you all to take extra precautions," Uncle Joey warned. "If someone is out to undermine our organization, then everyone is a target. Spread the word that we're looking for information on the killings." He unlocked his bottom drawer, and passed out stacks of money. "This should help loosen a few tongues. Call me if you find anything, otherwise, we'll meet again on Monday."

After everyone left, Uncle Joey locked his bottom drawer and turned to me. "Well?"

"I don't think any of them did it," I said. "Most of them seemed pretty upset, but if one of them did it, they sure didn't think about it."

"I see." He walked slowly around the room thinking about the enemies he'd made over the years. "I thought it was someone close to me, but I couldn't imagine any of my boys doing this. We're like a family—you know?"

I hoped he didn't expect an answer. I mean, most families don't think about killing each other, do they? "Maybe it didn't have anything to do with you. Maybe it was just some random thing."

Uncle Joey shook his head. "I don't think so."

"Maybe it was someone in his family. Wasn't the other guy that was killed the one Johnny was going to give the business to? Maybe a relative of his wasn't happy about it, and killed them both."

"Hmm... you're right. That's a definite possibility. I think we should pay our respects to his wife, and see what you can pick up at the house."

Maybe I should just keep my mouth shut. "I don't know if I have time. I really have a lot to do today."

"It won't take long." Uncle Joey was already leaving the room, and calling for Ramos to bring the car around.

I closed my eyes and moaned. What now? How long was this going to take? I checked my watch. It was nearly one o'clock, and I had to pick the kids up from school at three-twenty. I hurried back to the bathroom, and grabbed my make-up kit, then headed for the elevator where Uncle Joey waited.

"I'm going to have to follow you in my car so I can leave to pick my kids up from school. They get out at three-twenty." I tried to be matter-of-fact, so he wouldn't feel threatened.

"There's no need, we'll be back by then."

I had the sudden feeling that Uncle Joey had no intention of letting me out of his sight for a very long time. He was singing a tune in his head, so I couldn't know for sure. Very clever. We exited through the main doors of the building where Ramos waited with the car.

My heart started to pound when we drove off, like I was having a panic attack or something. I suddenly wanted to go home more than anything in the world. What was I doing in this car with these men? How in the world had this happened?

I could have lived with the mind reading thing, but now I was at the beck and call of a mobster. All because of Kate. Here I was with her Uncle, and she was in an office with my husband, who was waiting for a phone call from me that I couldn't make. I should have told Dimples what was going on this morning, and now it was too late. How was I ever going to get out of this?

We pulled up in front of a beautiful colonial mansion and Uncle Joey helped me out. We weren't the only ones here to pay our respects, as cars were parked all along the driveway. Ramos followed behind us, alert for any signs of treachery.

A maid showed us to a large open room where a solemn group of people were gathered at one end. Seeing us, a woman detached herself from the group and came to Uncle Joey who gathered her in his arms. She cried delicately against his chest, and Uncle Joey assured her that he would not rest until Johnny's murderer was found. She drew him to the couch to sit and talk, leaving me standing alone in the middle of the room.

Ramos touched my shoulder and motioned me toward the opposite end of the room where a buffet was set up on a long table. He gave me a plate, got one for himself, and began to fill it with food. "Might as well eat since we missed lunch," he explained. He never let business interfere with his appetite.

I wasn't very hungry, but once I tried the crab canapés and creamy cheese bread, I changed my mind. Good food always helped me relax. We sat at a small table in the corner, and I scanned the crowd, trying to pick out thoughts that would tell me anything about the murders.

It didn't take long to recognize defeat. No one here had wanted Johnny dead. They all felt bad about it. One of them wondered if Uncle Joey had done it, but I couldn't tell who that thought came from. After trying to get more information, I figured that coming here had been a waste of time, except for the food. I nearly said as much to Ramos, but caught myself. Uncle Joey was still talking, so I told Ramos I had to find the bathroom before we left.

I wandered down the hall, but passed the bathroom door and kept on going toward the kitchen. It was like my mind had switched to survival mode, and all I wanted to do was get away. Without even thinking about it, I opened the back door and walked out.

I took a few steps then jerked to a sudden stop. A low growl came from the area to my right, and my heart just about jumped out of my chest. The biggest dog I had ever seen bared its teeth and growled at me. With a startled cry, I flew back inside the house so fast I ran right into Ramos. I would have kept on going if he hadn't grabbed my arms and held on tight.

"There's a really big dog out there," I tried to explain. My legs had turned to jelly, and I was shaking like a leaf.

"Why did you go outside?" Ramos asked. "I thought you went to find the bathroom?"

"I did, but something made my feet carry me out the door. I guess I just needed some fresh air. Is Uncle Joey ready to go? I really need to get home."

Ramos didn't believe me. He knew I was trying to escape. "Look, I won't tell Mr. Manetto you tried to run away. It would be bad for you. I told you he doesn't like people who run or grovel."

"No you didn't. You only told me about the groveling part, not the running part."

"Well, that's probably because I didn't take you for a runner."

"Oh? Just a groveler?"

He shook his head, thinking this was an argument he didn't want to have. "Come on. Mr. Manetto's ready to leave."

My legs were still a bit shaky, so I didn't mind that Ramos kept hold of my arm.

He let me go when we got back to the crowded room. Uncle Joey disengaged himself from Johnny's widow and met us at the door. When we were sitting comfortably in the car, Uncle Joey asked me if I had any success.

"No one there wanted Johnny dead," I answered. Then I realized that Ramos was listening. "We should probably talk about this in your office." I inclined my head toward Ramos.

"Oh," Uncle Joey said, unconcerned. He trusted Ramos completely. "Yes, of course."

I wanted to know what he was thinking, but once again, he started singing a song in his mind. He was doing it on purpose, and it irritated me. I knew he was planning something I wasn't going to be happy about. It made me mad, but worse was that other feeling I'd been trying to bury under layers of anger. Deep inside where I didn't want to admit it, I was scared to death.

Chapter 9

Ramos let Uncle Joey and me out at the curb, and we entered the building through the revolving doors. I was tempted to keep going around and come back out, but what was the point? I mean, how far could I get anyway? Uncle Joey might be old, but he was in great shape. Once we were alone in the elevator, I decided to ask him something that had been bothering me.

"Why do you say you're Kate's uncle when you're not related?"

He was shocked and surprised. "How did you know that?" I tapped my head. "Oh yeah. Umm, well, it's a long story. Maybe someday I'll tell you."

I didn't really think he would tell me in the first place. I mostly just wanted to stop him from singing that stupid tune. Maybe talking would help. "You need to figure out the motive behind Johnny's death. How many enemies did he have? Who would want him dead? Is it because of something he did? It could even be something from a long time ago. You've been friends for a while. Did anything happen in all those years that would make someone want to kill him?"

Uncle Joey didn't say anything, but I caught a feeling of regret that he'd had to kill someone, and that Johnny had helped him do it. The image was so powerful it was like I was there. I actually caught a glimpse of a man falling at Uncle Joey's feet, with a knife protruding from his chest. There was shock on the dying man's face while Johnny held him from behind. I blinked back to the present when Uncle Joey pushed the memory away.

This was bad, and I tried to cover it by asking, "So, have you thought of anything yet?"

His sharp glance pierced me to the quick, and the skin around his eyes tightened. He was pretty certain I'd just witnessed his crime. "Shelby, what am I going to do with you?" My stomach plunged. Had I just sealed my fate? Again? Just then, the elevator doors slid open. "After you," he said smoothly.

As we entered his suite, his secretary smiled and gave us a cheery greeting. At least someone was happy. "There's a Mr. Hodges here to see you," she said. "He's in your office."

"Come with me Shelby. Let's hear what he has to say." Since I was in disguise, I could hardly refuse. Besides, I was as good as dead anyway. Uncle Joey greeted Hodges, and introduced me as his assistant. I took the other seat in front of Uncle Joey's desk next to Hodges, and kept my face averted. Luckily, Hodges was so preoccupied that he didn't really look at me, and I breathed a sigh of relief.

"I just wanted you to know that my case is going well," Hodges began. "The lawyers have worked wonders, and it looks promising that I'll get the insurance money. It's been hard going these last few weeks. Until I get the insurance money, I don't have enough funds to restock my store." He was nervous, but after discovering last night that his jewels were stolen, he was determined to find out if Uncle Joey knew anything.

"I suppose business has slowed down considerably. Do you need my help? I'm sure I can loan you a fair amount until the money comes in."

"That's what brings me here. You see, I had a few jewels in my safe at home that I was planning on using to restock, but last night I discovered they'd been stolen."

"How strange. Did you call the police?"

"No. I couldn't involve them because of my case. They might think they were some of the jewels I'd reported stolen, and it wouldn't look good."

"Were they?" Uncle Joey wasn't in the mood to beat around the bush.

"No," Hodges quickly denied it. "I wouldn't do that. I just thought that maybe with your connections, you could look into it."

Uncle Joey took his time answering, and Hodges started to fidget. "I'll do that as a favor to you, but just remember that I have very little tolerance for double-crossers." He stood, signaling that the meeting was over. "I'll let you know if I find anything."

"Thank you." Hodges left quickly, holding back his anger. He knew that Uncle Joey had his jewels, and there was nothing he could do about it.

After the door closed, Uncle Joey turned to me. "Well?"

"He panicked when he found that his jewels were gone. It's ruined everything, and now he's got a pretty good idea that you have them."

"Ah. Well, I hope he's learned his lesson." He took a deep breath, considering me from under his bushy eyebrows. "It's true that I don't like double-crossers." He was worried that I knew too much, and he was trying to decide what to do about it.

I nearly groaned, knowing I was going to my doom. Would he kill me? He reached in his desk drawer, and my heart skipped a beat. Was he getting out a gun?

"What's the matter?" Uncle Joey said. "You're white as a ghost." He drew out a stack of money, and placed it on the desk. "Here, I forgot to give this to you earlier. It's for all the extra time you've put in."

"What?"

"It's yours. You've earned it."

I was shocked, and more than a little confused. What was this all about? I didn't trust him for one minute, but I didn't know what to do. If I took the money, it might make things worse. I could get sucked in so deep, that if I wasn't killed, I would probably go to prison. What could be worse than that? "I think I'd rather put it in my account as a direct deposit," I improvised. "I don't really like going to banks anymore."

That startled a laugh from him. It was a loud, booming sound, and it relieved some of my anxiety. He caught his breath, and put the money back in his drawer. "I'll have Jackie get the paperwork, and you can give her a voided check."

"Okay. Well, I'd better get going." I checked my watch. "I have to pick my kids up from school in half an hour. Call if you need anything." I almost made it to the door before his commanding voice stopped me.

"You can't go now," he said. "I need you here."

I whirled around and faced him, desperation feeding my anger. "I can't stay. It's my responsibility to pick up my kids from school." He opened his mouth to object so I cut him off. "Look, I've done everything you asked, and more. I've listened to all your men, and told you everything they were thinking. I went to Mr. Hodges house, and found all his jewels for you. I told you everything I learned at the police station this morning. I even went to Johnny's house, and listened to his family, who were pretty pissed off, by the way. And I've given you some great advice. I think the least you could do is let me pick up my kids like I'm supposed to."

Uncle Joey blinked at my audacity to contradict him. It threw him off-guard. He wasn't used to anyone who didn't grovel most of the time. He hated it when people groveled, but this was almost more than he could take.

"There's not a lot I can do for you here," I said, in a soothing tone, inching closer to the door. "And I've got my phone. You call, and I'll come right back. You know I will. Have I ever let you down? Now I've really got to go." I rushed out the door before Uncle Joey could say anything.

Ramos stood in the hallway like a guard. I smiled as I rushed past him, and pushed the call button for the elevator. It surprised him that I had managed to escape. It was hard to believe that the boss would let me walk out of there. When I stepped onto the elevator, he followed, thinking that maybe he should come with me.

"No!" I blurted.

Ramos crammed his arm in the elevator door so it wouldn't close. "What did you say?"

He knew what I said, and I knew I'd better do some quick thinking. "It looked like you were wondering if you should come with me. I could tell by the way you hesitated, and looked around for Uncle Joey. I said no because I didn't want you to waste your time asking me when you didn't need to. Okay?" He grunted but didn't move, so I swatted his arm. "Let me go. I've got to pick my kids up from school, and I'm going to be late." When he still hesitated I added, "It's okay with Uncle Joey, I promise."

Nobody had swatted him like that for a long time. Not since his grandmother, and she had died when he was a kid.

I sure hoped he liked his grandmother. After a second of indecision, he pulled his hand away, and the doors swooshed closed. I let out my breath and nearly collapsed. That was close. It wasn't until I was driving out of the parking garage that I let myself relax. I did it. I got away.

I pulled up in front of the school just as the bell rang. Finally, something was going right. I glanced in my rearview mirror to make sure no one had followed me, and got a shock. I still had my wig on. I whipped it off, then wondered what I was going to do with it.

The glove box. I threw it in, and tried to pull out all the bobby pins that held my hair back. I got one side undone when the car door opened. Savannah slid in next to me and did a double-take. "Mom? When did you get glasses?"

"Umm... just the other day. How was school?"

"Fine." Besides my weird hair and glasses, she couldn't help but notice my short skirt and boots. Why was I wearing that? It suddenly dawned on her that I must be having a midlife crisis. It was the only thing that explained the way I was acting. Wow, she didn't realize I was so old.

Old? Me? The car door opened, effectively stopping me from telling her how wrong she was. I wasn't old. The other kids started piling into the car, but I'd learned my lesson and blocked their thoughts. I didn't need to hear how old I was again.

It was a relief to drop each of them off at their houses and get home. Home. I never wanted to leave again. So far, all my strategies had just gotten me into more trouble. If I wasn't such an optimistic person, I could easily get depressed.

It was time to try a different tactic. Now that I had 'seen' Uncle Joey commit a murder, all I needed to do was find out whom he had killed. Then I could put him away for good. I'd seen the victim's face so that was a good start. There was something else. Johnny was involved. He must have been an accomplice, and since it was on Uncle Joey's mind, he must have thought it was tied to Johnny's murder.

Besides the murder victim's face, and Johnny's involvement with Uncle Joey, I had one more clue. In Uncle Joey's memory, Johnny wasn't bald or fat. He was young. That meant it had happened at least twenty years ago, maybe more. So now I had to find an unsolved murder that had happened in the last twenty years.

Of course, maybe afterward, Uncle Joey had made it look like an accident. Then it wouldn't be recorded as a murder. Maybe he dumped the body somewhere, and the guy's a missing person. Or he could have covered the whole thing up, and nobody even knew the guy was dead. No, somebody knew, or Johnny wouldn't be dead, right? Unless Johnny's death was totally unrelated. My heart sank. With so many different possibilities, how would I ever find the truth? I had to find out what happened. It was the only way out of this terrible mess.

I pulled the car into the garage feeling drained and discouraged. Savannah rushed inside, and I envied her youth and innocence. It was hard to believe that just a few weeks ago, my life was simple and relatively stress-free. I was happy taking care of my family and doing all the little mundane things I did. I didn't care about having a career like Chris thought. I was making a difference in my own way. Now, after barely escaping death from a deranged bank robber, I was trying to keep a mob boss satisfied enough to let me live. All because I had stopped at the grocery store for a few carrots! Ugh! I slammed the car door, and stomped into the house.

"Hey, mom," Josh was drinking milk out of the bottle. It started to run down his chin, and he wiped it off with his sleeve. He opened his mouth, and let out a huge belch.

"Joshua!" I scolded.

He grinned like a maniac, happy he'd gotten a response out of me. Lately, I'd hardly noticed him, and he wondered if something was wrong with me. "Nice boots." He took in my short skirt, and was surprised that I looked so good for someone my age. All except for the hair. It looked pretty stupid. "I didn't know you needed glasses."

"I don't. I just like the way I look in them, so I got them for fun." Telling the truth was probably not the smartest thing to do, but I was tired of lying.

"Oh." He considered how I looked. "You look good in them." He thought I'd look better if I fixed my hair different.

"I had my hair pulled back earlier, but some of the pins fell out, that's why it looks funny. So, how was school?"

He stilled. How did I know he was thinking about my hair? It must be women's intuition or something like that. "Uh, school's fine."

"Good." I wasn't going to get any more out of him. His mind had wandered, and it was making me dizzy trying to keep up. Mostly, he was thinking about food. "Why don't you get your homework done, and I'll make those chicken enchiladas you like so much?"

"I was just thinking about chicken enchiladas!" he exclaimed. "Weird."

"Yeah, isn't it?" If he only knew.

I pushed my worries about Uncle Joey aside as I changed my clothes, and got all the pins out of my hair. I fluffed it up and put on some lipstick. That's when I realized that my jeans weren't too tight; in fact, they were a little loose. Elated, I put on some perfume, and a low-cut cotton shirt. Chris would be coming home soon, and I needed him distracted.

He'd been upset with me last night, and I knew he was not going to be happy with me today, since I hadn't called him back. To top it off, Kate had spilled the beans about my "consulting business" and it would look like another deception to him. I hoped looking and smelling sexy would make him forget.

I put the chicken in to defrost and started cutting up an onion. This dinner was something Chris really liked, so that was a plus. He'd be so distracted by the food and my sexy body, he'd forget his anger, right? My heart lightened, and I got lost in preparing our dinner. It was a relief to forget my troubles in this simple task. I popped the enchiladas in the oven, and started to clean up.

The air was heavy with the smell of roasted chicken and enchilada sauce with cheese when Chris walked in. I could tell he appreciated the aroma, when he closed the door and inhaled deeply. I was cutting up tomatoes for a salad, and practically threw down my knife.

"Hi." I quickly wrapped my arms around him while he was distracted, and hugged him tight. He dropped his briefcase, and his arms closed around me. So far, so good.

"What are you cooking?" he asked. "It smells wonderful."

"Chicken enchiladas," I smiled up at him. "They'll be done in about fifteen minutes." He looked into my eyes, and I leaned up to kiss him. Our lips met and he groaned. I deepened the kiss, giving him a promise of what was to come.

He pulled back, out of breath. "I know what you're trying to do."

"Is it working?"

"Yes."

This time he took control, and pinned me against the counter, capturing my lips with bruising force. It was a few seconds later that the shrill beeping of the timer went off and we pulled apart.

"Hold that thought," I said, and breathlessly turned off the oven. Before I could grab him again, he picked up his brief case and held it in front of him like a shield.

"What are you doing that for?" I asked, disappointed.

"You know exactly why I'm doing this. You think you can use your body to get out of talking to me. Well, you can't."

"Are you sure about that? It looks like it's working to me."

Chris held back a smile, and shook his head. "Shelby, I wasn't even sure you'd be here when I came home. Why didn't you call me back?"

"I didn't have a chance, and by the time I got through with the meeting, I barely had enough time to get Savannah from school. I guess I could have called you when I got home, but I figured you'd be home soon, and I put it off. I guess, mostly because I knew you'd be mad since I didn't call you. So I probably just made it all worse, but you have to remember that you weren't happy last night either."

I probably shouldn't have reminded him, since he'd nearly forgotten it himself. In fact, the main thing overriding all his thoughts was worry. He'd been worried about me, and by not calling, he'd been afraid something was wrong, and this time, maybe I wasn't coming home. It was something he didn't want to admit, even to himself.

"Oh, Chris," I reached for him. "I'm sorry."

"Did you just... you're not supposed to do that." He wasn't really mad, but he was tired of blocking his thoughts all the time. Something had to give.

I smiled at him. "Let's eat and then we can talk."

He was thinking of something else he'd rather do, and my heart skipped a beat at his sudden change of direction. He leaned down to kiss me when Joshua breezed through.

"Is dinner ready?" Josh saw what we were doing, and was filled with embarrassment. "I'm starving here."

"Yes." I turned away from Chris. "I just need to finish the salad. Why don't you guys set the table?"

The next half hour things seemed almost normal. I kept my mental shields up and realized I was getting better at it, although I couldn't totally relax. I was also learning not to respond when I did pick something up. That was harder to do, especially when what they were thinking needed to be straightened out. The urge to correct them was hard to suppress, but I found there were other ways to do it that didn't ruffle any feathers.

It wasn't until we were getting ready for bed that Chris and I could finally talk without interruption. "So," Chris began. "Kate said she saw you at the police station. What were you doing there?"

"You told me Dimples called yesterday. I couldn't get through to him, so I went down to the station to see what he wanted. That's when I ran into Kate. Do you know what kinds of clients she has? I didn't think your firm handled those kinds of cases."

"What kinds of cases?"

"The ones where the guy you're defending is guilty. That's what Dimples needed me for, to find out if the guy was guilty. Since I'd been able to help him before, he decided to ask again. Kate turned out to be the guy's lawyer and she came in for the questioning. When she asked what I was doing there, I told her I was starting my own consulting business. See how easily it happened? That was the only thing I could think of to say."

"Yes." Chris let out a breath, thinking how easy it had become for me to tell a lie. "So, I take it he was guilty?"

"Yes." It hurt me that he thought I was becoming a liar and I couldn't squelch the simmering indignation. "I only lie because I have to cover up the fact that I can read minds. But I don't enjoy it. I hate it. It's hard to know things about people."

"Shelby... I'm sure it's hard. I wish it had never happened. I keep hoping that maybe it will go away."

"Me too." I leaned into his arms for comfort, and hoped our conversation was over. He had questions about Thrasher Development that I didn't want to answer, so I decided to take his mind off them the best way I knew how.

He pulled away from my kiss with a raised brow. "You're distracting me again."

"I know."

Instead of protesting, he pushed me onto the bed, and grabbed my arms. I yelped, realizing his intentions a second too late, and he began tickling me without mercy. One thing led to another and it wasn't until much later that I was resting peacefully beside him. His breathing deepened and I congratulated myself that I'd accomplished my goal. Then his deep voice startled me. "Did you know Thrasher Development is owned by Joey Manetto?"

His unexpected question gave me a shock, and my heart sped up. It took me a minute to answer. "Mr. Manetto's first name is Joey?" I tried to put as much unbelief in my voice as I could.

"So, you know him?"

"I've met him. Briefly." If Chris could hear my heart pounding, he'd know I was lying through my teeth.

He rose up on one elbow, and leaned over me. "Shelby, this guy's bad. He's a mob boss, and I don't want you working for him."

"What?" I tried to act surprised.

"I want you to quit your job."

"Wow, a mob boss? How did you find out?"

He was thinking that was a pretty dumb question since he was a lawyer, and knew stuff like that. "It doesn't matter. What matters is that you quit working for him. I don't want you getting involved in any of his business. I know you just started, but there's got to be something else you could do."

"Umm... I guess I could quit. I certainly don't want to be involved with criminals."

"Good, do it as soon as you can."

"Sure, first thing Monday morning."

He lay back down, relieved I hadn't put up a fuss. "I've been thinking about your new talents. Since you seem to be stuck with them, it might be a good idea to put them to use, and make a little money while you're at it, since you want to have a career and all. What do you think?"

"You mean, like a detective agency?"

"No, nothing dangerous, but I'm sure there's something else. We'll have to think about it." Thoughts of playing poker in Las Vegas briefly crossed his mind, but he wasn't sure I knew how to play. He was right, but I could learn, couldn't I? "Oh, before I forget, we probably ought to turn in the rental car tomorrow."

My heart sank. "I don't want to turn it in until I have another one to replace it."

"Maybe we can look for a car tomorrow," Chris replied.

"Yeah, if there's time, that would be good." We said goodnight, and I spent the next few hours tossing and turning. I should have known Chris would find out who owned Thrasher Development. Maybe he'd known it all along.

Somehow, I'd have to figure out a way to keep the car until Monday. Hopefully by then, I'd know who Uncle Joey had killed so we could put him behind bars permanently. In truth, it was about the only way I could quit my job.

The next morning was Saturday, and after my unsettled sleep, I woke up late. Chris and Josh had already left for Josh's soccer game, and I decided it would be a good time for me to go to the library. It was the best place I could think to do some research on the man Uncle Joey killed. I just had to find out who he was. I showered and got ready, dropping Savannah off at her friend's house on the way.

The archives were in the basement, and it took a while to get settled in and find the newspapers in the files that I wanted. I decided to go back twenty-two years to make sure I didn't miss anything. The first two years of newspapers, I spent way too much time reading everything. After that I decided to just check for murders, and if there wasn't a picture included, I checked the obituaries as well.

I went through eight years in three hours with no luck, and my heart fell. How could it not be there? Uncle Joey couldn't have covered the whole thing up, could he? Maybe I hadn't gone back far enough.

This time I went back thirty years and started over, pinning all my hopes of success that I would find something. Another hour, and two years later, my heart skipped a beat when I scanned the page and there was a photo of him. Stephen Cohen. He was a handsome man, with dark blond hair and a nice smile. Uncle Joey's memory had faded some, but I recognized his eyes. They were deep and penetrating in the picture, like he was looking into your soul. Just as they had when Uncle Joey stabbed him.

The headline read, "Prominent Lawyer Murdered" and stated that he had been killed in his own home when he walked in on a burglary. Luckily, his wife and young child were away at the time.

I gasped and fought off a chill when I read the name of the law firm he had worked for. It was Cohen, Larsen, and Pratt, the same firm where Chris worked. The article continued, saying that the victim had died of a stab wound. At least they got that right. The knife had been found along with several stolen articles in the trunk of a known thief, and they had the man in custody. The police said it was an open and closed case, given all the circumstantial evidence. I cringed, knowing they'd sent the wrong man to prison.

Could this man be out of prison by now? Was he the person who had killed Johnny for revenge? It probably had nothing to do with it and I was grasping at straws. Even so, that didn't change the fact that Uncle Joey had killed Stephen Cohen. That knowledge had to be good for something, right?

I put everything back, and was shocked it was so late. What excuse could I give Chris? It always took me a long time to go shopping, and since I couldn't think of anything better, I stopped at the mall and looked through all the clearance items. I found some really cute clothes on sale. A black skirt with turquoise paneling, paired with a turquoise v-neck cardigan looked fantastic. When I tried them on they fit so well that I had to buy them. Of course, I had to get some black pumps to go with the outfit. But they were on sale too, so altogether, I saved more than I spent. Is that even possible? There's nothing like a good shopping trip to make me happy.

I was putting my new purchases in the trunk when my cell phone rang. Chris was probably wondering what had happened to me. My excuse was cut short when I realized it was Uncle Joey instead. What did he want? I almost didn't answer, but knew I didn't really have a choice.

"Hello?"

"You left so fast yesterday that you forgot to leave a cancelled check," he said.

"Oh, that's right," I started to apologize, but he cut me off.

"It's okay. I've opened an account for you at my bank. You can pick up the paperwork on Monday. That's why I'm calling. It's Johnny's funeral on Monday and I want you there. A lot of times the killer will show up at the funeral, and it would be helpful if you could use your talents to locate him for me. The funeral's at noon."

He rattled off the name and address of the funeral home and disconnected before I could say anything. Damn. My good mood evaporated, and I wanted to throw my phone across the parking lot, instead, I just stomped my feet a few times. I got in the car and slammed the door, then sat for a minute and took some deep breaths. I could get through this. I just needed to keep it together a little while longer.

When I got home, Chris was ready to go car shopping. He had even found a few cars in the paper he wanted to look at. He was excited to use my mind-reading talents to get the best deal possible, and I had to go along with it.

We spent the next few hours looking at cars. I told Chris I didn't want another van, even though that was probably the most practical kind of car for us. I mean, how do you pick up a bunch of kids in a cute, sexy sports car? So that's what we ended up looking for. Most of the dealers were pretty straight-forward. We told them what we wanted and how much money we had to spend, and they showed us the cars in that price range.

There were a couple of dealers that tried to sell us some bad cars, and we couldn't get away fast enough from them. Along the way, I got a headache trying to keep all the numbers straight. High book, low book, it was kind of confusing, and I'm not the best at numbers in the first place. Still, I was surprised at how much the cars were marked up. We came home empty-handed, which was my goal since the car I was using wasn't really a rental. I kind of felt guilty, but Chris just smiled and said we'd try again tomorrow.

The next day, between going to church and looking at cars, I asked Chris about his law firm. I couldn't get over the fact that he worked for someone so closely tied to Uncle Joey.

"So, tell me something," I began. "I've met the partners Larsen and Pratt from your law firm, but never Cohen. How come?"

"That would be Stephen Cohen. He was the force behind the establishment of our law firm, a real smart and talented guy. Unfortunately, he was killed about twenty-five years ago. Murdered, actually, and from what I know, his murder was a real tragedy," he said. "Apparently, he surprised a burglar in his home, and ended up getting killed. At least his murderer was put away for it."

"Wow, that's awful."

"Yes," Chris agreed. "The senior partners have been around a long time, but they're thinking of adding to the list and retiring. I'm hoping I can move into one of those spots."

"So, you think it's a good firm?"

"Of course," he said, surprised. "Why are you asking me that?"

"It's just that Kate seems to represent some clients that aren't the best. Even you think that Mr. Hodges is guilty, right?"

"Well, yes at first, but now I'm not so sure. We went to court on Friday, and he seemed pretty desperate. I haven't seen him like that before. He told everyone that no matter who stole them, his jewels were gone, and if he didn't get the insurance money, he was ruined. It didn't seem like he was lying to me."

"When will you find out the verdict?"

"Monday, or Tuesday. We still have more witnesses to call." He could see I was still troubled. "Hey, in this business sometimes you can't choose who you represent. It's not always a matter of who's guilty; it's a matter of representing your client to the best of your ability under the law. If everyone does their job right, the guilty are caught. But sometimes it doesn't work that way."

"Doesn't it bother you?" I had to ask.

"Yes, but I try not to think about it too hard."

"Just don't make any enemies or you could end up like Stephen Cohen."

He sensed that I knew more than I was saying, but he didn't pry, and I was grateful. I didn't think telling Chris about Stephen Cohen and who really killed him was a good thing to do. At least not yet. First, I had to figure out how to use this information to my advantage, but for the life of me, I couldn't come up with anything.

Chapter 10

Monday morning began rainy and wet, perfect for a funeral. I donned my wig and glasses, but decided not to wear my black clothes even though they were the right color. I was getting tired of black. Besides, I wanted to wear the new clothes I got at the mall.

As I drove to the funeral, a sinking feeling settled in the pit of my stomach. I didn't care much for funerals in the first place, but I was worried that with my abilities, I would pick up a lot of the family's grief and sadness. I really didn't want to cry, but some funerals were sad with all the goodbyes, even when the deceased wasn't someone you knew. That, along with listening to all those minds, could be disturbing. I mean, wouldn't most of them be thinking about Johnny? Of course, the murderer probably would be too, and that was what I wanted, right? If I actually heard the murderer, I sure hoped I could figure out who it was in the crowd.

I arrived about ten minutes early. Not early enough for the viewing, but hopefully in time to get a good seat in the back. Usually those were the first to go, but if I was the murderer, that's where I'd sit, and I was hoping the proximity would help me 'hear' him. Or her if it was a woman, I mean, who knew?

The place was filling up, and there weren't many seats left. So much for my plans. Uncle Joey and Ramos were sitting up front, but I didn't want to go up there. I scanned the back again, hoping to find a small space I could squeeze into. Number Five was sitting on a row close to the back, and he caught my eye. He motioned me over, and I happily squeezed in beside him.

"Thanks for letting me sit here," I said, truly grateful.

"No problem," he answered. "I have to admit I am surprised to see you here. I didn't think you knew Johnny that well."

"Oh, I'm not here for Johnny as much as for Uncle Joey. He was pretty upset about Johnny's death."

Number Five smiled. "I didn't know Mr. Manetto was your Uncle."

Oops. "Oh, yeah...on my mother's side." My mother would kill me if she ever found out I'd said this.

"Ah...I thought you were involved because of other reasons." He was thinking it was because of things I had no control of.

"Oh, I am... I mean... well... you know how it is." I was trying not to say too much, but if he was a cop, I didn't want him to think I was really working for Uncle Joey of my own free will. I smiled and he just smiled back. Maybe now was a good time to do a little probing of my own. I whispered, "I think Uncle Joey has a good idea about who killed Johnny."

"Really? Did he tell you?" Number Five was suddenly tense. His whole body tightened up, and he focused all of his attention on me.

"No," I said quickly, hoping he'd calm down. Why was this upsetting him so much? "But he has informants everywhere, even in the police department." I hoped he took that as a warning.

"Oh." He relaxed, and I let out my breath. I puzzled him. He was wondering why I'd bring up the cops, since he was the one who took care of them. Maybe I didn't know as much as I thought. Or maybe I knew a lot more than he was giving me credit for. Whatever the case, it was time he did some real checking up on me.

Oh great. Now I'd just made things worse. What was I thinking? The funeral services began, and the conversation around us stopped. Everyone stood as the funeral directors brought the casket down the aisle with the family following behind. I didn't want to listen to any of them, their grief and anger was too fresh. Besides, I already knew none of them did it.

After everyone sat down, I got down to business. I tried to pick out individual thoughts, and concentrated on the back row. I figured I'd move forward row by row, that way I wouldn't miss anyone.

At first, all I got were random thoughts, none of them telling me anything important. I scanned up through the crowd, listening for anything that sounded remotely incriminating. There were a lot of people who would miss Johnny. He was a good person even though he was a bad guy. Everybody seemed to agree about that, but I wasn't sure it made sense. Many were angry that he'd been killed so violently, but that came with the territory. They just hoped Uncle Joey would take revenge.

Soon, my mind began to overload. I could no longer pick out individual thoughts because there were so many. It was like being in a crowded room with everyone talking at the same time. I used all of my concentration to pick up those stray thoughts that told me they were glad he was dead, but it was almost like looking for a needle in a haystack. I tried blocking out thoughts and then listening again, but that didn't make them any clearer.

I tried everything I could think of, but all it got me was a pounding headache. The funeral was nearly over when I knew I had to get out of there, even if it was just for a few minutes. I excused myself to Number Five, realizing I didn't even know his name, and nearly collapsed when I got outside the doors.

I found a drinking fountain, and swallowed some aspirin, then wandered around until I found an empty room. I sank into a soft chair, and closed my eyes, grateful for the silence. After a few minutes my headache dulled to something bearable, and I could breathe again. I relaxed and decided I couldn't go back in there. The stress was too much. I wasn't sure what I'd tell Uncle Joey, but I'd figure that out later.

After a while the voices of people leaving the service reached me, and I knew it was over. I reluctantly left my chair, and searched for Uncle Joey. He would probably want a report, and if I gave it to him here, then maybe I could go home.

I wandered into the foyer and spotted Ramos standing beside Uncle Joey in a watchful stance. He looked like a bodyguard, and it hit me that Uncle Joey was a standing target for the killer. If someone took him out now, my troubles would be over.

That didn't make me feel as glad as I would have thought. I didn't like Uncle Joey, and I hated being in his service, but I still didn't like the thoughts of him being gunned down in cold blood. What was wrong with me? Was I showing signs of that hostage syndrome thing? I hoped not. It was probably just that I didn't like to see people get killed. Now if he were holding a gun to my head, it would be different.

The crowd had thinned considerably when Uncle Joey spotted me. His smile was friendly, and he motioned me over with an outstretched arm. "I'm glad to see you made it. You look a little pale, are you all right?"

"I'm okay now. It was a little stressful in there."

"I didn't see you come in."

"I sat in the back by Number Five, but I got a headache, and had to leave for the last few minutes of the service."

"Number Five?"

"Yeah, the guy you saw me talking to in the parking garage, on your surveillance camera. I don't know his name, so that's what I call him."

"Oh, yes I remember now. Why don't we head over to my office? We can order some food, and discuss what you found."

"Well, I really didn't find anything—"

"That's okay. I have some other things I need to talk to you about." He held the doors open for me, and I took a breath of fresh air. The rain had stopped, and the sun was shining. A big rainbow hung over the cemetery like a benediction, and took my breath away.

"That's something isn't it?" I said.

"Yes. Somehow, it makes me feel okay about Johnny. I hope he's in a better place." I was surprised to hear that coming from a hardened crime boss like Uncle Joey. "I'm not all bad, Shelby." He didn't like the look of surprise on my face.

"Oh... no, of course not."

"You can come with us, my car's over there."

"No, wait. I brought my car. I might as well meet you at the office."

He looked around until he spotted it. "I know you went car shopping over the weekend, did you have any luck?"

Did he know everything? "No, not yet."

"I know someone who can get you a good deal. You can have anything on the lot for less than half of what they're asking. I'll call him, and tell him you're coming. I just got a new car myself. It's right over there." He pointed it out, and we started walking toward it.

"Oh, you mean that black one? Now why doesn't that surprise me? You know, you really should try a different color some time."

"But I like black. He's got another one on the lot just like it that you could get. It's a great car with all the bells and whistles. It even has a remote start. Ramos, show her how it can start from here."

Did he really think I'd want a car just like his? I had to admit, however, that it looked pretty sleek, lots more fun to drive than a van. Ramos pulled the keys out of his pocket and pushed a button. The engine sputtered for a second, and then sprang to life with a huge unnatural roar. Why did it sound so strange?

Suddenly, the car exploded in a fiery blast of shattering glass and metal. The blast threw me to the ground, and I cringed as showering sparks and metal fell around me. Ramos and Uncle Joey were beside me, and before I knew it, Ramos pulled me under him, shielding me with his body.

We stayed like that until the last of the flying debris came to rest. For a fleeting second Ramos's eyes met mine, then traveled to my lips. I could feel a rush of pure desire pulse through him before he quickly jerked to his feet. He turned to Uncle Joey, checking to see if he was injured.

"I'm all right," Uncle Joey muttered. Ramos helped him to his feet. "Check Shelby."

Ramos dutifully took my hands and pulled me up. I was shaking so bad it was hard to stand without his help. "Are you okay?" he asked.

My mouth didn't seem to be working so I just nodded. What was going on? What had happened? We all stood there in shock, watching flames shoot out from the car. The black smoke billowed up, and the air was thick with the smell of burning rubber and gasoline.

Soon people were gathering around us, and I heard a siren in the distance. Someone asked if that was our car, and Uncle Joey nodded. His hair was sticking up on one side, and there was a smudge of dirt on his face. A trickle of blood ran down the side of Ramos's face, making him look more dangerous than ever. His hair was sticking up too, and I panicked, hoping my wig hadn't blown off my head.

I frantically reached up and let out my breath to find it was still there. It seemed a little crooked so I straightened it the best I could, and caught a fleeting smile from Ramos. He nodded, then quickly turned away, puzzled and uncomfortable with the protective feelings I aroused in him.

I took a deep breath, and let it out slowly. It was good he felt that way, wasn't it? At least it would make it harder to kill me, and that was a plus. I inspected my new skirt and cardigan and gasped. Not only were they spotted with something black, but covered with charred holes where the material was burned away. That's when it hit me that I'd almost been killed. Again.

A fire engine pulled into the parking lot, and started hosing down the car. Luckily, it was the only one sitting in that part of the parking lot at the time of the blast, or others probably would have gone up with it. One of the firemen asked if anyone was hurt, and proceeded to look us over. The back of Ramos's jacket was singed, and he had a cut in his scalp over his temple. It looked like he took the brunt of the blast protecting me. I wondered if Uncle Joey had noticed what he'd done. Ramos was supposed to be his bodyguard, not mine.

After being prodded by the fireman, Uncle Joey lost the dazed look in his eyes, and started telling everyone what to do. Someone had planted a bomb in his brand new car, and he wanted a full investigation by the police. He wanted to know who did this, and he wanted them caught.

The parking lot was starting to get crowded, especially when three police cars roared in with their lights blazing. I thought they were getting a little carried away, but what's the fun of being a policeman otherwise? I was starting to get tired of standing around when another car pulled in, and I recognized Dimples. Yikes!

"Ramos," I grabbed his arm. "I'm going to go now." His eyes tightened. "Or maybe I should just wait in my car. Is that okay? I guess you guys will need a ride back to the office. I'll wait." I hoped he would leave me out of the police report, but I couldn't come right out and say it.

He knew something had rattled me, and he searched the crowd to see who it was. Not finding anything he decided to trust me. "Go ahead. Just don't start your car until I check it."

"Are you serious?" He was thinking that was as good a reason as any to keep me from leaving.

"You never know," he said, adding, "I'd rather be safe than sorry." He figured it was a possibility, remote, but it could happen.

"Okay." I slipped behind the crowd before Dimples got there, and tried to walk nonchalantly to my car. When I was still several feet away, I hit the unlock button and cringed. Of course nothing happened, except that the door unlocked. I climbed behind the steering wheel and sagged into the seat.

I sat there staring morosely at the scene when movement from the funeral home caught my attention, and I noticed two people standing in front of the doors arguing. With everyone out in the parking lot, no one saw them but me. Shock ran through me when I recognized them as Kate and Number Five. I hadn't seen Kate at the funeral. In fact, I thought her relationship with Uncle Joey was supposed to be a secret, so what was she doing here?

She jerked in anger when Number Five tried to touch her. He shook his head, and said something that seemed to calm her down. In a moment she nodded, and after glancing at the crowd, disappeared into the building. Number Five ran a hand through his hair, looking like a man who had bitten off more than he could chew. He hurried toward the opposite end of the parking lot. I kept him in my sights all the way to his car, and watched as he drove away.

Interesting. She had been angry at something, but what? Did they plant the bomb? It was obvious they were working together, but what were they trying to accomplish? What would either of them gain by killing Uncle Joey? Especially if Kate was his successor? All she had to do was wait a few years, and the business would be hers anyway. Why risk killing him now? Should I tell Uncle Joey I'd seen them together?

I leaned my head against the steering wheel and closed my eyes. This was getting way too complicated. I relaxed for a few minutes until a tap on the window startled me. It was Ramos. I fumbled to open the door and realized I'd fallen asleep.

"They told us we could go," he explained.

I glanced at the burned out shell of Uncle Joey's new car. The fire truck was gone along with most of the people. Only one police car remained.

"Can you pop the hood? I just want to check the engine."

"Sure."

While Ramos checked the engine, Uncle Joey came over to the car. He seemed a lot older than he had a little while ago. He opened the back door, and settled in with a sigh. "It sure feels good to sit down. What's Ramos doing?"

"I think he's checking for bombs."

"Oh." He hadn't thought of that. It was a good thing he had Ramos to watch out for him. Ramos was worth every penny he paid him. He glanced back at the smoldering remains of his new car and cursed. "Damn, I really liked that car."

"You said there was another one just like it," I reminded him.

"That's true. I'll have to have my secretary call when we get back to the office."

He was serious. How could he be thinking about getting another car when he just about got blown to smithereens? It must be his way of coping.

"I know you really like black," I said, deciding to put in my two cents worth. "But would it hurt to get a different color? What about red? That's a power color. Or how about a metallic gray? I've seen cars that color, and I think they look great. They even sparkle in the sunshine."

Uncle Joey shook his head. "I don't want a car that sparkles."

"I guess not," I answered.

Ramos had crawled under the car and came back out, dirtier than ever. He checked the engine once more, then let the hood fall with a boom that made me jump. Pulling open my door, he said, "Scoot over, I'm driving back."

"No way," I blurted. "You're filthy. I don't want dirt and grease all over the seat, especially when I have to drive home." He couldn't believe what he was hearing. It caught him off guard, and he was speechless. It was kind of funny. "I guess if you take off your jacket and your pants you could get in."

His eyes narrowed dangerously, and I knew he was about to pop. Uncle Joey surprised me with his laughter, and it relieved the tension. "Ramos, get in. She's just joking."

Ramos began to sit down and I had to move over real fast. I cringed when he settled into the seat. What made Uncle Joey think I was kidding? Didn't he know it would take a special cleanser to ever get that seat clean again?

Ramos glanced at me, and I tried to smooth the grimace off my face. He studied me for a minute before saying, "Something's wrong." He turned the key to start the car and I panicked.

"Wait! What is it? Is it the car?"

"No. It's you."

"Me? What do you mean?"

"Mr. Manetto, don't you think there's something different about Shelby?"

Uncle Joey studied me for a minute. "Now that you mention it... yes, but I'm not sure what it is."

I had a sneaking suspicion that Ramos was trying to get back at me. He put the car in reverse while I pulled the visor down to look in the mirror. Maybe it was my wig, and it was crooked or something.

"I know." Ramos stepped on the brakes. "It's your glasses. They're gone. You must have lost them in the blast."

I touched my face. He was right. "Damn, I really liked those glasses." Was I starting to sound like Uncle Joey? I was certainly cursing more than I used to. I glanced out the window just in case I could spot them, but the parking lot was covered with debris. "Do you think—"

"Not a chance," Ramos cut me off. "Too many people and cars. They're probably smashed by now."

I sighed. "Oh well. I'm kind of getting tired of this disguise anyway." My head itched and I really wanted to take the wig off. Maybe it didn't matter anymore.

"I think you look nice with black hair," Uncle Joey said. Of course he would say that, after all, it was his favorite color. "And you can get another pair of glasses. There's plenty of money in your new account for a lot of things."

I groaned. He was sure making it hard not to take his money, which reminded me of a question I wanted to ask. "Does Kate know she's your successor?"

"Why do you want to know?" Uncle Joey was suddenly suspicious.

"I'm just trying to piece things together. If she knew she was going to take over the business, there would be no reason for her to bomb your car, but if she didn't—"

"Don't be ridiculous. Kate would never harm me. I've raised her like she was my own daughter. She owes everything to me. She's not going to throw that away. I've told her many times I was thinking of turning the business over to her. She'd never do anything to jeopardize that."

"Okay. So who do you think did it?"

"The same person who killed Johnny. Someone's trying to take over my business."

"Does anyone else know you're leaving your business to Kate?"

"Besides you? No." We sat in silence for a few minutes. Uncle Joey was real bothered about something. "I'm not planning on retiring anytime soon anyway." He was mad that I thought he was so old.

"You're not that old, I just thought that maybe you were getting tired of this life. I mean, not life in general, but this part of your life, you know, the bad part."

He hated it when I read his mind like that. "The bad part? I know you don't think much of what I do, but it's not all bad. I help a lot of people who have nowhere else to turn. Granted, some days like today are hard, but most of the time I enjoy it. So no, I'm not going to retire for a while."

What could I say to that? Good? I'm so glad? When was he going to let me quit? Probably never. All at once I was struck with a brilliant idea. The best way for me to get out of this was to lose my mind-reading abilities. Not that I really had to lose them, but maybe I could fake it. It could work, couldn't it?

We pulled into the parking garage, and parked in Uncle Joey's spot by the elevators. It was the first time I'd taken a good look at Uncle Joey, and I was surprised by how rumpled he was. I glanced at Ramos, and noticed he had washed the blood off his face, but there was a splash of red on his collar and shirt. I couldn't look much better with all the burn holes and black grease in my clothes. The explosion had rattled me, and all I wanted to do was go home. The only problem was Ramos had my car keys.

"Well, that was an adventure wasn't it?" They both looked at me like I'd lost my mind. "Could I have the car keys?" I felt like a teenager. "If you don't need me anymore, I think I'll go home. I could use a shower."

Uncle Joey considered it. "Okay, but before you do, why don't you come up and sign the papers for the bank account. It will only take a few minutes."

I listened to his mind for hidden messages, but Uncle Joey wasn't thinking any further than that. Ramos was thinking I could use a shower. The dirt on my nose was driving him crazy. He wanted to wipe it off, but that would mean touching me, and after what had happened in the parking lot, he didn't think that was such a good idea.

"Sure, I'll come up." I rubbed my nose, wishing I had a mirror. Ramos swallowed, what was I doing? He was just thinking about the dirt on my nose... *wait... now she's looking at me like she knows...* I quickly slammed my mental barriers shut, and lowered my gaze.

We got on the elevator and I avoided looking at Ramos while I tried to get my heart rate back to normal. I didn't want him to know my secret, but I could tell he was getting close to the truth, and the way Uncle Joey kept asking me things in front of him didn't help either.

"I had Jackie order some food," Uncle Joey said. "There should be plenty if you want some."

Now that wasn't fair. I was hungry, but it was late, and I wanted to get out of these clothes and showered before the kids got home. "Thanks, but I can't."

Uncle Joey just nodded. He was tired, and he didn't feel like asserting his authority over me. Maybe he'd call it a day too. We entered the office and Uncle Joey explained to his secretary that we'd had an accident, but we were fine. He asked for the paperwork I needed to sign, but Jackie interrupted him. "Sir, Mr. Hodges is here to see you. He's in your office."

"How long has he been here?"

"Almost an hour." Uncle Joey wasn't happy that Hodges had been in his office that long. Sensing this, Jackie explained. "He waited about half an hour before asking if he could work in your office on his laptop where it was quiet. I didn't see any harm in it, and the door's been open the whole time."

The door wasn't open now. Uncle Joey nodded to Ramos, who moved silently toward the door. He pulled a gun out from under his jacket and burst inside, startling a cry from Mr. Hodges.

"Stop. Don't shoot!" Mr. Hodges held both hands above his head. Ramos moved aside, and I followed Uncle Joey into the room. Hodges paled, and broke into a sweat. He was shocked to see Uncle Joey alive. "Your secretary said it was okay to work in here while I waited for you."

"What do you want Mr. Hodges," Uncle Joey asked.

"I just needed to ask if I could have more time on my rent." Hodges lowered his arms, and quickly put his laptop into his briefcase. "Things went well today in court, and I'll probably get the insurance money, but not until after the due date. If it wouldn't be an imposition, I was hoping you could extend it for another week." Hodges stood ready to run. Ramos charging in with his gun had frightened him badly. He thought he'd have plenty of time to get the jewels out of the safe. Why hadn't it worked? Manetto should be dead.

"All right," Uncle Joey conceded. "I'll give you an extra week, but you'll owe me double for the favor."

"Sure, that's fine." Hodges would agree to anything since he already had his ticket to Mexico, and never intended to pay anyway. He just hated to leave without the jewels. "I'll get the money to you as soon as I can." He nodded at Uncle Joey, and hurried out the door.

Uncle Joey turned to me. "What was that all about? He's lying, isn't he?" I cleared my throat and motioned to Ramos. Uncle Joey sighed, and turned to Ramos. "Why don't you get the food set up in the other office while I talk to Shelby?"

Ramos nodded, and, with a pointed look at me, he left. Uncle Joey sat down heavily in his soft leather chair. "It's been a long day."

"You can say that again."

"So what did he want?"

Should I tell Uncle Joey that Hodges was the one who planted the bomb? "He was in here trying to open your safe. He had a lot of hardware in his briefcase, enough to crack your codes. He's convinced that you have the jewels, and he doesn't want to leave town until he gets his hands on them. To him, they represent years and years of work." I hesitated, but decided I might as well tell him. "He's the one who planted the bomb in your car."

Uncle Joey stiffened. "Are you sure?"

"Well, he was certainly shocked to see you here alive. He was hoping you'd be dead, and all his troubles would be over. Plus, he thought he had plenty of time to crack the safe and get the jewels. Doesn't that sound like somebody who planted a bomb?" I let that sink in.

"Do you think he'll be back?"

"I don't know. I guess it depends on how desperate he is."

"Hmm..." Uncle Joey growled under his breath. "Thank you, Shelby. I can't tell you how relieved I am to know who planted the bomb. I never would have thought it was him."

"Me either."

"It still doesn't solve Johnny's murder. Did you find out anything at the funeral?"

"Most people were pretty sad about Johnny's death. I scanned the room several times, but I never did get anything close to a confession. If the killer was there, he wasn't thinking about how he killed him or anything like that."

"I see. Well, it wasn't what I was hoping for, but I guess it was worth a try." He stood, and politely followed me out the door. "I won't keep you, but you're welcome to get some food before you go. And don't forget to sign the paperwork for the account." He was getting tired of this whole business. Maybe retirement wasn't such a bad idea. Only that was out of the question. He wouldn't rest until he found out who had killed Johnny.

I wanted to tell him that maybe he'd better have a long talk with Kate, but then he'd want to know why I thought that, and I'd have to explain that I saw her at the funeral. I wasn't quite ready to share that information.

I decided it wouldn't hurt to see what kind of food was in the other office. If there was a sandwich, I could eat it on the way home. Besides, I was starved. Before I got down the hallway, numbers two, three, and four came hustling into the office.

"Mr. Manetto, we just heard the news," Number two said. "Are you all right? Who did this?" He was worried that Uncle Joey might think it was him.

"I'm fine," Uncle Joey said. "But my new car's gone." The guys all exclaimed vehemently. They were really upset about that. Uncle Joey ushered them into his office and closed the door. They were all there except Johnny and

Number Five, and Johnny was dead. So where was Number
Five?

I grabbed a turkey croissant sandwich and a Diet Coke.
There was no sign of Ramos, which was probably a good
thing since he was starting to guess what I did. I checked
my watch, and almost choked on my sandwich. How did it
get so late?

I rushed out the door, but before I could push the call
button for the elevator, Jackie came after me. "Shelby... wait!
You can't go until you sign these forms." When I hesitated,
she pleaded, "All you have to do is sign this. It won't take
long." I wrapped my sandwich in a napkin and, after signing
the forms, she handed me a checkbook and the account
information. I slipped it into my purse along with my
sandwich, and dashed to the elevator.

I spent the time on the elevator looking for my car keys.
Ramos had handed them over, but I couldn't remember
where I put them. I finally dumped everything out of my
purse and found the keys just as the doors opened. Luckily,
no one was there to see me kneeling on the floor. I pushed
everything back into my purse, inadvertently smashing the
sandwich, and stepped off the elevator.

The parking garage smelled faintly of exhaust, like
someone had just driven off. I started toward the car and a
sudden chill went down my spine when I realized the sign
above the space said: Reserved for Joe E. Manetto. How
long ago had Mr. Hodges left? Could he have planted
another bomb in my car thinking it was Uncle Joey's?

I glanced around the lot and my neck tingled with
sudden apprehension. It was dark in the far corners, and I
couldn't see into the shadows. Anyone could be hiding
there. I stood for a few seconds, wondering what to do. Was
I being paranoid? All at once, it felt as if someone's eyes

were boring into my back. I whirled around, but no one was there. I was getting totally freaked out. I took one more look at the car and decided there was no way I could get inside and start it. Not without having it checked first.

I hurried back to the elevator and sighed with relief when the doors closed. When they opened on the twenty-sixth floor, I was more in control. I marched confidently into the office, startling Jackie. "Is Ramos here? I forgot something."

"Um... sure. Just a minute." She dialed a number on the phone, then told me he'd be right out. A minute later he came down the hall. His hair was wet and curly, and he had on a clean set of clothes.

"What's up?" he asked.

"I... um... I was just wondering if you would mind looking over my car. You know, for bombs? It's parked in Uncle Joey's spot."

He smiled. "Hmm, I don't know. I just changed my clothes." He wasn't going to make this easy.

"Well, maybe you don't have to crawl underneath it. You could just look under the hood with a flashlight or something." He thought I was being paranoid. He was probably right. "Please?"

"All right. I'll take a look." He wasn't real happy to spend any time with me after what had happened earlier, but he didn't want me to get blown up either. From now on, he'd probably have to check all of Mr. Manetto's cars for bombs. It was one more thing to worry about.

The realization hit me that it wasn't safe to drive one of Uncle Joey's cars. I needed my own car. Maybe I should take Uncle Joey up on his offer, and get a new car from his dealer. It would be at a good price, and I wouldn't have to worry about getting blown up. That probably made it okay, and I was sure if Chris knew, he'd agree with me.

"Wait," I stopped Ramos. "I think I want to get my own car. Uncle Joey might need the car I've been using now that his got blown up. Do you think it would be okay to ask him?"

Ramos glanced toward Uncle Joey's office and shrugged. "Sure."

I took a deep breath and knocked before sticking my head in the door. "Excuse me, but can I ask you a question?" At his nod, I continued, "You probably need the car I've been using, so I was wondering if I could take you up on the offer of getting a car from the person you spoke of earlier."

"Of course," Uncle Joey replied, a little surprised that I'd accept his help. "Have Ramos take you, and he can check on the other car for me."

"Great. Thanks." I gently closed the door, and smiled at my good fortune. Ramos waited for me by Jackie's desk. "He said you should take me to the car dealer, and you should look at the other car he wants while you're there," I told him.

"I thought you needed to get home." He thought about the had dirt on my face, and my ruined clothes.

I checked my watch. It was too late to beat the kids home now. "I have some clothes in the trunk. While you're checking the car, I can change and wash up in the bathroom, okay?"

He nodded, resigned to the idea that he was taking me car shopping. He liked looking at new cars, but he'd never gone with a woman like me before. He was a little worried about his reputation, but he figured he'd survive, as long as I didn't want to buy a van.

Chapter 11

Ramos had just finished checking the car when I came back from changing my clothes. My face was now mostly make-up free, but without the dirt, it was an improvement. I also got rid of the wig, since without the glasses it just didn't work. Besides, I didn't need my disguise any more today. I'd pulled my hair back into a ponytail, and wearing jeans and a t-shirt, I felt more like myself than I had in days.

"No bombs," Ramos said, thinking I looked a lot younger with my real hair, or maybe it was the ponytail. "You ready?"

"Yes," I hesitated. "You're sure the car's okay?" I really wanted him to start the car before I got in, but it might hurt his feelings to ask.

"The car's already running."

"Oh, you're right. Silly me." I tried to cover my embarrassment with a little laugh. How had I not noticed that the motor was on? Ramos opened the trunk, and I stashed my things inside before getting in.

The car dealership was only a few blocks away, so it didn't take long to get there. When we pulled in, a salesman hurried out before we had even opened the doors. He took one look at Ramos, and turned right back around.

"They know me here," Ramos explained. "He went to get Tony."

Sure enough, an older man in a tan sports jacket and open-collared shirt ambled over to us. He wore a thick gold chain with a cross around his neck, and a gold stud in one ear. He shook Ramos' hand, and the gold ring on his little finger glimmered in the sun. "Nice to see you, Ramos, how's the new car working out? I told Mr. Manetto he'd love it."

"That's the problem Tony. The car got blown up earlier today. Mr. Manetto was very upset."

"What? Someone blew up that beautiful car? Are they insane?"

"Yeah, something like that. Anyway, he sent me back to see if you still had the other one that was just like it."

"Oh, yeah I do." He was thinking that another guy was looking at it, but if Uncle Joey wanted the car, he'd have to tell the other guy it wasn't available. He hated doing that, since it was bad for business, but Joey "The Knife" came first.

"Good, he'll be relieved. He really liked that car." Ramos nodded toward me. "This is Shelby. Mr. Manetto wants you to fix her up with something she'd like."

"Hi." I shook his hand, feeling a little guilty that I was taking advantage of him. He greeted me warmly, thinking Mr. Manetto was robbing the cradle, and I let out a little laugh while a blush crept up my neck. I kind of liked Tony.

"What kind of car are you looking for?" he asked.

"A van," I replied, and stole a glance at Ramos. His eyes widened and he dropped his head, thinking he should have known. "Do you have anything like that?"

"You know... I don't." Tony was trying not to smile. "But I'm sure there's something else here that you'd be happy with. Why don't you take a look around while I get the paperwork started for Ramos?"

"Okay." They left and I started my search. There were a lot of nice cars, but I couldn't tell one brand from another. To me, they came in three sizes; small, medium, and big— that about covered what I knew about cars.

I preferred the medium size, with more of a sporty look, something that would get good gas mileage, but had enough power to go fast in a pinch. Did they even make cars like that? If I could fit three people in the back and two more in front, I wouldn't need a van. Besides, people with vans ended up driving more because they had so much room to cart all the kids around, right?

I checked some of the sticker prices, and cut them in half to see how much a new car would cost with Uncle Joey's 'discount,' and could hardly contain my excitement. At half price, the insurance money could get me something really classy.

Tony caught up to me, and started explaining all about the different cars. We'd covered most of the lot when I spotted a cream colored beauty in a different area. When I expressed an interest, he opened the gate and I followed him in. "This is just like Mr. Manetto's car except for the color. Would you like to see the inside?" He found the keys, and unlocked the door.

The first thing that came to me was the fresh scent of new car and leather seats. I sat down in plush luxury, and took a deep breath, reveling in extravagance. Tony showed me how the seat adjusted to my body, and explained the different features. It came with stuff I didn't even know what to do with. "Do you want to take a test drive?" Did I ever.

The engine purred to life, and I took to the streets in cultured elegance. It was the smoothest ride I'd ever experienced in my life. And the power! A tap on the gas and we were off! This car was a dream, and I could see why Uncle Joey liked it so much. How could anyone in their right mind blow up something like this? It was unthinkable.

When we got back to the dealership, I had stars in my eyes. This was the car I wanted. It was the only car I could ever be satisfied with. It didn't matter that it only seated five people. Who needed more room than that anyway?

We found Ramos, and he frowned at the glazed look in my eyes. When I told him I wanted the car, he understood where the look came from. "I thought you wanted a van," he couldn't help teasing. "Besides, what will your husband think when he sees you driving home in this car?"

I didn't want to think about that. "How much?" I asked Tony. He quoted me a price that was higher than the insurance money. I nearly groaned before I thought of the bank account Uncle Joey had given me. I pulled out the account book, and nearly fell off my chair. Ten thousand dollars? He'd given me ten thousand dollars? I couldn't accept that. It was way too much.

"Shelby?" Ramos caught my attention. "Do you want the car?"

"Yes." I did, didn't I? It was a great deal. When would I ever have another opportunity like this?

"I'll get the paperwork started," Tony said. "One thing you should know. When I do this for Mr. Manetto, I require that you sign a contract that states you'll sell the car back to me if, for any reason, you don't want it. It wouldn't be good for business if you turned around and sold it for full price. I'm sure you understand."

"Of course." It seemed like a reasonable request. I couldn't detect anything in his thoughts to tell me otherwise. Ramos thought I was getting a good deal too. He was glad that Manetto was helping me out, maybe that meant he was planning on keeping me around. He also knew I was providing valuable information for Manetto, but the way I did it was uncanny. It was almost like I could read minds, but that was impossible, wasn't it? He glanced at me, wondering if I was 'listening' right now.

"What?" I asked. "Do you think I'm making a mistake?"

"No, it's a great deal." He was a little disappointed, but let it go, thinking he could always try to catch me off guard another time. I relaxed, knowing I was off the hook for now, but I'd better be careful in the future.

Tony had all the papers ready and, after I signed them, I got out my checkbook. I wrote the first check from the account where we'd put the insurance money, and the second check from Uncle Joey's account. I figured that the amount I was spending from him would pretty much cover all the work I'd done for him. That was fair. As for the rest, I wasn't touching it.

Tony handed me two sets of keys, and stuck a temporary license on the back window, telling me he'd call when he got the real plates. The car was officially mine. I remembered to get my stuff out of Uncle Joey's car, and I was ready to go. Ramos smiled when I waved at him, and I sat back, relieved not to worry about being blown up.

It was after five when I pulled into the driveway. Chris wasn't home yet, but I knew he would be there soon. When he found out about the good deal I got, he was sure to be impressed. Even though it cost a little more than we'd wanted, I could explain that I'd used the money from my job to make up the difference. After he drove the car, I was sure he'd be convinced I'd done the right thing.

I left the car sitting in the driveway, and took my singed clothes out of the trunk. They were ruined, so I threw them directly into the garbage. I salvaged my wig and hurried into the house and put it away. Although, at this point, I didn't want to keep it either. I put on some lipstick and a hint of perfume while I waited for Chris. My stomach was doing little flip-flops, and I wondered why I was so nervous. I hadn't done anything wrong.

Savannah was in her room talking on her phone, so she just waved at me when I checked on her. Josh was playing a video game. "I got a new car," I said.

"Cool," he replied.

"Do you want to come see it?"

"Umm... is it a van?" He was thinking that if it was a van it didn't matter if he saw it or not. They were all alike as far as he was concerned.

"No, it's something else." Right then I wished I knew what kind of car it was, not that it mattered to me, but it might make a difference to him.

"Sure. I'll be there in a minute." Which meant he'd come when he came to a stopping place in his game, if he remembered.

I went downstairs to the kitchen to fix dinner, and my shoulders tightened when Chris walked in.

"Whose car is that?" he asked, setting down his briefcase.

"Do you like it?"

"Yeah, it's great..." The rest of what he was going to say died in his throat. He jerked his eyes to mine in sudden suspicion, and I swallowed. "You didn't just buy that car did you?" he asked before I could say anything.

"Come and look at it," I tugged at his arm.

"Oh no," he said, closing his eyes. "You did."

"I got a great deal on it, and I'm sure after you drive it, you'll understand why I couldn't pass it up."

"You bought that car? Do you know how much cars like that cost?" His voice rose with each word.

"I got a good deal. I only had to pay a little more than the insurance money, and I used the money from my job to make up the difference. See? So you don't have to be upset."

He couldn't believe what he was hearing. Maybe the car wasn't as expensive as he thought it was. It had to be a different make or something. Otherwise, it would cost a lot more than what I could afford.

"Come on," I cajoled. "I've got the keys right here. Come take it for a spin, you'll love it!" Now I knew how a car salesman felt.

"I thought we were going to get a van." He still couldn't believe I'd bought a car. On my own. Without him. "I thought we were going to talk about this first."

"Yeah, but when I found this, I couldn't pass it up. You'll understand when you drive it." This time he let me pull him through the door to the driveway. I hurried over to the driver's side and opened the door. "Here, sit down. Isn't this great?" I suddenly felt like Eve in the Garden of Eden, trying to get Adam to eat the apple.

He sat down, and I handed him the keys. "It even has a remote start button." I shut the door and hurried to the passenger side. He ran his hands over the steering wheel, and the dashboard, taking in all the features.

"This thing's loaded." His voice was quiet. He pierced me with a stare full of worry and disbelief. How? How had I managed to get a car like this for the price of the insurance money and the little I'd made at my job? He knew it wouldn't begin to cover the full cost. Had I lied to him?

I started to panic. How did he know how much cars like this cost in the first place? This was not going well. "I've got all the paperwork in the house. You can look it over if you don't believe me."

He flinched. "I forgot you were reading my mind. I thought you weren't going to do that."

What could I say? "I know. I'm sorry. I shouldn't have been listening, but you seemed so upset, and you don't need to be. Everything's fine." He closed his eyes and shuttered his thoughts, not trusting himself to speak. "We don't have to keep it," I ventured. "I can always take it back, but since it's here, you might as well take it for a spin."

He took a deep breath and started her up. We backed out of the driveway and down the street. I felt him relax as he took the corner, and I sat back in my seat. He kept his thoughts quiet, and I concentrated on blocking them. We got on the freeway, and he relaxed even more. After ten minutes, he was enjoying the smooth handling, and was curious about all the features.

"Does it have GPS?" I asked.

"Yeah." He started explaining how it worked, then went on to tell me about some of the other features. It amazed me that he knew so much about cars.

By the time we pulled in the driveway, he had loosened up. He wasn't gushing about the car, but he wasn't mad either. "I'd like to look over the paperwork."

"Sure." We went inside without a word, and I gently placed the paperwork in his hands. He retreated to his study and closed the door, shutting me out. I knew I was partly to blame for that. He wanted to be someplace where I couldn't 'listen' to him.

I washed my hands to get dinner ready, and noticed my palms were tender with abrasions from the blast. I also had a new bruise on my hip and knee from where I'd landed, but I was learning to take it in stride, almost like it was just another day on the job.

For the rest of the evening Chris kept to himself, and I was careful not to intrude. In a way, I was glad he was so preoccupied. It kept me from having to lie about my day, since there was no way I was going to tell him about the explosion. When it was time for bed, I couldn't wait for his verdict any longer. "Well? What do you think about the car?"

"I'm not sure. It's hard to believe you got it for that price."

"I know. It's crazy, huh?"

"Yes. I guess we can keep it. For now. I just hope it's not stolen or something."

Alarm buzzed through me. Could it be a stolen car? Was Chris right? I hadn't even thought about that. If it was, how had Tony been able to sell it to me? Didn't he have to have all the right paperwork to get a license and everything?

It was hard to get to sleep after that. Every time I shut my eyes, I kept seeing my new car blow up. When I finally drifted off, dreams of falling off a cliff plagued my sleep, and when I wasn't falling, I seemed to be drowning in a pool of muck. I woke the next morning exhausted. If I didn't know better, I'd think the stress was getting to me.

I got out of bed, glad that Chris hadn't left for work yet. For some reason, I had an overwhelming urge to hold him, and tell him what was going on. He hugged me, but he was preoccupied, and running late.

"What's on your schedule for today?" I asked.

"We're wrapping up Mr. Hodges' case. The kid accused of stealing his jewels is probably going to go free, but Mr. Hodges shouldn't have any problem getting the insurance money. I think we established that the jewels were definitely stolen."

"Oh, that's good." I took a deep breath. "Could we talk tonight? There's something I need to tell you."

His gaze jerked to mine. "You're finally going to tell me what's going on?"

"Yes. I need your help."

Hope surged through him, and then wrapped around me like a blanket. I was shocked by the intensity of his feelings. He'd been waiting for this for such a long time. "Finally. I wish I didn't have to go."

I smiled. "It's okay. Tonight's soon enough."

"All right." He kissed me, and hurried out the door, relieved to know I had finally come to my senses.

"Wow," I said, aloud. "What an idiot I am. How could I be so stupid?" I should have been talking to Chris all along. I closed my eyes. It would be such a relief to tell him everything. I didn't know if I had enough to stop Uncle Joey from using me, but maybe there was something Chris could do. All I needed was some leverage of my own.

After the kids left for school, I got some toast and orange juice, and sat at the table to read the newspaper. A picture on the bottom half of the front page caught my attention. It looked like a burning car, and my heart stopped when I spotted Uncle Joey in the background. Standing next to him in a black wig and no glasses was me.

The caption read, 'Car Bomb Explodes in Parking Lot of Sunset Mortuary.' I quickly scanned the article. At least there was no mention of my name, but it was clear that the car belonged to Uncle Joey.

I stared hard at the picture, wondering if anyone could possibly recognize me. It looked a lot like me, but wouldn't the dark hair throw people off? No one would expect me to have dark hair and bangs, so if they saw the picture, they would probably think it looked like me, but it wasn't me because of the dark hair. Besides, what would I be doing with Uncle Joey at Sunset Mortuary?

Panic washed over me, and I felt the blood drain from my head. Dizzy, I put my head between my knees, and took deep breaths. After a minute, I felt more calm and rational. This wasn't as bad as I thought. I just needed to calm down.

I jerked when the phone rang. I checked the caller ID. It was my mom. Should I answer it? If I didn't, she'd probably call Chris. That would be bad. "Hello?"

"Shelby? What are you doing on the front page of the newspaper?" How did she know? Should I act dumb? Before I could answer she continued, "Of course the dark hair and bangs aren't you, but the face is you."

"I noticed that picture too," I said, improvising. "I guess it kind of looks like me, but I don't see that big of a resemblance."

"You don't think so? I think it looks just like you." She wasn't going to back down.

"That's kind of creepy isn't it? To think there's another person that looks like me running around? Thank goodness we have different hair—otherwise I'd be really freaked out."

Silence from the other end of the line told me she wasn't buying it.

"Anyway, I'd better go. I've got to get ready for work."

She sighed. "Fine, but just for the record, I know it's you. So how is your new job going anyway?"

This topic wasn't any better, so I said the first thing that came to mind. "Oh that? I'm quitting. It's not working out too well. I'll probably finish out the rest of the week, but that's it."

"Why? What happened?"

"I just don't get along very well with the boss. I mean he's nice enough, but I think I'd rather try something else. Like flower arranging. Something more creative and artistic. That sounds a lot more fun to me."

"You'd be good at that," she said. We talked for a few more minutes and then hung up. I hated lying to her, but it was better for her that she didn't know the truth.

Between the funeral and the car bomb, I'd been distracted from my goal of getting something on Uncle Joey. What kind of leverage would make him back off, or better yet, put him in jail? If I could expose him as Stephen Cohen's murderer, that would do it.

I tried to think of another way, but I kept coming up blank. Since I had decided to tell Chris, maybe it would be helpful to have more background information on Stephen Cohen. I was also curious if the police had anything more on Johnny's murderer. Maybe I should pay a visit to Dimples and find out. After that, I could drop in at Chris' office, and do some poking around.

I drove to the police station in decadent luxury, feeling like a million bucks. I had taken extra care with my hair, scrunching it to curl softly around my face. I'd also found my cream colored jacket and jeans outfit that matched the car perfectly. With a light blue shirt to match my eyes, I looked like I belonged to that car, and it belonged to me.

I pulled into the police station with a slight twinge of unease, hoping the car wasn't really stolen. If it was, I was pretty stupid to drive it here. When I walked inside, the officer at the desk recognized me from before, and ushered me right in to see Dimples.

"Shelby. Good to see you." He was pleasantly surprised.

"Hi. I was just driving by and thought I'd check up on that lead about the guy who robbed that store. Did you find his stash?"

"Yes, we did. I was just going to call and thank you for your help."

"Good, I'm glad it worked out. He sure was cocky wasn't he?"

"Yes. We've still got a lot to do for a conviction, but I think we have all the evidence we need to put him away for a few years."

"Great. Glad to help." I was trying to think of a casual way I could ask about Johnny's murder investigation. "I noticed it was Johnny Falzone's funeral yesterday."

"Yeah, there's more about it in today's paper." Dimples pulled out the newspaper and set it on his desk. "After the funeral, there was an attempt on Mr. Manetto's life. Someone planted a bomb in his car. We think it's probably related." He was studying the picture, then studying me. "This lady sure looks an awful lot like you, except for the hair."

I looked at the picture like I hadn't seen it before. "Wow, that's weird isn't it? Kind of gives me the creeps."

"Yes, I'll bet it does. Do you have any premonitions about this?" He motioned his hand to indicate the article.

"Umm... this might seem strange," I lowered my voice. "But there was an unsolved murder that happened a long time ago. I keep getting impressions that it has something to do with this case."

"Who was murdered?" Dimples asked.

"I'm not sure, but I think the last name starts with a C. It's something like Coburn, or Cohen. I know it's not much, but maybe you could check it out."

"Sure. I'll look into it." I'd never steered Dimples wrong yet, so he was willing to take a look.

"Well, I'd better get going." I stood and shook Dimples hand.

"Thanks for your help," he said, standing. "I'll call you if something comes up."

I left quickly, hoping I'd done the right thing. If Uncle Joey found out, I was dead. I hurried to Chris' office, thinking it was almost lunchtime and maybe we could go to lunch together. I was also going to ask him if he could find out more about Stephen Cohen. At this point, what did I have to lose?

When I arrived, Chris' secretary told me he was still in court, and would probably be there for quite some time. I'd forgotten he was there for Mr. Hodges' case. Maybe I'd go over and see how it was going. "That's okay," I told her. "I'll just leave a note in his office."

I found some paper and quickly explained what I wanted in the note, then I wondered if I should leave it there. What if someone else saw it? Someone like Kate? She would probably wonder why I wanted Chris to look into the death of Stephen Cohen. With her connection to Uncle Joey, she might even know why Stephen Cohen was killed. Either way, she was sure to tell Uncle Joey, and I didn't want that to happen. I needed to protect Chris as long as possible. I stuffed the note in my purse, and walked down the hall.

As I passed by Kate's door, I realized she was in court with Chris. Maybe now would be a good time to take a look in her office. I checked the hall and, since no one was around, I opened the door and slid inside. I stood quietly by the door listening for footsteps, but when none came, I let out my breath, and hurried to her desk.

There were several files scattered there, along with a half-full mug of coffee. The files looked like cases she was currently working on. Nothing I wanted to see. I moved to the filing cabinets by the wall and opened one. These files were in alphabetical order, and I scanned down until I found the C's. After going through them twice, and not finding a thing, disappointment lodged in my chest.

I sat back down at her desk, and started opening drawers. The top drawer had pencils and pens along with paper clips and erasers. The one below it was a large file drawer. I tried to pull it open, but it was locked. I rummaged through the top drawer again, and hit pay dirt when I found the key under a small notepad.

As I inserted the key, my heart pounded, and my hands started to sweat. I knew I was taking a chance of getting caught, but I couldn't stop now. I turned the key, and the lock clicked. Holding my breath, I carefully pulled the drawer open.

There were several files inside. One had Mr. Hodges' name on it, another I recognized from my encounter with Kate at the police station. These were the files that had something to do with Uncle Joey.

I sucked in my breath at the name on the last file. It was Stephen Cohen. The file contained two manila folders, and I carefully placed the first one on top of Kate's desk. The first few pages looked like cases he had worked on. They were dated over thirty years before, and many had his personal notes attached. As I turned the pages, the cases got closer to the date of his death. Next, in red letters someone had written the date of his death over the newspaper article I had already read, with a copy of the obituary. The last part of the file contained the name and picture of the man convicted of Stephen Cohen's murder, along with transcripts from the trial.

Why would Kate have such an extensive file on the man Uncle Joey had murdered? Did she know Uncle Joey had murdered him? I checked the clock, hoping the secretary was right, and Kate wouldn't be back for a while longer. My hands were already shaking with nervousness. Still, I had to check the second manila folder while I had the chance.

This folder had totally different information. It looked like bank accounts, with numbers circled in red, and crossreferenced to other pages. Were they money transfers of some kind? Someone had written Uncle Joey's name next to one of the account numbers, and Stephen Cohen's name beside the other. It looked like Uncle Joey was giving Stephen Cohen a lot of money. Was Cohen blackmailing Uncle Joey?

Next was information on an actual case Stephen Cohen was working on. Thrasher Development was the plaintiff and Berkley Construction was the defendant. I couldn't understand all the legal jargon, except that it looked like Thrasher Development won a huge settlement against the construction company. Had Stephen Cohen transferred the money from Uncle Joey's account to his own? Would Uncle Joey have killed him for that?

I checked the clock again, realizing I'd been there for a little more than half an hour. It was time to go, but what should I do with the files? I decided to put the bigger file back, but I couldn't bring myself to part with the smaller one. I knew the information was important, and taking it might be a really dumb thing to do, but still, how could I pass it up? When would I get another chance like this?

Footsteps and talking came from outside the door, and I froze. The doorknob turned and Kate's low voice spurred me into action. I dove under the desk, and pulled my knees up to my chin. I held as still as I could and tried to calm my pounding heart.

"I can't believe I left it on my desk," Kate called to someone in the hall. The carpet muffled her footsteps, and I cringed when she came closer. The tips of her shoes were visible under the desk, and I held my breath. If she came any further, she'd find me.

She picked something up off the desk, and thought about how satisfying it was to finally get Chris to go to lunch with her. She undid another button on her blouse, and expertly applied some lipstick, glancing in a mirror she pulled from her purse. Then she turned, and walked back toward the door. "I found it," she called.

My heart sped up when I heard Chris at the door. "I don't have a lot of time for lunch." He sounded hesitant, clearly trying to get out of going with her.

"Nonsense," Kate replied. "You have to eat, and it won't take long. Besides, it's my treat for winning the case. We can go to the Italian restaurant. It's just down the street, and it will be a nice walk." She closed the door on Chris' reply.

I scrambled out from under the desk, ready to follow. How dare she make Chris go to lunch with her. The devious little bitch. Before I got to the door, I stopped in my tracks, realizing I couldn't go charging after them right now. How would I explain what I was doing in Kate's office? I leaned against the desk to catch my breath and steady my trembling legs.

At least she hadn't noticed the file. I snatched it up and stuffed it into my purse. If she was trying to steal my husband, then I might as well steal this. It could be days before she'd miss it, and even then, she wouldn't know I had it.

Feeling better, I gingerly opened the door, and peered down the hall. It was quiet and, since I didn't want the secretary to see me, I went around the back to the staircase. It was a relief to start down the stairs and know I was almost out of there. The stairs came out on the main floor, and I turned toward the revolving doors, wondering if I could catch a glimpse of Chris and Kate as they walked to the restaurant. Did she have her arm through his? Was she looking up at him through fluttering lashes?

Before I knew it, I was on the sidewalk, craning my neck to catch sight of them. I started down the street, but could see nothing of them in front of me. By now, they were probably already at the restaurant.

I slowed my step, wondering vaguely what I was doing, but unable to stop. It wasn't long before I stood in front of the restaurant like a lost puppy. Now what? A hostess opened the door, and invited me inside. Since I couldn't just stand there like an idiot, I went in.

They sat at a table near the window, and a waitress was taking their orders. Kate's back was to me, so she didn't know I was silently observing them. At first, Chris didn't either. Then he caught sight of me, and his eyes widened with alarm. As I walked toward their table, Kate turned with a puzzled look on her face that quickly vanished into a calculating smirk.

Guilt flooded over Chris, and he opened his mouth to speak, but Kate beat him to the punch. "Why Shelby... what a surprise," she purred. "What brings you to this neck of the woods?"

"I just stopped by the office to talk with Chris, and his secretary told me where you were. Since it wasn't far, I thought I'd join you."

"Well, this is a nice surprise." Inside, Kate wasn't too happy that I'd spoiled her plans. "Please sit down."

"Thanks." I turned to Chris, who stayed unusually quiet, and brushed his cheek with a quick kiss. "So what are we celebrating?"

"The Hodges' case." Chris got his voice back, and resigned himself to being involved in an uncomfortable confrontation between two hostile women.

"Yes," Kate broke in. "We won."

"Congratulations," I said, then couldn't help adding, "Although I really think that Mr. Hodges set the whole thing up and took the jewels himself."

Kate's curiosity flared. "Why would you think that?"

"I don't know. Just a hunch, I guess," I shrugged. "Of course, the irony would be if someone else stole them from him."

Kate wondered if I knew what really happened, or if it was a lucky guess. "If that were the case I don't think he would be very happy about it."

"No, I'm sure you're right about that," I quickly agreed.

"I suppose we'll never know," she replied. "Mr. Hodges doesn't strike me as the devious type, but some people are really good at deceiving others." She was thinking about me, and I tensed with alarm. What did she know?

She smiled with satisfaction, realizing she'd hit a sore spot, then turned her attention to Chris. "Did you see the paper this morning? There was a picture on the front page of the car that got blown up yesterday at the funeral home."

"Yeah, I heard something about that," Chris replied.

"The article says that the car belonged to Mr. Joseph Manetto, and in the picture, he's standing next to a dark-haired woman. They're looking at the car as it's burning up." She paused for breath. "It's funny. There was something about the woman that seemed familiar, like I knew her from somewhere. Did you happen to see it Shelby?"

"Yes, I did." How did she know it was me? I glanced at Chris. He wanted to find a paper real bad. He focused on me, wondering if his suspicions were correct. I wanted to deny it, but I couldn't lie to him, so I didn't say anything. Besides, I was supposed to have my shields up around him.

Chris started to get angry, thinking that whatever was going on was all my fault. If I was mixed up with Manetto, it was worse than he thought. Why hadn't I confided in him before now?

"Too bad about the car, but at least no one was hurt," Kate said, in a placating tone. She thought it was too bad I hadn't been blown up along with the car.

I was sick to death of her and her attitude. I nearly groaned with frustration, but I managed to hold it in check. She was annoying, obnoxious, and overbearing. And now Chris was ready to kill me. After this, would he ever listen to me again? It was all her fault. I was in this mess with Uncle Joey because of her. Damn. I had to get out of there before I did something stupid.

I made a show of checking my watch. "Oh no, it's later than I thought! I'm sorry, but I have to go. I promised my mom I'd stop by before the kids got home." I stood and grabbed my purse, nearly knocking the file out of it. I tucked it up under my arm where Kate couldn't see it and said goodbye. "I'll talk to you later, honey." I leaned over and gave him a kiss. He was still upset and figured I was leaving to get away from him. He wanted to confront me right then and there, but not with Kate watching.

"Call me as soon as you get home," he said.

"Okay." I glanced at Kate, and she smiled maliciously, knowing she'd scared me off. Now she had Chris all to herself, and I was leaving.

"Oh, Chris, don't forget about that other thing I asked you to do."

"What other thing?"

"You know... the thing about Stephen Cohen. You were going to ask the senior partners about him." I glanced at Kate. Her eyes went wide and her face got splotchy. Chris didn't have a clue what I was talking about, and his temper started to boil.

Oops. "Okay. Well. Bye." I hurried out before he could stop me.

Outside, I realized that was probably the dumbest thing I'd ever done. Why couldn't I keep my mouth shut? She'd probably ask Chris why I wanted to know about Stephen Cohen, and he'd have to make something up. At least, I hoped he'd cover for me.

As I walked back to Chris' office, a plan began to formulate in my mind. I had something on Kate that could be very valuable to Uncle Joey, and if I told him about it before Kate did, it would look better for me. And he might do me a favor in return. I took out my cell phone, and pushed his number. His secretary put me through to him.

"Shelby. What a pleasant surprise. What can I do for you?"

"I have some information that might interest you, but I need a favor in return."

"I'm listening," he said.

I suddenly realized that talking to him over the phone was probably not in my best interests, since I needed to know what he was thinking. "Maybe I'd better come over. Is that all right?"

"Certainly," he replied. "How's the new car?"

"It's fantastic."

"Great. See you soon."

He disconnected, and I felt a little off balance. Why did he have to bring up the car right then? Did it mean I was more in his debt than he was in mine? I was sure he would want to know about Kate's file on Stephen Cohen, I just hoped it was enough for the favor I had in mind.

Chapter 12

When I arrived at Uncle Joey's office, Ramos was sitting at Jackie's desk. "Jackie left for an appointment, so I'm filling in. Mr. Manetto's visiting with a client, but he should be done in about fifteen minutes. Do you want some coffee or something?"

"Have you got a Diet Coke?"

He smiled. "Come on back." He led the way down the hall and I followed, expecting a break room or something. He turned left into a private corridor, and unlocked the door at the end of the hall. Sunlight spilled into the hallway from a wall of windows covered by filmy white curtains. The large room was airy and bright, and filled with white leather furniture and glass tabletops. My feet sank into the deep, white shag carpet, and I suddenly wanted to take off my shoes. Everything was done in black and white, with splashes of color in the paintings and flower arrangements.

Ramos had disappeared through a doorway into the kitchen. Here, the cabinets were white and the countertops black, with black tile underfoot. He held the refrigerator door open, and handed me a Diet Coke.

"Thanks," I said. "Who lives here?"

"This is my place," he said, easily. "Sometimes I stay on the estate, but mostly I'm here."

"Very nice," I said, knowing that was an understatement.

"Come in and see the view." He led me back to the windows. The view of the city was breathtaking. After a moment I caught an undercurrent of concern. Something was bothering him, and he'd brought me here to tell me.

"How do you like your new car?"

"It's great."

He nodded, then decided to quit beating around the bush, although it would probably make me mad. "Mr. Manetto told me you were coming in to make a deal, and I just wanted to warn you to be careful. He does seem to like you, so it should be okay. Just remember that he doesn't like people who grovel, run, or double-cross him, and he would know if you were trying to double-cross him." Somehow, he'd found out I was at the police station earlier, and he was worried that I was informing on the boss.

"How would he know?"

"He has connections."

"You mean like with the police?" I asked. He nodded, cautious about revealing too much. "You know I went there this morning, don't you?"

"Umm... Yeah."

"How did you find out?"

"Tony put a device on your car so we could keep track of you." This was the part he knew I wouldn't like. He was right.

"Look, I only went to the police station to see if there was anything new about Johnny's case. I don't think Uncle

Joey would be mad about that, but thanks for your concern. It was nice of you to warn me."

"Sure." Now he was embarrassed, he didn't want me to think he cared or something. "We'd better get back." He followed me out the door and, although he was somewhat relieved, he knew I was out of my league when it came to dealing with men like Manetto.

He hated to admit that the real problem came down to the fact that he didn't think he could kill me anymore. That would be bad since he didn't want to lose his job, although he had been thinking about a different career path, just in case. He leaned toward starting his own business. Something with security. He knew a lot about that, and there was good money in it.

It encouraged me that his attitude was changing. Who knew? Maybe there was hope for him after all. I looked over my shoulder and smiled my approval. He seemed puzzled at first, then his eyes widened. It was like I knew what he was thinking. Could it be true?

Oops. "Thanks for the Diet Coke." I hoped that would answer his unspoken question, and cover the reason for my smile.

"Sure." He was still suspicious, but chided himself. What was he thinking? Reading minds wasn't possible.

Uncle Joey's client had left while we were gone, and I hurried into his office. My legs trembled, and I hoped I knew what I was doing.

"So, what have you got?" Uncle Joey asked, after we both sat down. He was very interested in my information, and thinking that by asking a favor, I showed a lot of promise for the business. He was more than willing to mentor me through the process, and hoped I wouldn't disappoint him.

"Well…" I swallowed, hoping I was doing this right. "I was at Chris' law office this morning, and came across a file that had your name in it." He nodded encouragingly, and I continued. "I can tell you the name of the person on the file, and who compiled it, if you'll agree to leave my husband and kids alone."

"That's easy, Shelby. I never intended to harm them. That threat was just to get you to cooperate. Why don't you think of something else?" He really wanted me to do this right.

"Okay. How about that you don't kill me?"

"That's better," he encouraged. "But you're not quite there yet."

This was harder than I thought. "I know. How about that I don't have to work for you anymore?"

He smiled broadly. "That's the spirit. You need to remember that when you're negotiating, you should always go for the thing you're least likely to get first. Then you can always back off to some of these other things if that doesn't work."

"But if you have really good information, then why wouldn't you get what you wanted?"

"Because once you share that information, you lose your bargaining power," he reasoned.

"But then I'd never get what I wanted, because you could always renege on the deal once you had the information," I said.

"That's why you should always have a backup plan. It ensures that both of us will hold up our end of the bargain."

"Okay, I think I know what you mean."

"Good." He smiled. "So, tell me what you have."

"If I do that, I'll lose my bargaining power. You have to agree to my terms first."

"I can't do that without knowing how good your information is."

"So what do I do?" I was really getting confused.

"Okay, let me help you," he said. "On a scale of one to ten, if your information is a nine or a ten, then you'll get what you want. Less than that, and you'll have to back down."

Was he serious? "But aren't you the one who determines how good the information is?"

"Of course, but that's because I'm the one with the most power. You match me in power, and it goes differently. If your information puts you in the driver's seat, then you can call the shots."

"Well, I'm not sure it will do that, but I guess I have to take the chance. I do have a backup plan though, so I guess I'll have to rely on that."

"Great. So what have you got?"

"All of the information in the file is about Stephen Cohen, and a case he was working on before his death, along with certain banking transactions." Uncle Joey's mouth dropped open in shock. This wasn't what he was expecting. I was better than he thought. That gave me courage, and I continued. "This information could be damaging to you, but even if the file isn't worth a nine or a ten, I think the name of the person who compiled the file is."

"Who is it?" he asked, his brows drawn together.

"Kate," I blurted.

Uncle Joey smiled to hide his confusion and surprise. "What if I told you that I asked Kate to keep a file on Stephen Cohen for me?" He was good. He almost pulled it off.

"I'd know you were bluffing."

He'd forgotten I could read his mind. "Uh..." he did a mental head bang, then slumped in defeat. "All right, Shelby," he confessed. "This information is valuable to me. I'd like to see it." If he could get his hands on it... he jerked away from that train of thought, but it was too late.

"Not yet. That's my backup plan. I've got the file in a safe place." If you could call the trunk of my car safe.

"Hmm... it looks like you've got me at a disadvantage."

"That's good, right?" Would he really give in to my demands?

"I hate to admit it, but yes. Even without the file, just knowing that Kate had it, puts a different slant on things." He wondered how Kate had managed to put it together, and why I was tracking her.

"I saw her today, you know. She was making goo-goo eyes at my husband."

"So that's what this is all about? I wondered. Now I think I understand." He was sizing me up, and making calculations in his mind that I couldn't quite catch. "This is great work. You've done an excellent job, but I can't let you go until it's cleared up. I'm going to have to talk to Kate, and I'm going to need your talents to help me."

"Of course." I agreed, then the realization hit me, and I gasped. "I can't believe it. I just agreed to help you without being coerced. Why would I do that?"

"Because it's personal," Uncle Joey smiled. "Kate's after your husband and you're determined to stop her. You can only do that if you help me."

"That still doesn't get you out of our bargain. Once this is all cleared up, I'm out of here. Right?"

"Yes, of course." He was covering his thoughts, and I couldn't tell if he meant it. "I wouldn't mind if you came back and helped me once in a while, but it's totally up to you." He was counting on my feelings of obligation for the car and the money in my bank account. He did have me there.

"Did you tell Kate I was working with you?" I asked. "I didn't think you were going to tell her."

"No, I didn't tell her anything about us."

"Well, somehow she found out. I followed her and Chris to a restaurant today, and spoiled her little celebration. She wasn't very happy I showed up, so she mentioned the picture of you and me in the paper this morning. She threatened to tell Chris. She didn't, but it sure made me mad. Mad enough that I may have mentioned a certain name when I left the restaurant."

Uncle Joey stilled. He hoped it wasn't the name he thought it was. "What? You didn't... tell me you didn't..." He could see from my stricken expression that I had.

"It's not that bad." I tried to defend myself. "And she'd never believe I'd come to you. She doesn't know how well we get along. Besides, all I did was mention his name in passing."

Uncle Joey sighed. "So, now she knows you know about Stephen Cohen, even though you don't really know what it is she thinks you know."

"That's right, because I really don't know."

"What is it you do know, Shelby?" He was quiet and watchful, deciding that my response would determine my fate.

I took a deep breath and made my choice. I wanted to live. "I know that Stephen Cohen was killed a long time ago because he walked in on a burglary. They found the man who killed him, and he was sent to prison. I think the guy's still in prison, but I could be wrong."

Uncle Joey let out his breath. "That's right. That's exactly what happened. I'm glad you know the truth."

I relaxed my tense shoulders, knowing I'd barely escaped with my life. Ramos was right. I wasn't in the same league as Uncle Joey. Somewhere along the way I'd forgotten that he was dangerous, and that was something I couldn't afford to forget. Ever.

Having my life spared almost made me want to grovel, but I held back, then remembered something else. "By the way, Mr. Hodges won the case, or at least, he'll be getting the insurance money. I think he might try stealing the jewels back before he leaves the country."

"Yes, I thought the same thing, but I haven't had a chance to move them. I'll have Ramos take care of it today."

"Well, if that's all, I think I'll go." I stood, but Uncle Joey held up his hand.

"Wait." He waited until I sat back down before he continued. "I'm concerned about what might happen to you once Kate realizes you've taken the file. Are you sure it's in a safe place?" He hurried on before I could answer. "Because it might be in your best interests to give it to me."

"But what about our bargain?"

"You don't know Kate like I do."

"You might be surprised," I murmured.

"Let me keep the file where it's safe, and I'll consider us even. I'll no longer have any hold over you. In return, all I ask is that you never reveal anything about me or my organization to anyone."

Wow. I must have all the power since he was giving in to every one of my demands. The file was more important than I thought. "You'll keep your word?"

"Yes. I really do need that file." He meant it. In fact, he was desperate for it. "As long as you keep your end of the bargain, I will never harm you or your family."

I couldn't help it. I was still skeptical. How could this be so easy? "What's in that file? No, wait... don't tell me. I don't want to know."

"Believe me Shelby, if there was any way I could keep your services, I would, but this file is too important, and I can't pass it up. You've done well." He seemed sincere. I could detect nothing sinister in his thoughts, but since he knew I could pick them up, he could probably hide something. Weighing my options, I felt this was my best chance at freedom. It was a risk worth taking.

"Deal," I said, before I could change my mind. "I'll go get it. It's just in the trunk of my car."

Surprise flickered over Uncle Joey and he shook his head. "The trunk of your car? You think that's safe?"

Smiling sweetly, I said, "I'll be right back." I dashed out of the office to the elevator. There was no sign of Ramos, and I was glad. This was something I wanted to do on my own. If he came, it would be like I was forced into it. This time I had the power, not Uncle Joey, and I liked the way it felt.

I stepped off the elevator into the parking garage and smiled. My car was easy to spot since all the others were black. As I started toward my car, someone grabbed me from behind, and a gloved hand stifled my startled scream. Kate stepped around the corner, triumph gleaming in her eyes.

"I believe you have something that belongs to me." The cold fury in her eyes chilled me to the bone, and I struggled to break free. A knife flashed in her hand, stilling my movements. "You're going to tell me what I want to know, or you'll wish you had after I get through with you." She held the knife menacingly, and I thought she was a little bit crazy to expect an answer with my mouth covered up.

I glanced over my shoulder at the man who held me and my suspicions were confirmed. Number Five. He tightened his grip, forcing the remaining air from my lungs, and dragged me back toward the elevator. Kate pushed the call button and the doors swooshed open. I half hoped to see Ramos inside ready to save me, and my heart sank to find the elevator empty.

"There's a wonderful, little interrogation room in the basement. Uncle Joey never uses it anymore, but it will suit my purposes perfectly." I didn't care if she had a knife, I started kicking and screaming for all I was worth. Number Five pinned me against the wall while Kate pulled a roll of duct tape out of her purse and tacked a strip over my mouth. Number Five grabbed my wrists in front of me, and she wrapped tape around them as well.

He shoved me into the elevator, and I fell to my knees, angry and scared. Kate was enjoying this way too much, and Number Five was content to let her do whatever she wanted. His mind was ordered and methodical, making it difficult to pick up his thoughts.

I knew one thing for sure. I would find no ally in him. His allegiance was toward Kate, not Uncle Joey, and I wondered what was in it for him. What could possibly drive him to become her henchman? If I knew that, I might have some leverage, but with his mind so shuttered, it was hard to tell.

The doors opened, and Number Five roughly dragged me to my feet before pushing me into a dark corridor behind Kate. The musty smell of damp cement and dust assaulted my senses. It didn't seem as if anyone had been down here in a long time. Kate brushed her fingers along the wall until she hit the light switch.

There were several doorways in the hall, but Kate continued until she came to the last one. The hinges squeaked loudly as it swung open. I did not want to go in there, and I dug in my heels, but Number Five forced me through the doorway. Kate flipped a switch, showing a bare cement room with a wooden chair placed in the center.

I was no match for Number Five and, against my protests; he forced me into the chair. He cut through the duct tape holding my wrists together and then taped them to the arms of the chair. After that, he taped my legs together at the ankles and I quit struggling. I wasn't going anywhere.

Kate stood in front of me. With a jerk, she quickly ripped the tape from my mouth. I gasped in pain, and licked the blood on my lips where my skin had come off.

"You took something from me today," she said. "And I want it back. Where is it?"

I could have denied knowing what she was talking about, but she wanted an excuse to hit me, and I wasn't about to give it to her. I tried a different tack. "How do you know I didn't just give it to Uncle Joey?"

"You wouldn't be that stupid. I think you came to make a deal with him."

"And if I tell you where it is, what will happen to me?"

"You're in this too deep for me to let you go. I don't know what your bargain with Uncle Joey is, or why he's keeping you alive, but one way or another, you're going to get killed. What you should really be concerned about is your family. You don't want anything bad to happen to Chris, or Josh, or Savannah, do you?"

This again? How could Kate follow through with a threat like that when she wanted Chris so much? She had to know that Chris would never have anything to do with her if she hurt our kids. She was bluffing, but I had to make her think I believed her.

If I could just keep her busy for the next few minutes, I was sure Ramos would rescue me. Uncle Joey would expect me back by now, and with my car still there, he'd know something had happened. The surveillance cameras in the garage would have picked up my abduction, so they should have a pretty good idea where I was, and who I was with... as long as they were looking at them. I just needed some time.

"I suppose if that's not enough of a persuasion," Kate said. "I'm sure we can come up with something else." She nodded at Number Five, and he quickly stepped close to me, a knife in his hand.

"All right," I said, frantically trying to come up with a plan. "I left the file in Chris' office. I put it in his filing cabinet because it looked like a good hiding place, and I didn't want to get caught taking it."

Kate wasn't sure she believed me, but it made sense in a strange way. "If it's not there, you're going to wish you were dead by the time I get through with you." She turned to Number Five. "I'll get it. You stay and keep her company. I won't be gone long." She checked her watch. "Chris is probably still in his office, but he won't mind if I look through his files. I'll just tell him I misplaced one of mine. And if it's not there... well, maybe I can persuade him to come back with me. Shelby might be more forthcoming if he's hurting."

Right then, I'd never hated anyone as much as I hated her. She laughed tauntingly in my face, and I had to bite my lip to keep from screaming at her. She left with a satisfied smile, and I gritted my teeth. She was not going to win. I was not going to let her get away with this.

I had to think, but what could I do? I focused on Number Five. He was seething with irritation. He didn't like Kate telling him what to do, but he'd let it pass for now.

What did he mean by that? There had to be some reason why he was helping her. What was in it for him? "So," I began. "How long have you known Kate?"

Suspicion flowed from him, although he didn't think I was a threat. "Long enough." He didn't like Kate that much, but she was a necessary part of his plan.

"Why are you helping her? Uncle Joey's the one with the power."

He smiled and sat on his heels next to my chair. I caught sight of a gun inside his jacket, and unease washed over me. He was trying to figure me out, but his control was wearing thin. "What do you really do for Manetto?"

What could I say? I read minds? He'd never believe me. "What were you talking to Kate about after the funeral?"

He rocked back. "You saw us, huh?"

"Yeah, but I didn't tell Uncle Joey. I probably should have. I thought maybe you'd planted the bomb, but you didn't."

"Yeah? So who did?"

"Some guy Uncle Joey cheated." I wasn't going to give him any details.

He was thinking he was glad it didn't work since it would have spoiled everything. He got up and started pacing, wishing Kate hadn't insisted on taking me. I was one more person he'd have to silence, and it was getting out of hand. Especially if she decided to bring my husband into it, then he'd have to kill both of us.

"I'll be right back." He needed to call Kate and make her leave Chris out of it. There were easier ways to make me talk, and the less people involved, the better.

He really meant it. I squeezed my eyes shut while a shudder ran over me. My heart was pounding so hard I almost missed the soft swish of the elevator doors opening and closing, then silence. I was alone, and Number Five was going to kill me. I took a deep breath, and tried to keep away the panic, but something inside me snapped. With desperate energy, I jerked at my bonds for all I was worth. I had to get out of here.

The duct tape refused to cooperate, and I cursed at how strong it was. Then an idea occurred to me. I was taped to the chair but that didn't mean I couldn't move. If I could get to the elevator before he came back, I could go all the way up to Uncle Joey's office. I immediately tried scooting the chair toward the door but it wouldn't budge. Looking down, I realized it was bolted to the floor. Damn. Now what? The only thing I could try now were my teeth.

It was difficult to bend over far enough to reach the tape with my mouth, and when I did, it was like chewing on rubber. My heart sank. Soon, he'd be back, and there was nothing I could do about it. I tried to chew through the tape again, but it was hopeless. Unless I had razor sharp teeth, it wasn't going to work. At least I could hope he made sure Kate didn't involve Chris. Why did I tell her the file was in his office? Stupid, stupid, stupid.

A whisper of sound jolted me out of my misery. It didn't come from the elevator, but I knew I wasn't alone. Someone was in the hall and coming closer. Was it Number Five, back already? Ramos appeared in the doorway and my heart nearly burst.

"Hurry! Hurry! He's making a phone call, but he'll be back." I jumped against my bonds like a crazy person.

"Calm down." Ramos sliced through the tape at my wrists, then bent to my feet.

"He's planning to kill me. I don't know what the rest of his plans are, but after Kate gets back, they were planning to make me tell them where I put the file, and then they were going to kill me." I started pulling the tape off my wrists. It hurt. "What took you so long? I was scared to death." I didn't mean to sound ungrateful or whiney, but I couldn't help it.

"I had to get the file out of your car. The boss has it now."

"Oh."

The door slammed open, and Number Five drew his gun. Ramos shoved me behind him and pulled out his gun, but he wasn't fast enough. A loud shot erupted from across the room and I screamed. It caught Ramos in the chest, and he fell back.

"Ramos!" He didn't move or breathe. I frantically called his name again, but got no response.

As I bent down to check him, Number Five grabbed my arm. "Shut up!" he shouted, and yanked me through the doorway and down the hall to the elevator.

"You killed him!" I screamed. "You bas—"

"I said, shut up!" He pulled my arm behind me, and I gasped in pain. Holding the gun to my head, he forced me into the elevator and pushed the button for Uncle Joey's floor.

"So you were lying. Manetto already has the file." He shoved me against the wall and hissed in my ear. "You know, I really don't care about that stupid file, but this should work to my advantage. Now that Ramos is out of the way, I can get to Manetto. So I guess I should thank you. This is working out better than I thought."

I froze in panic as the doors opened and Number Five shoved me into Thrasher Development. He dragged me down the hall to Uncle Joey's office, and slammed open the door.

Uncle Joey didn't even blink at the intrusion. With a gun in his hand, he must have been expecting us. "What do you want, Walter?"

Walter? Number Five's name was Walter?

"I want you to put your gun on the desk, and step aside." He shoved his gun to my head. "Do it now, or she's dead." Uncle Joey turned sad eyes to me. He was real sorry it had come to this. He hated to lose me, but he wasn't sure he had a choice. He couldn't let Walter get away with this.

My eyes widened. He was going to let Walter kill me? How could he do this?

Flooded with guilt, Uncle Joey looked away. Why did I have to look at him like that? Maybe he'd been in this business too long. Maybe a few years ago he could have called Walter's bluff, but today, he didn't have the heart to watch him kill me. He knew Walter, and knew he'd killed before. But if there was any chance of getting out of this alive, he owed it to me to try. With great reluctance, he put his gun on the desk. My knees wobbled with relief.

"Now move," Walter ordered, pleased with himself. "Over there, to the couch." Uncle Joey did as he was told and sat down. Walter shoved me toward Uncle Joey. I stumbled to the couch, shaken and trembling. Uncle Joey patted my arm, but didn't say anything comforting. He didn't want to give me false hope.

Walter kept the gun trained on us, and stepped over to the desk. "Is this the file?"

"Yes." Uncle Joey answered.

Walter opened the folder and rifled through the pages. Satisfied, he pulled out his cell phone. "Kate. I've got the file. It's here with Manetto... yes he's seen it... forget your lawyer friend. Just get here as fast as you can... Yes, I'm in his office." He ended the call, and I prayed that Chris wasn't involved.

"What's this all about?" Uncle Joey asked, raising his eyebrow.

Walter grimaced under Uncle Joey's scrutiny. It was hard to face Manetto as a double-crosser. The old man still had what it took to make him sweat, even with a gun pointed at him. "Let's just say Kate's been obsessed with finding her father's murderer for a long time, and now she has proof. It's all in the file." Her father? Stephen Cohen was Kate's father? And Uncle Joey killed him?

"This is foolishness. Stephen's murderer was sent to prison. I had nothing to do with it."

Walter shrugged. "I don't really care."

"Then why are you helping her?" Uncle Joey asked. I thought it was a good question.

"I don't think that's something you need to know just yet." He was thinking he wasn't really helping her, he was helping himself, and even though things had taken an unexpected turn, it could still work out. As long as Kate didn't ruin everything.

Walter kept the gun trained on us, but moved to look out the window. He wasn't too concerned that we would try anything.

Uncle Joey was wondering where Ramos was, and I couldn't hold back the tears. Ramos died saving me, and all I did was complain.

"Shelby, what's wrong?" Uncle Joey asked.

I took a deep breath to control my grief. "Walter shot Ramos while he was helping me escape." My voice trembled. Uncle Joey pulled a handkerchief out of his pocket and handed it to me. "Thanks," I whispered. He nodded, but didn't say anything. I was surprised that he took the news so well. In fact, he didn't seem concerned about Ramos. It was almost as if he believed he couldn't be hurt. Like he was in denial. The person he was most concerned about right now was Walter.

"Is he planning to kill us?" He whispered so low I could barely make out the question.

"Yes."

Uncle Joey straightened, and I felt him gather strength. He wasn't as helpless as Walter thought. He had a small gun in his jacket pocket, but he had to wait for the right time. Possibly when Kate arrived. He glanced at me and thought, *gun in my pocket, gun in my pocket.* I quickly nodded to let him know I heard.

"So," Uncle Joey began. "Kate is out for revenge because she thinks I killed her father."

"That's right, but she doesn't want to kill you. She feels too indebted to you for all you've done for her. So she's decided she just wants you to go to prison for the rest of your life. That's why she was compiling all this stuff."

"Did she kill Johnny?"

"No, that was me," Walter smiled with pride. "He wouldn't cooperate with our demands that he tell the police you killed Stephen Cohen. We knew he was there and witnessed the murder. When his nephew surprised us, I ended up killing them both. Kate wasn't happy with me, but it was them or me. You know how it is."

I noticed he said me instead of us. He wasn't acting like he and Kate were a team. What was he planning? What was it that he didn't want Kate to mess up? Uncle Joey was wondering the same thing. Only he was one step ahead of me. He was thinking that the only thing Walter would risk all this for was a shot at running the organization. That meant Uncle Joey had to die. So what did Walter need Kate for? I strained to listen to his thoughts, but nothing came to me.

We all heard the elevator doors open and someone walking toward the office. Uncle Joey nodded at me to be ready and I swallowed. Walter was watching the doorway, but something about our postures alerted him, and he pointed the gun at Uncle Joey's head. "Don't try anything."

Just then, Kate walked in, imbued with seething anger that seemed hotter than her red hair. "What happened?" She focused her anger on Walter. "How did Uncle Joey get the file?"

"Hey, it wasn't me." Walter motioned to Uncle Joey and me. "She gave it to him. He's had it all along. There wasn't anything I could do about it."

Kate turned her fury toward me. "I think I want to shoot you myself."

"Kate," Uncle Joey said. "What's going on here? Walter says that you think I killed your father. It's not true. I took you in like my own daughter, and I did it because Stephen and I had made a promise. I made a promise to him that if anything ever happened, I would take care of you and your mother. He knew there were risks in this business. I had nothing to do with his murder. He was one of my best friends."

"Then how do you account for everything in that file?"

"The information in that file was planted by a detective on the police force. He was an undercover cop who didn't like me much, and he managed to infiltrate my organization. He stole access to my bank accounts and created those records. It would have worked if the evidence hadn't been so clear that the real murderer was Lloyd Raines, the man convicted and sent to prison. He did it, not me." Uncle Joey almost had me convinced, but I had the impression he was making this up as he went. He was good.

Kate's anger evaporated. She wanted to believe him. In her own way, she loved Uncle Joey. "But... how can I believe you? Not all of that information could have been fabricated. Walter found some of it in your files..." She turned to Walter with a raised brow. "Unless he planted it."

"I didn't plant it, Kate. It's true. Don't believe him. It's just another way he's manipulating you. He killed your father, there's no doubt about it."

"What makes you so sure?" Kate asked.

"Because Lloyd Raines didn't do it," Walter said. "I should know."

"Oh yeah? How?"

"Because he's my Uncle."

Chapter 13

It was one of those moments that felt like time had stopped. For the space of a heartbeat, everyone froze.

Uncle Joey could hardly imagine how Walter had slipped into his organization with a past like that. Yet somehow, he believed him. "How is this possible?" he asked.

Walter shrugged. "My Uncle was into petty crime. He fancied himself to be a pretty shrewd dealer. I learned a lot of street smarts from him, and he was always bragging about how he never got caught. Then came the moment he was picked up for murder. To this day, he doesn't know how it happened, or how all the evidence was planted. I knew that whoever set him up was someone I could learn from—someone I could admire."

He faced Uncle Joey. "You were the only game in town. It opened my eyes to a whole new world of possibilities. I knew that someday, I wanted to be part of your group. I wanted to get to know the ins and outs of the kind of organization you ran. I got involved in little things at first. Once I proved myself, I moved up through the ranks. I've worked really hard for you, and I think I've proven myself savvy enough to run the company.

"But I didn't realize you had to be "related" to take over the business. Even though I've proven myself to be your best man, you were going to give everything to Kate. When she came up with this plan to send you to prison, I jumped at the chance to help her do it." He was also thinking that he couldn't pass up the opportunity to get rid of Kate at the same time. My pulse quickened, was he going to kill her too?

Kate could hardly believe that Walter was related to the man who was convicted of murdering her father. They had more in common than she thought. She totally missed Walter's underlying animosity toward her. "Why did you kill my father?" she asked Uncle Joey.

"Kate." Uncle Joey shook his head, his mouth drawn tight with disappointment. "How can you believe Walter over me? Especially after everything I've done for you? Has Walter taken care of you all your life? Has he paid for your education? Has he taken care of your mother, and paid all the bills? Did he buy your home for you? What about the car you drive? I've been with you through thick and thin, and you treat me like this?"

After that, even I was starting to feel guilty. "You should have come to me with your doubts. I could have cleared this up before it got out of hand. Now, the damage is almost irreparable. And killing Johnny. How could you do that? He was a good man. He didn't deserve it."

"I didn't kill Johnny," Kate blurted. "Walter did. It wasn't my idea." Tendrils of guilt threaded through her conscience. Was she wrong? Had Walter deceived her?

"Oh, so now you're going to blame everything on me?" Walter said. "That's not fair." Kate leapt to her defense, and soon, both of them were shouting at each other. I thought now might be a good time for Uncle Joey to do something. Like pull his gun.

"Stop it, both of you!" Uncle Joey commanded. "There's still a chance to do some damage control, but I need both of you to give up this ridiculous scheme."

My heart sank. That was not what I had in mind. I focused on Walter and, with sudden clarity, I knew he wasn't about to give up his plans. Now was the perfect time to kill Uncle Joey and set Kate up for it. Revenge for Stephen Cohen's murder was the best motive for both Uncle Joey's death and Johnny's murder. He couldn't let this chance to take over Uncle Joey's assets, and gain control over the organization, slip through his fingers.

Kate wasn't ready to give up either. Uncle Joey never said he hadn't killed her father. She hardened her resolve. "There's nothing you can say that's going to change my mind," she said. "You killed my father and I have proof." She grabbed the folder from Uncle Joey's desk. "It's all here in this file."

Uncle Joey rubbed his face in exasperation. "That file you hold so dearly is nothing but lies."

"I don't think so," Kate said calmly, all guilt gone. "But don't worry. I don't want you dead, especially when you've done so much for me as you so eloquently pointed out. But I think spending some time in prison would certainly make me feel better."

"What about her?" Walter pointed to me. "She's a liability we need to get rid of." He was wondering if he could goad Kate into killing me. He knew how much she hated me. "I never understood what she was doing here anyway."

"Yeah," Kate agreed. Turning to Uncle Joey she asked, "Why is Shelby involved in all this? Did you tell her to spy on me? You were supposed to take care of her. But next thing I know, she's working for you." That sparked Walter's curiosity, and he was willing to put off killing us to find out.

Uncle Joey knew something wasn't quite right. Why was Walter so willing to help Kate? What had she promised him that he was willing to kill for? Walter was dangerous and ambitious. The only thing he'd settle for was running the organization, and he wasn't sure Kate would give that up.

I needed to figure out a way to tell Uncle Joey what Walter was planning. I knew he would believe me, but how could I convince Kate? Would she believe Walter was going to double-cross her, especially if it came from me?

"I'll tell you," Uncle Joey said. "But first, I'm curious about something. If you were successful in pulling this off and sending me to prison, even though I'm innocent," he couldn't help adding. "Which one of you was going to run my organization?"

"Me, of course," Kate answered. "With Walter as my partner," she quickly added.

"And you're okay with that?" Uncle Joey asked Walter.

Walter gritted his teeth, but was careful to play along. "It's more than you were willing to give me." He was growing tired of all this talk, and Kate was getting too smug. Was she ever in for a surprise. Losing patience with it all, he started to raise his gun.

"Uncle Joey," I broke in. "You never told them why I'm here. I'm sure they will want to know." Walter lowered the gun, he'd almost forgotten about that. "Once you know the truth, you'll understand why Uncle Joey has kept me around."

Uncle Joey was surprised. Was I really going to tell them my secret? "There's no other way," I said to him. I got to my feet and took a few steps toward the window. I tried to look pensive so they would think it was hard for me to tell them the truth. But the real reason was to put some distance between Uncle Joey and me. I was hoping to keep Walter's attention on me so Uncle Joey could get to his gun.

"I have a gift," I said. "It's not something a normal person has. In fact, I don't think anyone else can do it and, so far, only Uncle Joey knows about it." This got their attention, and I turned to face them. "I found out about Uncle Joey from a conversation I had with you, Kate. You were thinking about how he put you through law school when we had lunch."

Her eyes narrowed as she tried to figure out what I meant. The only way that could happen was if I could read minds. That was impossible.

"It's not impossible, Kate. It's also how I know that Walter is planning to double-cross you. He's planning to kill both Uncle Joey and me, then frame you for it, along with Johnny's murder. You have to admit, you have the perfect motive, and Walter has it all figured out. Besides, if you really think about it, you'd realize that Walter would never share the business. He's only been humoring you. Even Uncle Joey can see that. Just look at him." I motioned toward Walter. "You can see it in his eyes. Walter wants it all for himself."

Walter was shocked. How did I know? "She's just saying that to drive us apart."

"Is this true?" Kate faced Walter.

He decided he'd waited long enough. He raised the gun and pointed it straight at me. I cringed and squeezed my eyes shut.

Just then, the door to Uncle Joey's office burst open, and Mr. Hodges came in yelling. "Get your hands up! All of you! Now!" Surprise rippled over me, and my heart raced. Mr. Hodges?

Walter hesitated, but lowered the gun when Hodges emptied a bullet near his foot. He jumped back and dropped the gun harmlessly to the floor.

"Move!" He yelled, slamming the door shut, and motioning with his gun. "Everyone... take a seat at the table!" As Walter and Kate backed away from him, he picked up Walter's gun, momentarily puzzled, then set it on Uncle Joey's desk. "Sit down... now! And put your hands on top of the table where I can see them."

What was going on? Had things just gotten worse, or had Hodges just saved me from death? I didn't think Hodges meant to kill any of us, but he was certainly scary the way he waved the gun in our faces.

At the table, Kate ended up sitting next to Walter. She tried to scoot her chair away from him without using her hands, but she couldn't get very far.

"I can't believe you were going to double-cross me!" Kate burst out, looking at Walter. "Now you've ruined everything! How could you?"

"If you think I could stand taking orders from you, you're nuts. You don't know how to run this business. You're nothing but a scum-sucking lawyer."

Kate inhaled sharply at the insult. "Why you no good, two-timing—"

"Stop it!" Hodges screamed. He was rapidly losing his cool. He hadn't expected such a crowd, and what was I doing there? "Shut up... or I'll shoot all of you!"

"He means it," I said. Both Kate and Walter glared at me.

"Mr. Hodges," Kate took a chance. "You may not know this, but you came at the perfect time." She started to stand, relying on her feminine skills to catch Hodges off-guard. "That man," she motioned toward Walter, "was just trying to rob Mr. Manetto."

"Sit down." Mr. Hodges turned the gun toward her. "I don't know what's going on here, and I don't care, but I'm not a fool. I'll kill you all unless I get my jewels back. I might just kill you anyway, if you don't do what I say." His hand was shaking, and Kate quickly sat.

"Manetto, I want you to open your safe. Do it slow and easy. The rest of you better not move a muscle, or I'll shoot."

With slow deliberation, Uncle Joey moved to the large painting on the wall. He tugged against it, and it swung open, revealing a black safe. As he fiddled with the lock, he was hoping that he could get to his gun before Hodges shot him. Too bad he hadn't moved the jewels. Now he'd have to give them back. Of course, it wouldn't matter if he got killed.

While Hodges had his gun trained on Uncle Joey, Kate tried again. "Look Hodges, we've worked together for a long time. You know you can trust me. I won your case for you, didn't I? You can't stand up to Manetto by yourself... you need me. Let me help you, I think we'd make a good team. The jewels are in there, but I know where he also keeps an enormous amount of cash. Take me with you, and we can both start over together."

"What? You've got to be crazy to think I would fall for that."

"Hey, it's a good deal for both of us. I have reasons of my own for cutting my ties with Uncle Joey. You know how he is. I don't want to end up dead, and that's what will happen if you don't take me with you."

Hodges had always found Kate attractive, but would she really leave with him? He didn't think he was her type, but she did sound sincere and frightened. Whatever was going on here must be pretty bad. Mexico wouldn't be so lonely if she was there.

"Hodges, I swear if you do this, I'll owe you big time. I promise to make it worth your while. Wherever you're going, I'm sure I can help you." Kate was desperate. She knew Uncle Joey didn't tolerate double-crossers, and she wanted all her ties with Walter cut. He was going down, and she didn't want to go with him. Maybe in a few years she could come back, but for now, she needed to disappear. Hodges was her way out.

Distracted, Hodges shook his head. "Let me think about it." He turned his attention back to Uncle Joey. "Aren't you done yet?" Just then the lock clicked, and the safe popped open. Uncle Joey started to reach inside.

"Stop!" yelled Hodges. He thought there might be a gun inside. He knew from experience that sometimes people put guns in their safes.

"Please, let me help you," Kate implored. "Keep the gun trained on him and give me the bag. I'll fill it up for you."

He could really use her help, especially with this crowd. He hadn't expected so many people. "All right." He threw her the bag. "Manetto, sit down."

Kate hurried over to the safe and began to push the contents into the bag. "You're in luck. It looks like it's all here. The rest of his money is in his desk. Do you want me to get it?"

"No, I'll do it." Hodges kept the gun trained on us as he inched his way to the desk.

While Hodges went through the drawers, Walter was trying to decide how to get out of this alive. He still hadn't figured out how I knew his plans. Was I like a psychic? Did I know what was going to happen next? That just gave him the creeps. Come to think of it, I did have bright blue eyes, and the way the light reflected off them was kind of eerie.

After that, I couldn't help staring at him with what I hoped was an 'otherworldly' look. I tried to convey an intimate 'I can see into your soul' moment just to freak him out.

He jerked his gaze from mine and decided to ignore me. It was just too weird. He'd better make his move soon. All he needed was a chance to grab his gun off Uncle Joey's desk, and he would be back in control. He couldn't believe that Kate was such a manipulator, especially the way she was kissing up to Hodges. It made his blood boil. Kate was always getting away with something, and it was time somebody stopped her.

Uncle Joey was assessing the situation as well. He didn't think he could pull his gun before Hodges could shoot him, and he had no doubt Hodges would. He needed to wait for the right moment. It was too bad that Kate was helping Hodges, but it showed initiative, something he had always tried to instill in her.

Uncle Joey also wondered what Walter had up his sleeve. Walter was probably waiting for his chance to rush Hodges and get his gun. That would be the perfect distraction for him to pull his own gun. It was bound to get exciting, and he was almost looking forward to it. Action of any kind was better than getting killed doing nothing.

Hodges was rifling through Uncle Joey's desk drawers by touch while he kept watching us. His arm was getting tired from holding the gun so long. Sweat trickled uncomfortably down his face, and he couldn't wipe it off. In fact, this whole ordeal was taking way too long. He touched something that felt like money and glanced down. There it was. A whole drawer full of large bills.

"Kate, when you're done with that, bring it over here," he told her.

She smiled. Her plan to get out of this was working. Hodges needed her and, with the jewels and money, there was enough to make a good start somewhere else.

Walter was getting ready to spring when Kate walked by, thinking he could use her as a shield if Hodges fired at him. I was just about to say something when Kate unexpectedly went around on the other side of the table.

Walter was about to go for her anyway, but before he made his move, the door exploded open. Ramos stood there like an avenging angel. His hair flew wild around his face, and his eyes held a wicked gleam. He was scary looking, but I'd never seen anything so wonderful in my life. Ramos was alive!

Hodges fired his gun, but Ramos was already in motion and the shot went wide. Ramos did a dive-roll and came up shooting. The room became a hotbed of gunfire. Hodges shot at Ramos while Walter jumped toward the desk, grabbed his gun, and rolled aside. Uncle Joey pulled his gun and, ducking behind the table, aimed at Walter. Kate was holding the bag of jewels in front of her like a shield, and tried to take cover behind a big potted plant.

I fell to my hands and knees. The sound of gunfire deafened me, and I wasn't sure where to go. A bullet whizzed past my ear and I let out a little scream. In a surge of desperation, I gathered my feet beneath me. Keeping as small as possible, I bolted for the half-open door.

Nearly there, someone came crashing through the doorway, slamming it open. I tried to stop, but couldn't get out of the way before the hard edge struck me in the head. I grunted and toppled over, unable to see around the swimming black dots that clouded my vision. Like a signal, the gunfire stopped, and I could hear people shouting, but it was lost behind the roaring in my ears and everything started to go dark.

I came awake hearing someone call my name.

"Shelby?" That sounded like Chris, but how could he be here? "Shelby? Can you hear me?" There it was again, but I knew it wasn't him. He couldn't be here. I must be losing my mind.

"I think she's fainted." Now that was Uncle Joey. At least I thought it was Uncle Joey. "I don't see any blood."

"No, actually, I clobbered her with the door when I came in. See that big bump on her forehead?" That was Chris again. Maybe he really was here.

"Oh... yeah. That's got to hurt. Wow, look at that. It's getting bigger by the second. Maybe we should get some ice on it."

"Is it over?" I tried to say, but it came out more like a groan.

"It's all right, Shelby. You're safe now."

I blinked my eyes. It really was Chris. He was here. Someone handed him something, and he gently placed it on my hurting head. I sucked in my breath. "Oww!" I yelled, suddenly awake. Tears leaked from the corners of my eyes, and I pushed the cloth away, struggling to sit up.

"You need to keep this on your head or the swelling might get worse."

"But touching it hurts!"

Chris helped prop me against the wall, then gently placed the ice on my head. Tears leaked out again, but this time it was easier to bear. After a few moments, the ice began to numb the pain, and I could finally open my eyes and focus on the room.

"Is that Dimples?"

"Yes." Chris sat down beside me.

"What's he doing here?"

Chris sighed. "Trying to save you. Same reason I'm here."

"How did you know?"

"Kate came to my office after our little lunch today, and told me she was looking for a file she'd misplaced. For some reason, she thought it might be in my filing cabinet. I told her to look all she wanted, and went out into the hall, then listened at the door.

"She got a phone call and went on and on about how you'd given her file on Stephen Cohen to Manetto, saying she couldn't wait to throttle you. I thought you might be in trouble, so I followed her here. I noticed your new car in the parking garage, and tried calling your cell, but you didn't answer. I started to get worried and called Dimples. He came right over, and when we got off the elevator, we heard the shots. I didn't even think. I just ran for the door."

"So, you're the one who slammed the door into my head?"

"I didn't know you'd be right behind it. At least you didn't get shot. How does it feel?"

"It hurts. Really bad." My head was pounding to beat the devil, and I still had trouble focusing. I could hear Uncle Joey talking, so I knew he must be okay. There were several more bodies in the room than before. Dimples was arguing with three other guys and I finally recognized them as numbers two, three, and four.

What had happened to Walter? Someone was lying on the floor. Was that him or Hodges? My head started to spin and I started feeling a bit nauseous.

"How are you doing?" Dimples asked, kneeling beside me.

"Awful." I couldn't move my head afraid I would throw up.

"I'm leaving for a minute, but I'll be back," he said to Chris. After he left, I heard the wail of sirens in the distance. Then Uncle Joey started arguing with the guys. With Dimples gone, it sounded like they were trying to decide what to do before he came back with more policemen. I scanned the room for Kate and Hodges, and found her wrapping something around Hodges' bloody arm. They were sitting in the corner by the potted plant.

All at once, EMT's and firemen flooded the room. They brought in a gurney and all sorts of equipment, making the room even smaller and more crowded. After a minute, one of them came to my side and started shining a light in my eyes.

"It looks like you might have a slight concussion." He removed the ice from my forehead and let out a low whistle. "Whew! That's huge!" He hurriedly put it back. "You need to keep ice on that, but you'll probably still have a couple of black eyes. Are you nauseated? Dizzy?"

"Just a little," I said trying not to move my head.

"Better sit tight for a few more minutes then. You might need to go to the hospital." He stayed by my side, but was clearly more interested in what was going on in the room.

"Man, what happened to this place? It looks like a shoot-out from The Godfather."

"Yeah, something like that," Chris said. The EMT got called over to the other group and someone else joined us.

"Hey babe," Ramos said. Chris stiffened at my side, but none of his thoughts came through.

"Ramos..." I got out. "I thought you were dead." Relief came so strong tears gathered in my eyes. He didn't look like he was at death's door, although there was blood on his shirt.

"I'm not that easy to kill."

"But I saw him shoot you," I protested.

He pulled his shirt open to reveal a black vest. "It's Kevlar. I don't wear it all the time, but when I saw them grab you on the monitors, I figured I'd better be prepared. I thought Walter would be gone longer than he was, or I would have had you out of there before he came back." He sounded apologetic, like he hadn't done his job.

"It's okay, I'm just glad you're alive." My arm was getting tired from holding the ice, so I lowered it for a minute.

"Whoa!" Ramos exhaled. "That's huge. How did that happen?"

I glanced at Chris out of the corner of my eye. He was frowning, and didn't seem to like Ramos very much. "I was trying to get away and ran into the door just as Chris was coming in." I wasn't sure Chris appreciated how nicely I said that.

"Oh." Ramos raised his brow at Chris. "You bring the cop?"

"Yeah." There was a challenge in his tone, but he was saved from further comment when the paramedics brought the gurney carrying Walter toward the door. There was an oxygen mask covering his face and an IV stuck in his arm. His face was pale and his shirt was covered in blood.

"Is he going to live?" I asked.

"Don't know," Ramos answered.

The paramedic that had looked at me before came back and shined the light in my eyes again. "Not quite so dilated this time. How are you feeling?"

"My head hurts pretty bad, and I'm still a little dizzy, but I'm not nauseous anymore."

"You should probably go to the hospital, just in case."

"No," I said forcefully. "I just want to go home."

The EMT frowned. "Well, then you should take something for the pain, and keep ice on your head. But you have to promise me if you start feeling worse, you'll go straight to the emergency room. Does that sound good to you?"

"I'll take care of her," Chris said.

Ramos grunted, then stalked over to Uncle Joey and the others. As soon as the paramedics left, Dimples entered the room with several other policemen, and I wondered what was going to happen. Would they try to arrest Ramos or Uncle Joey? Maybe they would arrest everyone, including me. What was I going to tell them? My head started to pound even worse and, at that moment, all I wanted to do was lie down and die.

"Come on Shelby," Chris said. "Let's get you home."

"Okay," I whimpered. He helped get me to my feet, and supported most of my weight. A wave of dizziness washed over me, but left as I got my balance. We got two steps toward the door when a burly cop blocked our way.

"Excuse me. No one is allowed to leave this room."

I couldn't help it. Tears started rolling down my face. This was just too much, and I couldn't take it anymore.

"Harris!" Chris called. Dimples excused himself from the group and came over. "He won't let us leave, and Shelby's had it."

Dimples took one look at me and nodded. "Of course, go ahead, we can talk tomorrow." He paused, then added. "Are you sure she doesn't need a doctor? That bump is huge."

Good grief, how bad could it be?

"She just needs to lie down and rest." I hated that they were talking about me like I wasn't there but, with the tears and headache, I couldn't trust myself to speak.

The brawny policeman let us go, and we were soon in the elevator. That's when I realized I didn't have my purse or my car keys. How were we going to get home? Through my tears I managed to tell Chris my worries.

"I've got my car," Chris soothed me. "I'll come back and get your stuff tomorrow."

"I don't even know where my purse is," I moaned.

"Don't worry, I'll find it." He helped me into his car and put the seat back. I closed my eyes and endured the pain in silent agony. We made it home, and Chris helped me inside.

He gave me one of my pain pills as soon as we walked in the kitchen. It didn't take long before I started feeling more relaxed, and the hard edge of my headache eased. I even felt mellow enough to take a look at the bump on my head, but every time I got close to a mirror, Chris got in the way.

Was he trying to spare my feelings? Wait a minute. Shouldn't I know what he was thinking? I tried to open my mind to his thoughts, but nothing happened. I couldn't 'hear' him. The only thing I got was a twinge of pain in my right temple where the door had hit me so hard. Was it gone? Did this mean I couldn't read minds anymore?

I didn't know if that made me happy or sad. Mostly, I was just tired and sleepy from the pill. Who knew what would happen tomorrow. It was hard to keep my eyes open, so I finally stopped trying and got into bed.

I only woke up once during the night, and Chris gave me another pain pill that knocked me out until midmorning. This time I woke up feeling mostly normal, although it hurt to lift my eyebrows.

I gingerly felt for the bump on my head. It was still there, but not nearly as big as it had seemed the night before. I was a little nervous about looking in the mirror, but the one on my dresser was far enough away that maybe it wouldn't be such a shock. I took a deep breath and sat up, only to find the mirror covered with a sheet.

If I hadn't been nervous before, now I was totally rattled. Why had Chris done that? I ran my hands over my face just to make sure everything was still in the right places. Were my eyes a little swollen? They seemed normal. At least, I could open them all the way. The rest of my face felt fine. The only thing that seemed unusual was the big bump on my forehead.

This was ridiculous, and upset me more than I liked. I should just look in the mirror and get it over with. I stood slowly. Then, taking my time, I wobbled into the bathroom. Good, no sheets. I glanced in the mirror and did a double take. Was that really me? I looked like something out of a horror movie, and the bump was huge!

My pale face looked like death warmed over, except for the skin around the bump, and around my eyes. It was totally black and blue, and I looked like a ghost who was having a really bad hair day. My stomach got queasy, and I had to steady myself against the bathroom sink. Taking slow and easy breaths, I tried not to panic.

This wouldn't last. Maybe a week, tops, and I'd be back to normal, right? I could handle looking like this for a while. Then it would go away. At least I was alive. I glanced at my reflection again and cringed. Maybe it was better if I covered up the mirrors. But what if I had to go out? I couldn't stand for anyone to see me like this.

There was always the option of wearing dark glasses. That would work. I teetered into the kitchen and opened the drawer where I kept them. With perverse satisfaction, I put them on my face and hurried back into the bathroom. To my great relief, the bruises were mostly hidden. It was a vast improvement. This I could handle.

I couldn't believe the irony that, with all the bullets flying around, the only injury I got was from my husband. How was I supposed to explain that to the kids? What about my mother? I could just imagine her reaction when I told her that Chris accidentally hit me with a door. She'd probably think I made it up.

I took a nice long shower, and threw on my standard t-shirt and jeans. I pulled some hair across my forehead to cover the bump and, with the glasses, I didn't look too bad. As long as no one took a closer look.

My stomach growled, and I meandered into the kitchen for breakfast. So far, I'd been able to keep my worries at bay, but while I ate, they all came back. I wondered what had happened after Chris and I had left. Had the police made any arrests? I was sure glad Ramos was alive, but I couldn't say the same about Walter. And what had happened to Kate and Hodges?

My main concern was what to tell Dimples. He'd let me go last night, but I'd have no such luck today. I wondered what story Uncle Joey had told him. Maybe I could blame everything on Kate. That would be nice. But if I did that, I'd have to tell them about the file, and I didn't think Uncle Joey would like that. So what should I do?

My phone rang and I jumped. I couldn't talk to Dimples until I knew what to say. I checked the caller ID and let out a breath. It was Chris.

"How are you doing?" he asked.

"Lots better, except I look horrible. The bump is still there, and now I have two black eyes! I look like I've been in a fight or something."

"You got hit pretty hard," he explained, then he seemed to realize it was his fault. "Uh... how's your head? Any headaches?"

"Not right now. Other than how I look, I'm feeling okay. So, what's going on? Have you heard anything? Is Kate there? Did Dimples arrest anyone?"

"I'm not sure about anything except that Kate didn't come in this morning, and no one's been able to find her."

"That's strange. Are you sure they didn't arrest her?"

"I don't know." Chris paused. "Shelby, I need to know everything that you've been involved in. Everything. You can't leave anything out. All right?"

"Well, sure. I was going to tell you what was going on anyway, but I never got the chance."

He hesitated, clearly contemplating if I was telling the truth. "Well, now the police are involved. Dimples called this morning and he wants to talk to you."

I took a sharp breath. "He's not going to arrest me or anything, is he?"

"No. But you're involved, and I need to know how much before you talk to him. It may not be in your best interests to tell him everything." He let that sink in for a second before continuing. "It's something I'll have to decide when I know the whole story."

At that moment, I was profoundly grateful he was a lawyer. "Okay. When did Dimples want to talk to me?"

"This afternoon. I've got a few things to take care of here, and then I'll come home and we can talk. After we decide how much you're going to tell him, I'll stay for the questioning."

"Okay," I agreed. "I'll see you soon." Chris was serious enough to make me nervous. I hadn't done anything wrong, had I? For some reason my head started to hurt, and I vaguely remembered that after being hit in the head, I couldn't hear Chris' thoughts last night. Had the injury somehow made me lose my powers? Were they still gone today?

I couldn't decide if I was relieved or not. What was wrong with me? If I couldn't hear thoughts anymore, that would be great, right? It was the answer to all of my current problems. Uncle Joey couldn't use me anymore, and I could go back to being normal.

I waited for the surge of relief I should've felt over that, but it never came. Part of me had enjoyed knowing other's thoughts. It gave me an advantage over them, but more than that, it made me unique and different from everyone else. It had also given me insights I never would have had.

Of course, it was better not to know some things. In fact, hearing people's thoughts had gotten me into more trouble than I cared to admit. Probably more than it was worth.

Who was I trying to kid? It had been a nightmare. I'd nearly been killed. My family had been in jeopardy. My relationship with Chris had suffered. I mean, look at me. I was a wreck.

Still, if it was gone, I would feel bad. How crazy was that?

The phone rang again. This time it was Uncle Joey. "Hello Shelby, I was just calling to see how you're doing. That was quite a big bump you got."

"Yeah, you should see it today. Not only is the bump black and blue, but I also have two black eyes. It scares me every time I look in the mirror."

He chuckled. "Well, if that's the worst of it, you should feel pretty lucky. For a while there, I thought we were both going to die."

I sobered instantly. "I know. I was pretty scared too. So what happened after I left?"

"It was quite a mess, but I think we got it mostly straightened out. I told the police that Walter was the one responsible for everything. Have they talked to you yet?"

"No, but Dimples is coming over this afternoon."

"Dimples?"

Oops. "I think his name is Harris, but I've always called him Dimples because of his... dimples."

"Oh... well. I guess that makes sense. I think I remember seeing some dimples." His kindness made me feel warm inside. "So... you've talked to him before?" Uncle Joey sounded suspicious and I knew I had some explaining to do.

"He's the officer that was involved with the bank robbery that got me into this mess. Anyway, Chris called and told me he's coming over to question me."

"Did Chris tell you anything else?"

"Just that he wanted to go over my story with me before I talked to the police. He said it might be a good thing if I didn't say too much."

"Good." Uncle Joey exhaled. "Those are my feelings as well. Why don't you tell them you do a little part-time office work for me, and you just happened to walk in at the wrong time. Make sure they know you heard Walter confess to Johnny's murder, and that he was planning on killing us as well."

"What about Hodges and Kate? What happened to them?"

"That's kind of a sore spot," Uncle Joey said. "In the confusion, they both got away."

"What?" I nearly shouted. "How could that happen?"

"It's true. They snuck out. None of us saw them go, and I haven't been able to find them since." Something about that seemed a little fishy to me. "So let's leave Kate and Hodges out of it. I want to take care of them myself." That sounded ominous.

"Okay. I won't say anything about them. I'll just concentrate on Walter's motives to take over your... what should I call it?"

"Company," he answered.

"Okay." I wanted to ask him about the file, and if he remembered our bargain, but maybe this wasn't the best time. "There's one more thing..." I hesitated, not sure how to continue.

"What?" He sounded cautious.

"Well... ever since I got hit on the head, I haven't been able to hear anyone's thoughts. I just wanted you to know... it's a possibility that my powers are gone." I waited for him to say something but all I got was silence. "Are you still there?" I asked.

"Are you sure?"

"It looks that way. I mean, since it was an injury to my head that brought it on, I guess it makes sense that an injury could make it stop. I just thought you should know."

"Do you think it could come back?"

"I don't have any idea." I didn't want to get his hopes up, especially when this could be my one way out.

"Maybe all you need is some rest.

"Yeah, maybe."

"Well, I guess we'll just have to wait and see. In the meantime, stay home and get better. If there's anything you need, anything at all, just let me know, and I'll see that you get it."

I thanked him and disconnected, relieved I'd told him. He had taken it pretty well, unless he didn't believe me. What would happen then? It didn't matter, even if I got my powers back, there was no way I would ever tell him the truth.

I checked the clock, knowing that once Chris got home, I would find out if my powers were really gone. It made me a little anxious, and I hoped I could deal with the answer. No matter what it was.

Chapter 14

I sat at the kitchen table, drinking a diet soda, when the back door opened and Chris walked in. I took a deep breath and tried to calm my pattering heart. This was it, the moment of truth.

"Hi honey," he said, coming into the kitchen. "What's with the dark glasses?"

I pulled them off with a flourish, and it surprised when he didn't flinch. I thought I caught a flare of shock, and my hopes soared. Maybe my powers were coming back.

"Wow, you've got the best black eyes I've ever seen." Was that supposed to be a compliment?

"It was either wear the glasses, or go into shock every time I passed a mirror. I went with the glasses."

"Makes sense to me." He stared at the swath of hair across my forehead and pursed his lips like he was hiding a smile. "How's the bump?"

"I think the swelling's gone down a little, but I've still got a bit of a headache."

"Maybe you'd better lie down."

"No, that's okay. There's something really important I need to tell you." Despite my best efforts, I hadn't been able to pick up any thoughts from Chris, and I decided that he needed to know I'd lost my powers. And if they came back? Well, I'd deal with that later.

"What's going on?" Chris took a chair across from me, his brows wrinkled in concern. I concentrated really hard, but I still couldn't sense anything. My heart plummeted.

"After you clobbered me in the head yesterday, I haven't been able to read minds. I think the ability I had to do that is gone." Enormous relief flooded over Chris. It seemed like a wall came down, and I realized he'd been blocking his thoughts from me all this time. It wasn't me at all, it was him. I managed to keep my mouth shut, but it was hard to hide my relief. Now I really had to play along.

"Are you sure?"

"Yup. I haven't been able to pick up a thing." The lie came to me so easily it was almost scary. "I guess since a head injury caused it, being hit in the head again took it away. Does that make sense? I don't know how else to explain it."

"Yeah, that makes a lot of sense. Wow. This is great."

"Uh-huh." I smiled, but he could tell it was half-hearted.

"What's wrong? Aren't you happy about this?"

"Sure. It's the best thing that could have happened."

"But..." he prodded.

"Well, I know I should be happy, and I think I am, but I'm also sad. I mean... it's stupid to feel that way when it caused so many problems, but... I don't know. It sort of made me special."

Chris shook his head and sighed. "Shelby, you don't need something like that to make you special. You are one of a kind... believe me."

Did he mean that in a good way? Then it came... and I understood a little of what he felt for me. He thought I was sweet, yet headstrong, exasperating on one hand, and completely loyal on the other. He loved the way I expressed myself, but I sometimes made him crazy. I had a zest for life that he'd never found with anyone else, and he'd be devastated without me.

"You think so?"

"Of course. You may miss it, but in the end it's really the best thing that could have happened."

"I think you're right," I agreed. "After all I've put you through, I'm glad it's gone." This time it was easy to be enthusiastic, especially since I knew how much it meant to Chris. Did that make lying about it okay?

"Well." Chris smiled, suddenly in a better mood. "We'd better get started before it gets any later. Harris is coming over in about an hour, and I want to make sure you know what you're going to tell him."

"Right." I was a little nervous about spoiling his good mood, but maybe he'd take it better now that he thought my powers were gone. "Let's see... I guess it all started when I had lunch with Kate. She was so into you, and looking at me like I was nothing. When I 'heard' her thinking about how Uncle Joey had put her through college and law school, I couldn't help but... well actually... I told her to stay away from you, or I'd tell everyone about Uncle Joey. At the time, I had no idea who Uncle Joey was, or I wouldn't have said anything."

Chris tried hard not to let anything I say bother him. It was water under the bridge, and there was nothing he could do about it now. "Go on," he prodded, unconsciously clenching his hands.

"That night when my car got rammed by that crazy bank robber, it was Ramos who killed him before he killed me. You met him yesterday, the one with the Kevlar vest?"

"Yeah, yeah, go on." Chris didn't like Ramos.

"Anyway, after Ramos shot the bank robber, he would have disappeared, except that Kate had called Uncle Joey and complained that I knew about him. So Uncle Joey made Ramos bring me to him so he could find out who had leaked the information. After he threatened to kill me, or you and the kids, I finally told him that I could read minds."

"You told him that?" He was appalled, realizing the position that put me in.

"It was the only way to keep him from killing me. Anyway, you can imagine how he took it. He made me go to all of his meetings and listen to people's thoughts, and then tell him what they were really thinking." As upset as Chris was, I didn't think he needed to know how I helped Ramos break into Hodges house and take all of his jewels, so I left that part out.

"After Johnny was murdered, things got a little tense. Especially after Uncle Joey's car got blown up."

"Who planted the bomb in his car?" Chris wasn't sure he wanted to know.

"That was Hodges. He was mad because Ramos had taken the jewels that Hodges had actually stolen from himself, and he wanted them back. Anyway, I saw Kate and Walter at the funeral and I picked up something about Stephen Cohen from them." I didn't think he needed to know that I 'saw' Uncle Joey kill him. That would be bad.

"When I stopped by your office yesterday and you weren't there, I thought that since I was already there, I might as well check Kate's files for anything on Stephen Cohen. I was in her office when you both came back from court, and hid under her desk. That's when I heard her talk you into going out to lunch with her. That kind of made me mad, so I took the file. I knew Uncle Joey would want to see it, and I thought if he wanted it bad enough, he would let me go."

"Then... how come you came to the restaurant?"

"I wasn't planning on going to the restaurant. I was just going to walk past it. But once I got there, I had to peek in. Then you saw me, and I had to come over and talk to you. It would have been rude not to."

Chris rolled his eyes. "Did you have the file then?"

"Um... yes. I know I shouldn't have said anything about Stephen Cohen, but I was so mad."

Even though Chris had decided not to get angry, he was having a hard time. At least he didn't have to worry about shielding his thoughts from me. "So what did you do next?"

"I went to Uncle Joey and made a deal with him. He said if I gave him the file, I wouldn't have to work for him anymore. It would have worked too, except for Kate. When I went down to the parking garage to get the file out of my car, Kate and Walter grabbed me. They taped me up and took me to an interrogation room in the basement. They wanted to know where the file was, so I told them I put it in your office. Kate left to get it, and Walter left to make a phone call. That's when Ramos came in to free me and Walter shot him. Only he wasn't dead because of the bullet-proof vest."

"I gathered that much." Chris didn't like it that Ramos had anything to do with me, even if he'd saved my life. In fact, he wondered just what was going on with Ramos. How much time had I spent with him anyhow? The guy seemed to know me pretty well. And he'd called me "Babe" yesterday. He didn't like that at all.

"Anyway, Walter took me to Uncle Joey's office where you found me."

"But why did Kate have the file, and what did Uncle... I mean Manetto have to do with it?"

"Stephen Cohen was Kate's father and she thought Uncle Joey had something to do with his death. All the information in the file pointed in that direction. She wanted Uncle Joey to go to jail, but Walter had other plans. He's the one who killed Johnny, and he was also planning to kill Uncle Joey and pin it on Kate. She had a great motive with the whole revenge thing. Then he was going to take over Uncle Joey's operation."

"And while all this was going on, Hodges showed up to get his jewels back?" Chris was thinking this sounded more incredible by the moment.

"Yeah. That's when Kate realized Walter was going to double-cross her, and she decided to help Hodges if he'd take her with him." I kind of left out the part where I hinted that I could read minds.

"Is that where she is? I can't believe Manetto would let them get away."

"I know, but I think he let her go on purpose."

"Why?"

"He told me he wanted to find her himself," I explained.

"You talked to him?"

"Yeah... he called today, right after you did. He wants me to tell the police that I was doing some office work when Walter came in with a gun and threatened me. Kind of like being in the wrong place at the wrong time. He wants me to tell the police Walter confessed to Johnny's murder and was threatening to kill both of us."

Chris took a deep breath, thinking it over. "I didn't think I'd ever agree with Manetto, but I think that's what you should do. If it was anyone but him, I'd say to tell it all, but who knows what he might do. It's better if you're perceived as an innocent bystander in all of this." He mulled it over then said, "You also need to tell Uncle Joey that you've lost your mind-reading abilities. I don't want you involved with him anymore."

"I already did. Sort of... I mean when he called, I told him I couldn't pick anything up. It seemed like he was hoping it would come back."

"Do you think it might?" he asked.

"I doubt it, but how should I know?" If I outright denied it, he might think I was lying, and I needed to be as convincing as possible.

"Look Shelby. Even if these powers come back, which I sincerely hope they don't, you have to make Uncle Joey think they're lost for good."

"Don't worry, I'm not stupid." He could see he'd hurt my feelings.

"I didn't mean that you were. It's just that this is a big deal. I mean, look what's happened. Look at this mess. Your involvement with Uncle Joey and that Ramos guy is... is... terrible. He had complete control over your life, and I don't think for one minute, he ever meant to let you go, even with all that bargaining you did. Then there's the rest of it. I mean, look at you. Your face is all black and blue. You've been shot at and practically run down. The truth of it is... you're lucky you didn't get killed." He was starting to get angry. He knew it wasn't my fault, but he wasn't sure I was completely blameless.

"I know." I agreed, wanting to calm him. "But we can work this out. Just tell me what I should tell the police."

We worked for several minutes on my story. Both of us thought it would be best to leave Kate and Stephen Cohen out of it, and just go with the basics. Then Chris questioned me as if he were a detective. "When they come, I want them to see your eyes and forehead. So make sure you take off your sunglasses, and comb your hair back."

"Okay." I thought that wasn't so smart, since he was the one who had caused my injuries, but he seemed to have forgotten that part. "You want them to take pity on me, right?"

Chris nodded. "Yeah, they'll definitely be more sympathetic when they see how you look today."

He didn't have to sound so enthusiastic, did he? Besides, Dimples knew that my injury was Chris' fault. "I hope so," I said instead, wanting to be agreeable.

It wasn't long before Dimples arrived with Detective Williams. As they entered, I took off my dark glasses, and was amply rewarded with the barely concealed expressions of horror on their faces.

It kind of made me feel bad, since I wasn't used to having people cringe when they looked at me. The hurt must have shown in my face because Dimples blurted out, "Those are like... the best black eyes I've ever seen."

"Um... thanks, I guess."

"Are you feeling better today?" he asked.

"Lots. I just look bad. How long do bruises like this last anyway?"

"Just a week... or two, tops." He really thought it would take four when they were that bad, but he didn't want to depress me, especially when I looked like... "Well, shall we get started?"

"Sure." I was real glad he hadn't finished that thought. I launched into the story Chris and I had gone over. Everything was going smoothly until he asked about Stephen Cohen. I realized it was something I had neglected to tell Chris, but I couldn't play dumb and act like I'd never told Dimples about him.

"Remember?" Dimples prompted. "He's the one you told me about. You thought he was connected to Johnny's death."

"Oh, right." I nodded. Chris closed his eyes. He wondered if there was anything else I had forgotten to tell him.

"Well," Dimples continued. "I looked up the case, but I didn't find a connection. Did you?"

"Yes, as a matter of fact, I found out when Walter was threatening us. It turns out Walter is related to the man convicted of murdering Stephen Cohen. He was Walter's uncle."

"Oh." Dimples was surprised, but he didn't know how that could possibly make a difference.

"So there was a connection," I reminded him. "I just don't know what it means."

Chris wondered what game I was playing, but wisely kept his mouth shut.

"Oh yeah, okay." Dimples figured it was one of my premonitions that hadn't panned out. He also realized that there was more to my story than I was telling, but when it involved Joey "The Knife" Manetto, he didn't blame me for being careful. "Well, I guess we're done here. If I need anything else, I'll let you know."

"What about Walter? How is he doing?" I asked.

"Umm... well, actually, he died during the night. That's why it's important that we have your testimony as an eye witness." Dimples was thinking that it wouldn't surprise him if someone had helped Walter along, but that was one can of worms he didn't want to touch.

"Oh." I was a little stunned that Walter was dead. "So now it's a case of self-defense?"

"Yes. We're going to continue our investigation, but with his death and your account, along with the others involved, it doesn't look like we'll be pressing charges against anyone."

I nodded, my shoulders sagging with relief.

They left right after that, and it wasn't long before Chris decided he needed to get back to work as well. I walked out to his car with him, and realized my brand new, beautiful car wasn't there. "I thought you were going to bring my car back."

"Uncle Joey's having it delivered after he gets it fixed."

"Oh no. What happened?"

"He didn't say, but if I were to guess, I'd say someone broke into your car to find a certain file you left in the trunk."

"Oh, that. Right. What about my purse?"

"It's on the counter. I brought it in when I came home." Before I could ask him how he got it, he explained. "A runner from Thrasher Development brought it over to my office this morning." He leaned down to kiss me, but hesitated. I was so black and blue that he wasn't sure it was all right.

"It's okay to kiss me. My lips aren't bruised." He immediately grew suspicious. Had I just read his mind? "Well? What are you waiting for?"

"So, you really can't hear my thoughts?"

I sighed so he'd know I thought he was being foolish. "Honey, if I could, I promise I would tell you. If you'll think about it, you'd realize that a person can tell what someone is thinking without hearing their thoughts. Like now, you're probably wishing you would have just kissed me and left, right?"

"No, actually, I wasn't." He was relieved and feeling optimistic. "I was thinking that once this is all cleared up, I'd like to spend some time away. You know. Just the two of us."

I smiled. "That sounds great to me." He kissed me then, and it felt pretty good. It even steamed up my dark glasses. After he left I went inside, feeling lucky to be alive. Maybe things were going to work out after all. With my 'powers' gone, Chris was acting more like his old self.

My head started to ache, and I got out an icepack, anxious for the swelling to go down. I was a little worried about keeping my secret safe. Now that I had lied about it, there was no turning back. I'd never considered myself a very good actor, but now I didn't have a choice. It was something I was going to have to get good at.

I was relaxing on the couch when the doorbell rang, and my first thought was to ignore it. Since I hadn't figured out a good story for my face, I didn't want anyone to see me like this, but when it rang again, I pulled the hair across my forehead, slipped on my dark glasses and answered it anyway.

"Hey babe." It was Ramos. "I brought your car back. Thought you might need it." He held out the car keys. "Let me have a look at you." He could see the bump between some strands of hair and he held back a smile. "That's looking better. What's behind the dark glasses?"

"If you must know, I have two of the best black eyes you've ever seen." I gently pulled the glasses away from my face, and was surprised when Ramos broke into a huge grin.

"Whoa! You're right. I've never seen any better." There was an awkward moment of silence when we just smiled at each other. I was glad he wasn't dead, but it wasn't something I could tell him. Then I realized he was thinking the same thing about me.

"So, how are things at the office?" I asked.

"With all the bullet holes, we're getting some remodeling done."

"I'll bet."

He took a deep breath. "Well, I'll be going. Mr. Manetto said you probably won't be working for him much." He was dying to know why. "Anyway, I'll see you around." He was really going to miss me.

Several days later, I had another visitor. The swelling on my head had finally gone down, but my eyes still looked awful. The black and blue had faded to a yellow-green that made me look like death warmed over. I tried to cover it with make-up, but that just made it look worse.

At least I had a new pair of dark glasses.

It was early afternoon, and I was trying to figure out what to fix for dinner when the doorbell rang. I looked out the kitchen window and spotted a black car just like mine sitting in the driveway. I'd been waiting for him to come, but now that he was here, my heart began to pound, and my knees went weak.

Uncle Joey smiled when I opened the door. "Shelby! It's so good to see you."

"You too," I lied. "Come in and sit down."

"Thanks. I can't stay long, but since I was in the neighborhood, I figured I might as well stop by and see how you were doing." He was lying through his teeth. What he really wanted to know was if I had my powers back, and if I did, how he was going to trick me into revealing it.

I smiled. "That was nice of you."

"So, how's your head?" He took a seat across from me on the couch. "The bump doesn't look so bad."

"Yes, the swelling's actually gone down. It's my eyes that are giving me grief. The greenish-yellow color is horrible."

"It's too bad that happened."

"Yes, but it's better than being shot." I paused and tried to look apologetic. "I hate to tell you this, but I still can't read minds. It never came back."

Uncle Joey hadn't known me for long, but he knew I wasn't a devious, cold-hearted kind of person. Like he was. Still, he wasn't sure I would tell him the truth.

"It probably makes you wonder if I'm telling the truth," I continued. "Since it would be better for me if I didn't have that ability. But I have to tell you. I really miss knowing what people are thinking. Sure, it got me into a lot of trouble, but it was really cool, too. Now, I'm just back to being plain old Shelby. There's nothing special about me anymore."

"I wouldn't say that." With all the trouble I'd caused, he thought I could never be considered entirely normal anyway. "I've actually grown quite fond of you." He hadn't meant to tell me that, but I looked so pathetic with my greenish skin and dark glasses.

"Anyway," he continued. "I just wanted to assure you that we're even. The file you gave me was worth the bargain we made, and I wanted you to know that I would stick to my end of the deal, even if you got your mind-reading abilities back."

"That's good to know, but I don't think they'll ever come back. For any reason." Oops. Maybe that wasn't quite the right way to put it.

Uncle Joey caught the underlying panic of my declaration and began to speculate. He thought I was sitting too straight to be telling the truth. Usually people with nothing to hide were more relaxed. I immediately leaned back against the couch and let out my breath. "So, what's next for you?" I had to get his attention off of me.

He looked down at his hands and smiled. "With my office getting a face-lift, I thought now would be a good time to take a little vacation."

"Really? Where?"

"Mexico." He looked at me and we both shared a grin. "Well, I'd better be going. It's been good talking to you, Shelby. Maybe we can do lunch when I get back. That way I can tell you all about my trip. You'd like that wouldn't you?" He was suddenly very pleased with himself.

"Yeah, sure."

He took my hand and patted it. "Until then."

With a courtly nod of his head, he was out the door in a flash, and I was left standing there with my mouth open. What had just happened? Why had he left so quickly? I got a sinking feeling in the pit of my stomach. Talking to Uncle Joey was like talking to a snake. He was way too cunning for me, and I decided it would be better to stay away from him. When he got back, I'd just have to be too busy to ever see him again.

That settled, I breathed a little easier.

I got my chance to tell Chris about Uncle Joey's visit that night. Chris was telling me they'd just hired someone straight out of law school to take Kate's place. "Is it a man or a woman?" I asked.

"Man," Chris answered, trying not to smile.

"Good," I said. "I don't think I could handle another Kate. Speaking of which, Uncle Joey came over today."

"Here?"

"Yup. He wanted to know how I was doing, but I really think he wanted to know if my powers had come back."

"I'm sure he did. What happened?" he asked.

"I told him the truth of course, but I'm not sure he believed me. Anyway, he said he was going on vacation to Mexico."

"After Kate and Hodges?"

I nodded. "I don't envy them."

Chris agreed, then caught me in a hug. "I'm sure glad you're not mixed up in all of that anymore."

"Me too," I said.

"Shelby." He rubbed my arms. "You'd tell me if your powers came back wouldn't you?"

"Of course." I'd learned a lot these last few weeks, both good and bad. What people think determines basically who they are. Putting a voice to thoughts doesn't change that. But there are times when we say things that aren't true. Not because we want to lie, but because the truth can cause more harm than good. There are times when a satisfying lie is better than the awful truth. That was why I could tell Chris that I couldn't read his mind. "Why do you ask?"

"Because of the way I acted before. I'm afraid you'd keep it to yourself when it would probably be better if you told me."

"Why do you think it would be better?"

"Because, sometimes... it just makes it easier if someone else knows." What he was really thinking was that sometimes I wasn't too smart about the way I handled things, and he didn't want me to get into any more trouble.

I smiled sweetly. "I know what you mean, and I don't want anything to come between us either. Especially not that. But honestly, you don't have to worry. It looks like I'm back to normal."

"That's good to know." He still had his doubts. It seemed like there were times when I knew more than I should.

"Though I have to admit," I continued. "That I think this whole experience has made me a little more sensitive to non-verbal communication. Did you know that ninety-eight percent of all communication is non-verbal? That's a lot."

"I didn't realize."

"So when you think I might be reading your mind, it's probably that I'm really just picking up on all of your non-verbal cues. Like this." I kissed him. "What do you think I'm thinking about when I do that?"

He smiled, and focused all his thoughts on the one person he loved more than anyone else in the world.

Me.

Thank you for reading **Carrots: A Shelby Nichols Adventure**. Ready for the next book in the series? **Fast Money: A Shelby Nichols Adventure** is now available in print, ebook and on audible. Get your copy today!

If you enjoyed this book, please consider leaving a review on Amazon. It's a great way to thank an author and keep her writing!

NEWSLETTER SIGNUP For news, updates, and special offers, please sign up for my newsletter on my website at www.colleenhelme.com. To thank you for subscribing you will receive a FREE ebook.

ABOUT THE AUTHOR

USA TODAY AND WALL STREET JOURNAL BESTSLLING AUTHOR

As the author of the Shelby Nichols Adventure Series, Colleen is often asked if Shelby Nichols is her alter-ego. "Definitely," she says. "Shelby is the epitome of everything I wish I dared to be." Known for her laugh since she was a kid, Colleen has always tried to find the humor in every situation and continues to enjoy writing about Shelby's adventures. "I love getting Shelby into trouble... I just don't always know how to get her out of it!" Besides writing, she loves a good book, biking, hiking, and playing board and card games with family and friends. She loves to connect with readers and admits that fans of the series keep her writing.

Connect with Colleen at www.colleenhelme.com